DV BERKOM

A LEINE BASSO THRILLER

TERMINAL THREAT

Terminal Threat

A Leine Basso Thriller
Copyright © 2023 by D.V. Berkom
Published by

First print edition July 2023
All rights reserved.
Cover by Deranged Doctor Designs

ISBN-13: 978-1-7348599-8-0

***Join my readers' list to be the first to find out about new releases and exclusive, subscriber-only special offers. (*See the back of the book for details*)

Website: dvberkom.com

WHAT READERS ARE SAYING ABOUT TERMINAL THREAT:

"D V. Berkom has once again created a fast-paced, action-filled, nail-biting story filled with intrigue and suspense." *~Lynda Custer*

"I regretted getting to the end so quickly but definitely didn't regret reading it. I just loved the book and can't wait for the next." *~ Julie Howard*

"DV has surpassed herself...The story is exciting, the pace is fast and the setting is perfect...another hit for me and one I won't hesitate to recommend to lovers of books that are full of action with a strong female lead." *~Hazel Howorth, Reading Stuff-n-Things*

"Get your copy of DV Berkom's sensational new Leine Basso thriller, Terminal Threat today...and sleep with a pistol under your pillow!" *~Rosemary*

"...non-stop action and intriguing characters...This is a page turner, folks, with our heroine using all of her skills to stay alive." *~James*

"...twists and turns and lots of 'badassery' that is typical from Leine and her partners in crime." *~Diane Wagner*

"Another thrill ride by D.V." *~Bob Gordon*

"Loved it. She is still a badass." *~Angel*

"...Her characters jump off the page..." ~*Joan*

"Another exciting Leine Basso non-stop thriller - when the action starts, it never stops." ~*Betsy*

"A great story full of action..." ~*Ellen White*

"Excellent!" ~ *Laurie Biundo*

"Fasten your seatbelts everyone...This is another excellent book in the Leine Basso series." ~*Gill Powell*

Other books in the Leine Basso Thriller Series:

A Killing Truth
Serial Date
Bad Traffic
The Body Market
Cargo
The Last Deception
Dark Return
Absolution
Dakota Burn
Shadow of the Jaguar
A Plague of Traitors
Fatal Objective

1

———

Gabriela deepened her breathing to calm herself as she raced to meet Eduardo. The warm October evening was mild for the northern Italian coast—more like early September. Perfect weather for an assignation with her *amore* along the waterside promenade known to locals as *la strada dell'amore*, "The Path of Love." Her heart still raced whenever she thought of being alone with him.

Lights gleamed from the windows of the brightly painted homes and businesses towering above her on both sides of the narrow cobblestone street, reminding Gabriela of warm nights sharing meals *al fresco* with friends and family in the middle of the thoroughfare. Traffic would be rerouted to a side street when that happened, giving everything a celebratory feel. Scivoloso was the quintessential northern Italian town, with ancient stone buildings filled with history, clinging to sandstone cliffs.

In her satchel she carried a liter of the local wine, trading wineglasses for the intimacy and practicality of drinking directly from the bottle. She'd also brought two different kinds of cheese —one bovine, the other sheep—redolent with the earthy fragrance of her beloved region, a package of flatbread, and a small jar of her family's olives.

Gabriela glanced at her phone. She was already late. Eduardo would understand. He always did. Business at the restaurant had been brisk that evening, and her uncle had asked her to finish folding the linen napkins for the next day's lunch service.

She hurried through the metal gate designed to keep errant tourists from stumbling upon the private walkway and stepped onto the stone path that led to her and Eduardo's special place. A full moon sparkled across the surface of the Mediterranean, playing hide-and-seek with scudding clouds as a gusty breeze tickled her cheek, bringing with it the briny scent of the sea. Partially hidden among a venerable grove of ancient olive trees, a semicircular stone bench materialized from the darkness. Here, the view of the sea set a mood for her meetings with Eduardo; they'd spent many evenings laughing, eating, drinking, and doing other things that would have made her grandmother blush.

Curiously, Eduardo wasn't there.

Gabriela set the satchel and wine on the bench, and was about to prepare the evening's feast when she heard a noise further down the path.

Perhaps Eduardo had been night fishing with some of his friends. Leaving the satchel, Gabriela made her way along the darkened walkway, a smile forming on her lips as she heard her fiancé's deep baritone rising above the relentless boom of waves crashing against the boulders below.

A storm was coming. Originating from deep within the Sahara, the *scirocco* was known to southern Italy as the "blood rain" for the red sand brought by the rain and cyclone-force winds. Here in the north, the system was no less destructive, bringing with it salt from the sea, damaging vineyards and structures built too close to the cliffs.

Rounding a concrete bulkhead, Gabriela stopped short at the sight before her. Bathed in moonlight, Eduardo stood below her on the sand with two men she didn't recognize. Held from behind, dark blood dripped from Eduardo's battered face as he struggled against the larger of the two men.

The shorter one leaned closer and said something. Eduardo shook his head, his protests obvious by his expression, although not loud enough for Gabriela to understand. The shorter man hunched his shoulders and delivered a blow to Eduardo's stomach, and her fiancé jackknifed forward. The waves stole Gabriela's shriek.

The shorter man stepped back. Something gleamed like a silvery fish as the man holding him reached from behind and slit Eduardo's throat.

Gabriela's scream ripped through her, its keening wail shrilling above the suffocating waves. Terrified she'd been heard, she slapped her hand over her mouth.

Too late.

The shorter man spun in her direction as Eduardo slumped to the sand. The man's malevolent gaze speared her as paralysis battled with flight.

Flight won.

Terror fueled Gabriela's escape. She didn't register the bench or the satchel as she raced past. At the entrance to the path, she hesitated, not knowing which direction to turn. The thought of bringing this evil anywhere near her family filled her with indecision. Should she hide or run?

The sound of heavy footsteps pounding up the lane behind her spurred her on. She careened toward the safety of the town's main street, panic clouding her memory—had any of the businesses she'd passed on her way to the beach been open?

Fighting for breath, Gabriela's hope sank as she reached the main street. The sleepy seaside town, normally so safe and welcoming, struck her as dead and barren of life. Her panic grew as she stumbled along the ancient cobblestones, praying for rescue. Tears streamed down her face. She was about to die. Not in her old age in a comfortable bed with her children and grandchildren surrounding her as she'd always hoped, but violently afraid, taking the secret of Eduardo's murderers with her to the grave.

She had to hide. Gabriela twisted to look behind her. The winding street was in her favor—for now. The men hadn't yet rounded the corner. She hurried past the closed restaurants and bakery, past the gelateria that had been there for as long as she could remember. A faint glow to her left caught her eye, and she veered toward it, a moth to a flame.

The sign hanging in the glass door read *Chiuso*. Closed. Her heart sank at the rows of empty bookshelves visible through the glass. A light in the back of the store lit a flame of hope that someone was there. She tried the handle.

Locked.

Stifling a sob, she knocked, gently, careful not to make too much noise, praying to the Virgin to deliver her from danger.

Between howls of angry wind, the sound of footsteps echoed in the street behind her. The men's pace had slowed. They were being cautious, aware a violent death in the street would bring attention in this small town.

Her violent death.

Her terror growing, Gabriela grasped the door handle and tried to shake the lock free.

The light inside the store momentarily dimmed as the silhouette of a tall, broad-shouldered woman emerged from the back. A sob of relief escaped Gabriela, and she waved frantically.

The woman opened the door and drew her inside, her other

hand cutting short the delicate tinkle of bells used to announce visitors to the store. The faint scent of jasmine and ylang-ylang mixed with a feeling of safety enveloped Gabriela and she instinctively relaxed. The woman closed and locked the door, then pulled the privacy shade before moving Gabriela swiftly to the back room where she turned off the light.

"Thank you, I—" Gabriela began, but the woman held a finger to her lips, and she quieted. Seconds later, the front door rattled, and the woman stiffened.

No, stiffened wasn't the right word. Gabriela detected no fear in her, only focus and self-assurance.

Gabriela leaned against the wall, her breath shallow as she tried to calm her racing heart. The woman stood and listened, hidden by shadow.

The door shuddered once more. Low voices floated toward them, then faded as the men continued their search. Gabriela and the woman waited in silence several more minutes. The ticking clock on the opposite wall echoed through the small room, marking the moment.

The immediate threat gone, the woman relaxed and lowered her arm. Gabriela hadn't noticed the gun. Her breath caught in her throat. Who was this woman? The weapon looked different than her uncle's pistol—the barrel was much longer. She thought it must be what her cousin on the police force had called a suppressor—something very difficult to acquire in Italy.

How was the woman—a stranger to Gabriela—able to obtain such a thing? Had Gabriela made the right decision to seek help here?

The woman took Gabriela by the arm and gently guided her through another door farther into the back.

A floor lamp cast light on an overstuffed, comfortable-looking chair with a tufted footstool. An open book splayed across one arm, next to a side table. Steam drifted lazily from a cup with a used teabag nearby, suggesting a quiet evening interrupted. Gabriela relaxed. Surely the woman only had the gun for her own protection.

"I'm so sorry," Gabriela began, the words coming out in a rush.

"Why were those men following you?" the stranger asked in Italian.

Gabriela's anxiety spiked. The grotesque scene she'd witnessed on the beach flooded her mind, and she closed her eyes. Fresh tears fell and she shook her head. "I saw something."

The woman offered Gabriela the chair, then sat on the footstool across from her. "What did you see?"

Gabriela stifled a sob, not knowing how much to tell her. She'd put this woman in danger. She deserved to know what happened. Afraid of being thrown out onto the street when she told her, Gabriela steeled her courage. "There were two men...they...they killed Eduardo." The sob breached the surface, the sound black and viscous, reminding her of the fiery car accident that had ripped her parents from her years before. A familiar despair.

One which she'd hoped never to repeat.

"Eduardo is your boyfriend?"

Gabriela nodded, too overcome with emotion to speak. The woman remained silent, holding Gabriela's hands as she sobbed.

Spent, Gabriela wiped her face and took a shaky breath. "I should leave. I don't want to bring you trouble." She glanced at several boxes stacked in a corner. The writing on them was in English. "You're the American."

"Yes." She held out her hand. "I'm Ava."

Gabriela shook it and replied, "Gabriela Mancini. Your Italian is quite good."

The American's arrival had been much anticipated. The town's realtor let it be known that she'd sold the vacant, historic building that once housed a bookstore and two small upstairs apartments to a wealthy American woman seeking a new life on the coast of Italy. Speculation ran wild as to why a woman alone would move from the sprawling metropolis of Los Angeles to their decidedly less exciting town. Had she divorced? Was she perhaps wanted by the authorities? Or maybe it was something far less gossip-worthy, and she only wanted a simpler life. The rows of bookshelves suggested that the woman was going to keep the shop in its former incarnation.

"Do you have family here in town?"

Gabriela nodded. "My father's family lives here. An aunt and uncle, many cousins."

"Do the men who killed Eduardo know who you are?"

"I don't think so. I've never seen either of them before."

"You need to be sure."

Gabriela stared at Ava, the implication of her words sinking in. "It wouldn't take long to find out. Not in this town. Everyone knows everyone."

"These men—what did they look like? Describe them in as much detail as you can."

"One was shorter than the other. He had a thick neck, like a bull, with sloping shoulders. Dark hair."

"And the taller of the two?"

"I didn't get a good look at him. He—he was the one who killed Eduardo." She shuddered at the memory.

"How did he kill him?"

"A knife across the throat."

Ava walked to a nearby coatrack and shrugged on a dark jacket. "Where is Eduardo?"

"On the beach." Fresh tears welled in her eyes at the thought. So young, so full of life, his heart filled with plans for the future.

Their future.

"Where, exactly? I'll go to the police—tell them I found him while out walking."

"No. I have to tell them what I saw. There must be justice for Eduardo's death."

Ava shook her head. "It would be best if you remained hidden. At least until the threat is identified. Do you have friends or family somewhere away from here?"

"My mother's family lives in the U.S., in Oregon. But I can't go there."

"Why not?"

"My home is here, in Italy." The thought of going back to the United States filled her with sadness. She loved her father's family, loved working in the restaurant and the olive groves. Oregon was beautiful, but Italy was home.

"You have to go somewhere they can't find you."

"I have a friend in Lucca." Emma would welcome her visit. They'd talked about meeting in Rome for a holiday. Perhaps she'd suggest it while she was there.

"That works. For now. You can't tell anyone where you're going."

"Not even my family?"

"Especially not your family."

"Are they in danger?"

"That depends on whether those two men find out who you are. Did they get a good look at your face?"

Had they? "I don't know. It was dark, but there was moonlight."

The panic came back with a force that took her breath. What if they found out where her family lived? Her uncle and his family were well known in the region. The Mancinis had lived there for generations. Would the murderers hurt them to find out where she'd gone?

Of course they would. They killed Eduardo.

"Then we have to assume they saw you." Ava studied her.

"Call your friend in Lucca and tell her you had a spat with someone in your family. Ask her if you can visit for a few days. You'll have to make up something. You can't tell her what happened to Eduardo. That could put you and your friend in danger. I'll take care of your family."

Gabriela thought of the gun the woman had earlier. How had she secured a pistol as a newcomer to Italy? Compared to the United States, Italian gun laws were draconian. Not that there weren't ways to get one—but there were a lot of hoops to jump through. No one she knew had access to something like a suppressor. She eyed Ava, her earlier doubt growing. Obviously, Ava knew someone. Why did Gabriela think she could trust her? Just because she was a woman?

It's the only path you have right now, Gabby.

Gabriela reached in her pocket for her mobile, but her hand came up empty. A knot formed in her stomach. She'd left it with the satchel.

"What's wrong?"

"My phone. It's still in my bag."

"Was there anything inside the bag that could point to you?" Ava asked. "Identification? Personal items?"

"Only my phone."

"What's on your lockscreen?"

Gabriela closed her eyes. "A photograph of Eduardo and me." A deep sob escaped her as she covered her face with her hands.

"I'll grab it before I call the police. Do you use a passcode to lock your phone?"

"Of course."

"That's good. They won't be able to access your contact list if they find it first. Here." Ava handed her phone to Gabriela. "Look up the train schedule. Then call your friend. You need to leave tonight."

2

———

Leine Basso moved silently through the darkened streets of the small Italian town, the suppressed pistol hidden in her jacket.

So much for a quiet life for her alter ego, Ava.

She checked her watch. The train left in three hours. That gave her plenty of time to locate the body, find the satchel with the phone, if the killers hadn't taken it already, and double back to the store where Gabriela waited.

She found the private pathway easily enough, given Gabriela's directions, and moved quickly past the lookout to the stone bench. The satchel wasn't there. Leine searched the surrounding area, but came up empty. The wind had kicked up again, pushing cold raindrops ahead of it, whipping her hair from her face. She smoothed it back and continued to the beach, allowing her sharpened awareness to lead her.

The sound of waves crashing below her muffled all sound—good on the one hand because no one would be able to hear her approach—but not so good on the other, as she couldn't hear anyone else, either.

The full moon shone between scudding clouds, creating

ghost-like shadows across the path, obscuring the landscape. She pulled out her gun as she reached the vantage point where Gabriela said she'd witnessed the murder, and eased forward, using a concrete bulkhead for cover. Partially obscured by a boulder, two men bent over a dark shape on the beach below. The clouds parted, allowing moonlight to shine through and giving her a clear view as the men hoisted a tarp-covered bundle —presumably Eduardo—over the side of an inflatable dinghy.

Leine considered dropping them where they stood. They'd killed a young man, and would hunt down Gabriela to get rid of any witnesses—but until she understood who they were and why they had killed Eduardo, she hesitated.

The two men worked as though familiar with the process; they hoisted what appeared to be an anchor onto the body and secured it, then dragged the boat to the water's edge with an efficiency that suggested practice.

The incoming tide had crawled up the beach, making it an easy job. The two men conferred before they climbed into the boat, and the taller of the two started the engine. He appeared to struggle keeping the boat on course in the buffeting waves, but eventually succeeded in moving past the shore break. The weather proved too much for the small boat—a wave almost swamped them. Evidently deciding against trying to move further out, the second man muscled the tarp-covered body and anchor over the side.

At that moment, the wind picked up in a powerful gust, shrieking through the trees. A downpour followed, soaking everything within seconds. Leine gripped the gnarled root of an ancient olive tree next to the bulkhead to steady herself.

The men fought their way back to shore, the cresting waves threatening to swamp the boat as they did. The shorter man jumped into the water and heaved the boat to shore, then picked up what was likely Gabriela's satchel from the sand and slid it over his shoulder, pulling his jacket over his head against the deluge. The other man disembarked, and the two of them darted toward the path.

Leine slipped into the shadows as they passed by.

"We need to find her tonight," growled the shorter man. He was speaking Albanian, a familiar dialect from a target she'd eliminated years before.

"Not until we speak to Lorik," answered the taller of the two. They continued up the slight rise.

She followed at a distance, keeping them in view, yet staying far enough back in case one of them turned around. At the top of the path, they climbed into a white delivery van and drove off. Leine memorized the plates, make, and model before heading back to Gabriela.

She entered the bookstore and walked to the back room. She knocked twice and said in a low voice, "It's me," before proceeding through the door. Gabriela sat at the desk near the window, watching the storm. She turned when Leine entered.

"Did you find him?"

Leine nodded. "The two men matching your description were there."

"Oh, my God." Her eyes widened. "Did you call the police?"

"No."

"But why? They killed him. They must be brought to justice."

"The men got to Eduardo first. They weighted down the body so it would sink."

"You must tell the police what they've done. They'll be able to find him."

"I'm not sure that's the best way to go about this, Gabriela."

The young woman's puzzled expression told Leine to tread carefully.

"How well do you know the police here?" she asked.

"My cousin is a member. It's a small force—he is one of four."

"If I were to report Eduardo's death, I would need to bypass the local police and go straight to the *carabinieri,* since it's obviously murder. But the *carabinieri* would contact the local police. That could alert anyone who has a connection between his killers and the local cops."

Gabriela shook her head. "That cannot be. I know the police here. They wouldn't be involved."

"You may be right, but do you really want to take the chance? Whoever I contact would be interested in how I know. I can't just tell them I was out for a walk during the storm and witnessed someone dumping a body. I also can't say that someone else found him. We need to assume the men who killed Eduardo are part of a larger enterprise, one that may or may not have contacts within the police department."

Gabriela gave her a puzzled look. "Then I will call and leave an anonymous tip."

"Using what? They have your mobile. I haven't noticed any payphones in town."

"Everyone has a phone. There is no need."

"Work with me here. No tipping off the police, no contact with your family, for now, okay?"

Leine went to a cupboard next to the sink, selected a porcelain cup, and poured her some tea. She grabbed a nearby box of tissues and set it next to Gabriela, along with the cup. "Tell me about Eduardo."

Gabriela stared at Leine, her eyes bloodshot and rimmed in red. "But what about my family? You said they may be in danger." She pulled a tissue from the box and wiped her nose.

There was no sense sugar-coating things. Leine would have to act tonight. "The two men who are looking for you are likely the muscle for someone higher up in the food chain of a criminal group. I overheard one of them say they had to find you, but the other one mentioned they needed to run it past someone named Lorik. Ring any bells?"

Gabriela shook her head. "That's not an Italian name."

"Albanian, I believe."

"I don't know any Albanians."

"You said your uncle owns a restaurant in town?"

"Ristorante d'Mancini. It's very good."

"I'll talk to him after you leave for Lucca."

Relief lit Gabriela's face. "You will?"

"I said that I would take care of your family." There was a good chance a long-time business owner like her uncle would know which organized crime syndicates were operating in or around Scivoloso.

"I saw the gun. Earlier."

Leine nodded. "And?"

"And I would like to know how you acquired this." Gabriela frowned. "You moved to a small, quiet village in Italy from a huge city in America. Why did you think you needed a gun?"

"Habit."

The young woman nodded. A blinding flash illuminated the window, followed by a loud crack of thunder. Gabriela cried out and squeezed her eyes closed, her face draining of color as she gripped the china cup. Leine moved to the chair and wrapped her arms around her. Gabriela buried her face in her shoulder, another sob escaping her as she did.

"Shh. It's just the storm."

"They slit his throat as though he was worth nothing."

"I know." Leine smoothed the other woman's hair. "I promise I'll find out why they killed Eduardo."

With some time until Gabriela's train, Leine engaged her in conversation, trying to take her mind off the murder. The ploy worked. Gabriela came alive describing the town's history.

"Scivoloso means slippery in Italian. I've been meaning to ask how the town got its name?"

Gabriela smiled. "It's because of the nature of the people who live here. Back in the old times, they were as slippery as eels. What you might call escape artists today."

"Escape from what?"

"Not what, but whom. Did Francesca tell you why there's an opening in your floor?" Gabriela gestured to a four-by-six-foot rug Leine had positioned underneath a window to cover a trap door.

"Pirates?"

Gabriela nodded. "Centuries ago, the townspeople grew tired of marauders pillaging them whenever they wanted. There are three buildings on this side of the street with 'escape hatches' as they came to be called. When the pirates came, everyone would hide their valuables and disappear through the trap doors to the beaches below. The pirates would leave empty handed."

"What did the townspeople do during high tide?" Leine had explored the natural crevice that led from the store to the sea and reinforced the ladder that had been built into the rock.

"Several kept boats tied nearby."

"Bet that pissed off the pirates."

"It did. One group of marauders tried to burn the town, but with most of the buildings made of stone, the ploy wasn't very effective. Soon, they stopped coming."

"So their trick worked."

A shadow crossed Gabriela's features. "It appears the pirates have returned."

Leine checked the clock on the wall. "We should leave for the station." She opened a desk drawer and counted out several hundred euros, which she handed to Gabriela.

"I can't take this."

"Consider it a loan. You can't come back until I tell you it's safe, all right?"

Gabriela's shoulders slumped. "All right."

Leine selected one of three burner phones she kept in the desk and handed it to her. "You'll find my number in contacts—it's the only one there. Remember, you mustn't call or text your uncle or anyone else." She studied the younger woman. "Do I have your word?"

Gabriela nodded. "You have my word."

Leine pulled a piece of stationery from the desk and handed it to her, along with a pen. "I need you to put something in writing that tells your aunt and uncle I can be trusted. A complete stranger showing up on their doorstep offering to protect them won't carry much weight without some kind of proof."

"Of course."

"Add something that only you and they would know."

Gabriela did as instructed and handed the letter back to Leine. "Thank you, Ava. I don't know what I can do to repay you for your kindness."

"Just stay safe."

3
—————

Leine waited until the train to Lucca left the station before she made her way back to the bookstore. In a tiny hall closet on the upper floor, she grabbed a set of security cameras still in the box. She'd intended to return the smaller set, deciding instead to use an 8-camera suite she'd ordered for the bookstore.

Downstairs, she woke up her tablet and reviewed the security footage from earlier that evening a second time. The video of the two men had turned out to be only somewhat useful—hoods obscured their features, although she was able to get a sense of each man's size and proportion. Gabriela hadn't recognized either of them. Because of the storm, the audio wasn't as clear as she'd have liked, but she did pick up a few words that sounded like one of the Albanian dialects, reinforcing her earlier observations.

Armed with the security setup, her tablet, and a backpack with several items she'd likely need, she set off into the night, headed for the home of Tomaso and Francesca Mancini.

Located at the north end of town, the stately Mancini home sat behind and across the street from the restaurant that bore the family name. Leine lifted the ornate lion's head knocker and let it fall. A few minutes later the front light flickered on and the door opened.

"Yes?" A man in his forties with dark hair beginning to gray at the temples squinted at her. The rumpled clothes, bags under his eyes, and five o'clock shadow suggested he'd either been working all night or she'd woken him up and he'd hurriedly thrown on clothes to answer the door.

"Tomaso Mancini?"

"*Sì?*"

"I apologize for the early hour, but I'm here about your niece, Gabriela." She opted for Italian rather than English to put him at ease.

A look of concern washed over his face. "Is she all right?"

"Yes, she's fine." Leine nodded toward the foyer. "May I come in?"

"Forgive me, but who are you?"

"My name is Ava Basso. I recently moved here. I own the bookshop in the older part of town." Basso was a common enough name in Italy, and allowed her some cover from old enemies.

Recognition lit his eyes. "The American. My wife and I have been meaning to stop by to welcome you. Please forgive our rudeness."

"No forgiveness needed. It's hard to find time for anything when you own a business."

Tomaso's relief was genuine. "Two businesses, but yes, it is difficult, even at the best of times. *Prego, entri pure.*" He nodded and stepped back, allowing her to enter, then closed the door behind her. "May I take your things?" He looked pointedly at the box of security cameras.

"No, thank you."

"Your Italian is very good. Have you lived in Italy before?"

"No, but I have done quite a bit of business here in the past."

Tomaso nodded. "May I ask what this is about?"

"Your niece is in danger. You and your wife may be, also."

Tomaso gave her an incredulous look. "What do you mean?"

"I'll explain. But I'd prefer to talk to both of you."

"I'll get her. Please, make yourself at home."

"*Prego*." Leine walked into the living area, but remained standing. The solidly built furniture sported worn upholstery but was of good quality, as were the rest of the pieces in the room. Framed family photographs adorned the walls, with a smiling Gabriela in many of them. Leine was perusing the bookshelves when Tomaso reappeared with a stunning redhead in tow.

"Miss Basso, I'd like you to meet my wife, Francesca Mancini."

Francesca extended her hand, which Leine shook. "Basso. You are Italian?"

"Basso's my married name."

Francesca and Tomaso exchanged looks. "So you are married? Is your husband here?"

"Ex-husband, actually. We divorced years ago." Not that it was important. Frank Basso and she had formed a truce to make things easier for their daughter, April. April now lived in South America with her boyfriend, and Frank lived in Los Angeles, so she barely had to think about him at all.

"I didn't mean to offend." Francesca smiled apologetically. "Tomaso says you told him Gabriela is in danger?"

"No offense taken." Leine placed the box of security cameras on a nearby table. "I'm going to be blunt. Last night, Gabriela witnessed a murder."

The Mancinis' eyes widened in surprise. Francesca gripped her husband's hand, her face white. "She what? Is she all right?"

"She is. At least for now. Does the name Eduardo mean anything to you?"

Francesca nodded. "Gabriela's boyfriend."

Tomaso frowned at his wife. "She has a boyfriend?"

"Of course she does, *caro*." Francesca rolled her eyes. Then the penny dropped. She stared at Leine. "No. It can't be."

"I'm so sorry."

"Oh, my God. Where? Why?"

"On the beach. Near the Path of Love. We don't know why."

Francesca's knees buckled, and she reached for Tomaso's arm. He guided her to the sofa.

"Who would do such a thing?" Tomaso's shock had morphed into anger. "Where is Gabriela now?"

"To answer your first question, Gabriela didn't recognize the men responsible. I can't answer the second."

"Why not?" Francesca asked.

"Because if anyone were to find out, it could put both Gabriela and your family in grave danger."

"What happened to him?" Francesca asked, her voice quiet. "Someone will have to ship his body home to Calabria."

"I'm afraid that may not be possible. The men who killed him dumped his body in the sea."

Francesca gasped.

"How do we know you are telling the truth?" Tomaso asked.

Leine rummaged in her bag and pulled out the letter Gabriela had written. "She asked me to give this to you."

Francesca studied the paper. "It is her handwriting." The Mancinis each read the letter. When they finished, Francesca asked, "What can we do?"

"For now, nothing," Leine answered. "I'll take care of everything."

Tomaso nodded at the security cameras. "What do you intend to do with those?"

"With your permission, I'd like to install them on your property. I assume you have wi-fi?" The Mancinis nodded. "We'll both be able to monitor them" –Leine held up her tablet— "to make sure you're safe. If either of the men come looking for your niece, I'll take care of it."

Tomaso narrowed his eyes. "What makes you think you would be able to 'take care of it' as you say? These men are clearly dangerous, and you are a woman alone."

Liam Neeson's line from the movie *Taken* about a very particular set of skills floated through her mind. "Let's just say I have training pertinent to the objective."

Francesca placed her hand on Tomaso's knee. Color was returning to her cheeks. "That isn't the right question to ask, my love." She studied Leine. "I believe that our new friend knows what she's doing. Please, install the cameras."

"Thank you, Francesca." Leine leaned forward, elbows on her knees. "As the owners of a restaurant here in town, you would be well-positioned to know of criminal elements that might be operating in the area. Anything you know or have heard would be helpful. Have any strangers approached you or your employees?"

Tomaso glanced nervously at his wife. "There is a man. His name is Jona." Francesca gave her husband a sharp look. "He comes in every week."

"How much does he ask for?" Leine asked.

"Too much. We can't continue to operate and pay him, too."

"Why have you not told me of this?" Francesca asked.

"I didn't want to worry you."

Francesca rolled her eyes. "How is this a partnership? I can't be expected to make decisions if you keep important things from me."

Tomaso glanced at Leine, then back to his wife. "We will discuss this later, *tesoro mia*."

"When did he start?" Leine asked.

"A few weeks ago. I hoped he'd go away once I paid him."

"Have you seen him in town before?"

Tomaso shook his head. "No one had. He threatened my staff with violence if we didn't pay."

"Has he threatened others?"

"Yes. Many of the businesses in town have been approached. My friend, Angelo, who owns the small grocery at the south end, refused to pay. The next night, his building caught fire. Thankfully, Angelo and his employees were able to put it out before too much damage was done. There was a note saying the next time would be worse."

"So, arson and extortion." Probably some low-ranking criminals, hoping for an easy payday. "What day does Jona stop by?"

"Tuesdays. He normally comes in the morning, before we open for business."

"Unless something happens in the meantime," Leine said, "I'll be there."

Tuesday was only two days away. Were Jona and Lorik operating from the same crew? In a town as small as Scivoloso, she doubted there'd be competing criminal organizations operating an extortion scheme. If so, the place would likely be a war zone as they fought for control.

"Have you ever met or heard of anyone named Lorik?"

Both Tomaso and Francesca shook their heads.

"Let me know if the name comes up."

"Of course," Tomaso said. "What should we do now? Are my employees at risk?"

"I don't think so, although they could threaten you in an attempt to find out where Gabriela is. If that happens, do what you can to put them off and call me right away. I'll monitor the cameras in case they show up, but it's possible they could attempt to contact you at the restaurant. In the meantime, I'll ask around about Jona, see if I can find out more about his operation."

"The people in town don't know you," Tomaso said. "I doubt they'll tell you anything."

"What would you suggest?"

"I'll ask," Francesca offered. "There is a group to which I belong that includes many of the businesswomen here in town. Although," she shot a look at Tomaso, "I can't say for certain that the ones who are married will have been told about Jona."

Tomaso had the decency to look chagrined.

Francesca nudged him. "You can talk to the men, can't you, Tomaso?"

Tomaso frowned. "What if our questions cause Jona to retaliate?"

"I'll take care of it," Leine said.

"Just how will you 'take care of it'? Did you train in the military? A spy, perhaps?"

Francesca gave her husband a look. "Don't be rude. Ava is our guest, and she has offered to help us." She turned back to Leine. "As I said earlier, please do whatever needs to be done."

Leine studied them both. "As long as you both agree." There was no way in hell she wanted to come between a husband and wife. Life was too short.

Tomaso nodded. "Yes, yes. I agree."

"Great. Do you have a ladder?"

4

Leine mounted and tested the cameras around the Mancinis' property, assuring 360-degree coverage as Tomaso followed her, asking questions and suggesting locations. Once she was satisfied with her work, she said goodbye to Tomaso and Francesca and returned to the bookstore.

Too wired to sleep, Leine lit the tiny gas stove in her back room and fried herself an egg. She'd wait until later in the morning to try to talk with some of the other shopkeepers in town. As darkness faded to gray, replaced by the pinks and blues of another gorgeous Mediterranean sunrise, she contemplated her next move.

Why was she getting involved now? And what was she getting herself into? She'd just moved into the small community, hadn't even introduced herself to the locals, although a couple of the shopkeepers on her street had made overtures, which she'd returned. After the last op she'd done for SHEN, the anti-trafficking organization she worked with, she'd reevaluated her life and realized it was time to retire. On impulse, she'd bought the ancient bookstore, wanting nothing so much as to be left alone.

How'd that work out for you, Leine? She did her grocery shopping in another town, and not only because of the superior tequila selection.

The chime of a video call interrupted her thoughts and she reached for her phone. It was Santa.

"Hey there." Santiago Jensen's deep baritone and relaxed smile drew her in, shutting out everything else. From what she could see in the background, he was on the balcony of his apartment in Los Angeles. Oddly, the distant sound of traffic made her wistful.

"Hey." She smiled at the detective. She couldn't help herself —because of the last op she'd suffered deep memory loss at the hands of an organization called the Association, and the two of them had to rebuild trust and intimacy. Maybe it was because they'd known each other before, but she found herself coming to trust him more than anyone else. Her move to Italy was reconnaissance for when he hung up his badge and could join her.

Santa took a swig of his beer. A ritual after a long day. "So how's our retirement looking?"

Leine turned her phone toward the sunrise. "Pretty good, detective." She wasn't about to tell him what happened with Gabriela. The whole reason she moved to Italy was to start a new, less stressful life. One they could share.

Santa whistled. "That's what I'm talking about. How's the bookstore coming along? Have you set a date for the grand opening yet?"

Leine sighed. "Not yet. The inventory still needs to go on the shelves, but I've been enjoying my quiet time." Well, it was partially true.

"It's not like you need the income." He took another drink. "I booked my ticket today. I arrive on the fourth."

A little under a month. That should give her plenty of time to take care of Jona. "That's great, honey. Can't wait."

"You sure? You seem preoccupied."

She shook her head. "No, no. I'm good. Just a lot to think about for the bookstore. I'll try to have things ready for the opening by then. I'd love for you to be part of it."

"I'd like nothing better." He took another long pull on his beer. "So really, what's bothering you?"

Leine sighed. He'd learned to read her moods too well. She'd have to work on that. "Oh, just moving pains. Scivoloso isn't L.A."

"Ah. Small town stuff. Amiright?"

"Exactly. I stick out—the new kid on the block. What the hell was I thinking? It's like I took leave of my senses when I decided to move here." She shook her head. "I used to be a private person."

"I get it. Growing up in a small town had its drawbacks, but there are some good aspects." Santa had an idyllic childhood—growing up in a speck of a town in Northern California. Before Leine bought the bookstore in Italy, there'd been talk of moving back.

"The only time I spent in small towns was when I worked for SHEN." Memories of an op in North Dakota where she'd helped a friend expose a child sex trafficking ring near the Bakken oil fields flitted through her mind.

"It's gotta be culture shock. Especially since most of your adult life was built around blending in so no one would remember you. Hang in there, doll. And hey, if it's not for you, we'll go someplace else."

"Any word on Jinn?" The surrogate daughter Leine had

rescued from the streets of Tripoli in Libya, Jinn now lived in L.A. with Leine's old Agency handler, Lou Stokes.

"She's thriving. That is one smart, capable kid. You did good bringing her into the fold."

Into the fold, meaning the SHEN academy Leine had started with Lou. Recruits from around the world learned self-defense, tradecraft, and other skills in an effort to build an army against the third largest criminal enterprise known to law enforcement: human trafficking. Academy graduates had been deployed to several continents, including the United States, where they worked with local anti-trafficking groups to stem the flow.

"I miss her. And you."

"One month. And then we'll be together."

They said their goodbyes, and Leine set the phone down. Feeling oddly restless, Leine brought up the camera feeds at the Mancinis', checking to make sure everything was working. The picture was clear, even detecting movement of a nearby tree branch in the wind. Satisfied, she leaned her head back and wondered again what the hell she was doing.

5

———

Later that morning, Leine canvassed Old Town, introducing herself to shopkeepers and townspeople and asking leading questions. Francesca was right—no one was about to trust the new arrival. At least she was putting herself out there, getting a feel for the general tone of the town.

She stopped at a small café for an espresso and struck up a conversation with the waiter. His name was Bruno, and he'd been working at the café for three years. He looked to be about Gabriela's age, so she asked him if he knew her.

His brown eyes lit up and he smiled. "*Si*, I know Gabby. She's a good friend. And her boyfriend, Eduardo." He continued to thread clean wineglasses on the rack hanging above the bar. "We go out sometimes on the weekend. Do you know her?"

Leine nodded. "I met her at Mancinis'." No sense letting him know more than he needed to.

"Funny. You're the second person to ask about her today."

"Oh?"

"A man with an Eastern European accent came in right after we opened."

"What did you tell him?"

"I told him I knew her, but that I haven't seen her lately."

"Did he ask anything else?"

"Is she in danger?" Bruno raised his eyebrows, concern obvious on his face.

"That's what I'm trying to figure out."

"He asked me to call a number if I see her." Bruno fished in his pocket and showed her a card. Leine glanced at the number, memorizing it as she did.

"Did he give you his name?"

Bruno shook his head. "No, but I've seen him before. You might want to talk to the owner, Manny."

At that moment, an older gentleman walked out of the backroom, carrying a case of wine on his shoulder. Silver hair framed a lined, intelligent face. His gray eyes matched his bushy eyebrows, and held a sparkle of humor. Leine liked him immediately.

"Manny," Bruno said. "This woman is asking about Gabriela. I told her about the man who came in this morning."

Manny's brows dipped together, and his demeanor changed. He set the box down. "And who might you be?" He said the words with a smile, but the wariness in his eyes told her a different story.

Leine held out her hand. "My name is Ava Basso. I own the bookstore in Old Town."

The sparkle returned, and he cupped her hand in his. "Ah. The American, yes?"

"Yes."

"I've been meaning to pay you a visit, but business has been brisk." He kissed her hand and raised his eyes heavenward. "Thank God. Usually, when the tourists leave, business goes with them." He turned somber as he pulled out a chair and sat across from her. "This man Bruno told you about—he is not a good man. I would steer clear of him if I were you."

"I'm afraid that's not possible."

"Oh? Why?"

"Let's just say I'm here to help. Could you describe him? Have you seen him before?"

"He was tall, with a thuggish air about him. I've never seen him before, but I believe he is one of the criminals who has taken up residence here."

"An associate of Jona?"

Manny looked at her in surprise. "Has Jona paid you a visit?"

She shook her head. "No, but I've been informed that it's only a matter of time. I haven't opened my store yet, so there's no money."

Manny sighed, sympathy evident on his face. "He calls it a *tributo*, a tax. This is normal in certain areas in Italy."

"Here?"

"No, not here. Not usually." He studied her, obviously uncertain how much he should divulge. "If he comes to the bookstore, you send him my way, yes? You should not have to pay someone protection money."

"Neither should you."

He smiled, the wrinkles of his sun- and wind-weathered face deepening as he did. "I agree." He spread his hands wide. "But what can I do? Violence is the only other option, and I'm too old to take a beating." He glanced at Bruno, who was busy stocking the wine from the box Manny had brought out. "And he is too young to learn such a lesson."

"What if I told you there's another way?"

"Then I would say go with God." He leaned closer, interest twinkling in his eyes. "Is there anything an old man can do?"

6

Leine had just turned out the lights in the backroom and was headed upstairs to bed when the security app on her phone chimed, indicating movement at the Mancinis'. She pulled up the video feeds. A white van idled in the street near the front of their house—the same white van Leine had seen the night of Eduardo's murder. The thugs hadn't wasted any time. She immediately called Tomaso to warn him, and was out the door and on her way in minutes.

Leine parked down the block from the restaurant and moved through the shadows toward the Mancinis' home. The two men were still inside the van, waiting. She paused in the shadows of a darkened doorway across the street, where she pulled a pair of night vision binoculars from her bag. Her suppressed pistol rode in a custom holster hidden by her coat.

Hopefully she wouldn't need it.

The scent of garlic wafted toward her from the open door of the restaurant as employees prepped for the next day. Leine called Tomaso to let him know she was in position. A few minutes later, he exited the restaurant and headed to the house.

Leine had told him to keep his mobile connection open so she could intervene quickly if things went sideways.

The thugs waited until he entered his home before both exited the van and walked to the front door, checking their surroundings as they did.

They were similar in size to the men who had disposed of Eduardo's body—one was taller and wore a familiar-looking hoodie, the other noticeably shorter with sloped shoulders.

Frick and Frack.

Leine slipped across the street to the van and placed a tracker on the chassis. The battery would be good for a few hours.

Tomaso answered their knock, his face a mask of politeness.

"We're looking for your niece, Gabriela," the shorter of the two said in passable Italian.

"I don't know where she is. May I tell her who is looking for her?"

"Our names aren't important." The one Leine had nicknamed Frick unzipped his jacket and spread it open. Tomaso took a step back.

"There's no need to threaten anyone." Anxiety laced Tomaso's voice.

Frick must have shown him a gun. Leine got ready to move. She assumed their visit was a scare tactic, one to inflict as much psychological damage as possible, priming him to give up information on Gabriela.

"That's up to you and your lovely wife."

Definitely a scare tactic, since Francesca wasn't home. At Tomaso's insistence, she'd left to stay at a friend's house after Leine installed the cameras.

"Leave my wife out of this."

Frick shoved Tomaso backward into the house. Frack followed and slammed the door shut.

"You don't *ever* talk to my associate like that, are we clear?" Frick's voice echoed through the cellphone.

"I—I didn't mean anything." Tomaso's composure appeared to be cracking.

"And where is your wife?"

"She's not here."

"I don't believe you. Make sure he doesn't go anywhere, Erwin."

"She's not here, I told you," Tomaso insisted.

"We'll see."

Leine placed her shoulder against the van and pushed. The van started to rock, minimally at first, but soon she had a good rhythm going, which tripped the van's security system. The lights flashed and the alarm shattered the serenity of the neighborhood with its ear-splitting warning. She ducked behind the van as an employee from the restaurant came out to see what was going on. Keeping the vehicle between her and the employee, she sprinted across the yard and melted into the shadows near the porch.

"What the fuck?" Frack growled. He'd slipped into his mother tongue. "Erwin—find out what's going on."

The door burst open, and Erwin appeared, keys in hand, mumbling what sounded like choice Albanian curse words. He raised the key fob and pointed it at the van. The alarm chirped, followed by silence. He squinted into the darkness.

Leine took a step toward him, but stopped as he moved off the porch toward the van.

"Stay here," Frack said to Tomaso over her earpiece.

Leine smiled at his annoyed tone. The front door opened, and Frack walked onto the porch.

"Well?" he called in a low voice.

"There is no one here," Erwin answered. "I don't know what set it off."

Fists curled, Frack descended the porch steps and strode to the van.

By now, several more employees from the restaurant had gathered outside to see what was going on. Frack grumbled something to Erwin, and the two climbed inside the van. After a short hesitation, the engine roared to life, and they drove away.

Leine waited until their taillights disappeared, then went inside the house.

"Tomaso?"

"Back here."

His voice came from down the hall, near the Mancinis' home office. Leine made her way to the room to find Tomaso zip tied to a desk chair. She quickly cut him loose.

"They're gone. For now."

Tomaso wiped his forehead with the back of his hand. "I thought he would kill me."

"Not until he's sure you don't have the information he needs. The only reason he didn't use you as bait for your wife is because there were too many witnesses who saw them outside."

"But what can we do?" Tomaso gestured toward the front door. "We have a business to run. I can't live my life afraid of criminals."

"Hopefully you won't have to."

"What does that mean?"

"Trust me. Would you be able to join your wife tonight? I'd like you to be somewhere else in case they decide to come back."

"Of course. When can we return?"

"Let's figure on tomorrow. If things don't go as planned, I'll let you know."

LEINE FOLLOWED THE BLINKING RED DOT OF THE VAN ON HER tracking software to a villa in the hills overlooking the town. A security camera covered the area from one of two brick pillars on each side of a wrought-iron gate. An ancient wall surrounded the property. The gate opened onto a meandering drive flanked by narrow cypress trees leading to a large home at the crest, its exterior punctuated by bright perimeter lights. The van was visible near the entrance.

She followed the brick wall until she found a place where the masonry had eroded enough to allow her to climb up and over the top. Staying low, she hiked the hillside through the barren vineyard to the villa, holding behind a cypress just short of the perimeter cameras covering the front from the roofline. She studied the camera positions, drawing a map in her mind of the probable dead spaces where the visuals likely wouldn't reach. Whoever designed the security had done a passable job.

Thankfully, there was room for improvement.

A gunman dressed in all-black and carrying an AK-47 appeared, checking the perimeter, his breath creating little clouds of condensation as he walked. Leine waited until he'd disappeared around the corner of the villa before she sprinted across the grounds to a side door.

She made quick work of the lock with her lock picks and slipped inside what turned out to be a cellar. A low, barrel-shaped ceiling arched above ancient stone floors. Dozens of bottles of wine stacked in alcoves surrounded her, and a wooden table stood in the center of the room with a decanter and several glasses. The scent of red wine permeated the space.

A quick scan through her night vision goggles revealed an interior door leading to the rest of the villa. Leine slipped through and followed the stone corridor to a set of shallow stairs that led into a cavernous kitchen with a large open fireplace. Dark wooden beams held well-used copper pots and pans hung from iron hooks. The pans looked like they hadn't seen a chef's hand since the turn of the century.

Leaving the kitchen, Leine followed another hallway toward the main part of the villa, past faded murals of sunflowers and olive groves, and crates of unlabeled wine bottles covered in cobwebs. Voices floated toward her from the other end of the hall, and she slowed, stopping near the doorway.

"—how many times, huh?"

Leine didn't recognize the man's voice, but he used the same dialect as the thugs on the beach.

"There were witnesses." Frack's voice.

"Since when did that stop you?" The other man scoffed.

"What do you want us to do?" Erwin asked.

"I want you to find the girl. Now."

Leine moved her position so she could see the three men. The third was tall and wiry with blond hair and a beak for a nose.

"We'll go back to the house tomorrow night," Frack said.

"Mancini is probably long gone by now. You said his wife wasn't home?"

"So he said. We didn't get a chance to look."

"Find out where she is. I assume she's not far—not with a business to run and her husband there."

"What do we do once we find her?"

The other man paced the room, obviously agitated. "Follow her. Do you really think she won't try to speak to her niece? With the Italians, family is everything."

"Good idea, boss."

"Of course it is. Now, what's happening with the tributes? I heard from Jona that the old man at the wine bar has been talking to the other business owners, telling them they should band together and not pay. You need to give him the same message as Angelo."

"His restaurant is popular, Lorik. How will he pay—"

Lorik picked up a half-full decanter from a side table and threw it against the wall. Red wine and shards of glass cascaded across the floor. "I don't give a fuck if the place has ten Michelin stars. Burn. It. Down."

"Yes, sir."

Both men started for the door.

"Donat. Wait."

The shorter of the two men stopped. Erwin left the room. So that was Frack's name.

"Yes?" Donat replied.

"Keep an eye on your brother. He's getting soft."

"You don't have to worry about Erwin, Mr. Rrahmani," Donat said. "He's loyal."

"You're sure?"

"I'm sure."

"You need to be. Understand?"

"Yes, sir. Understood."

"And next time, fuck the witnesses. If you scare them, they'll be more pliable."

"What about the police?"

"I'll handle the police."

"Yes, sir."

"Send someone in here to clean this shit up."

"Right away." Donat exited the room.

Leine slipped back down the hallway. Now wasn't the time to confront Rrahmani. She needed a plan before she did anything. And, she needed to warn Manny about the thug's orders to burn down his restaurant.

She was halfway through the cavernous kitchen when a door on the other side of the room opened. Leine pulled her gun free and ducked beneath the marble-topped wooden table as an armed gunman walked in and closed the door behind him. If he turned on the light, he'd see her. She didn't want to kill anyone, yet. And certainly not at the villa. That would only alert Lorik to her activity. In response, he'd likely grow paranoid and call in reinforcements, making the fight that was coming even more difficult. No telling how brutal he'd get.

Leine tracked the gunman through the NVGs as he walked past. He paused at the large refrigerator and opened the door. Leine closed her eyes to preserve her vision as light spilled across the brick flooring.

The gunman selected a beer, popped the top, and closed the door. Then he leaned his head back and guzzled the beer. Leine tensed, expecting him to turn around, maybe head for the table. A few agonizing seconds later, he crumpled the can and tossed it into a nearby trash bin, then exited the room.

Leine exhaled the breath she'd been holding and moved from under the table. She made it to the cellar and cracked the door open to the outside. The perimeter guard wasn't visible. Easing out of the house, she closed the door and sprinted back the way she came.

WHEN SHE GOT BACK TO THE BOOKSTORE, SHE CALLED LOU.

"Great to hear from you, Leine. How's small town life?"

Why does everyone ask me that? "I need intel on a small-time Albanian crime boss named Lorik Rrahmani. See what you can dig up."

"That good, huh?" Lou's sigh could have been heard across the Atlantic without the mobile. "I seem to remember a certain someone claiming she wanted to live a peaceful, uneventful life in Italy. What's going on?"

"The guy had somebody killed and he's extorting business owners in town. I want to stop him."

"Your bookstore?"

"I'm not open yet. But it's only a matter of time."

"Who'd he kill?"

"Why does that matter?"

"Well, if he killed another criminal, that's one thing."

"It was a young guy. According to his girlfriend, he wasn't a criminal."

"I'll do it if you promise me one thing."

"What's that?"

"Steer clear of this guy."

"Not gonna happen."

Another sigh. "I sense that you've already blown past the whole low profile thing."

"Come on, Lou. It's not my fault. I really, really, really want to make this work. But I can't stand by and let some douche bag run roughshod over innocent people."

"I get it. Give me a day or two. I'll see what I can find."

"Thanks, Lou. And keep this just between us, all right?"

"I take it you haven't read Santa in on the situation?"

"Yeah, that wouldn't be a good idea. The town's amazing—exactly what we're looking for. I just need to take care of business before he gets here."

"Ah. His arrival is imminent?"

"Less than two weeks."

"He retired?"

"No, it's just a visit. He's got a little over a year before he can pull the plug."

"Like I said, I'll see what I can dig up. But let me impart a nugget of wisdom from thirty-something years of marriage to the same woman. You don't want to start keeping secrets. That's a recipe for destroying a good thing."

"I know, Lou. Just this once, all right?"

"Yeah, all right. Just this once."

Leine ended the call and stared into space. He was right. She hated keeping things from Santa. But this was a blip on the radar screen of life. A small distraction. She'd take care of things, and all would be well.

Right?

7

Francesca Mancini's phone vibrated on the desk in front of her. She looked up from the lunch menu she was planning and glanced at the screen, but didn't recognize the number.

"Hello?"

"*Tita*? It's Gabriela."

Francesca's heart skipped a beat. "*Cara mia!* How are you? Tomaso and I have been so worried."

"I'm fine. I know I'm not supposed to call you, but I needed to hear your voice. Are you okay? Nothing bad has happened?"

"No, nothing bad happened. Your friend Ava has been helping us. She's been helping the whole town."

"They went after the town?" Gabby's anxiety was palpable.

"Don't worry, *cara mia*. Everything is under control." A small lie, but one to soothe her niece.

"Then I can come home?"

"I don't think quite yet." Francesca closed her eyes and took a deep breath, relieved that Gabriela was safe. "Do you need anything? Are you far?"

"I'm—no, I'm not far. I'm visiting Emma. Ava lent me money so I could stay away until things calm down."

"You're in Lucca?" Francesca did a quick search on her phone. "There is a train this afternoon. Tell me what you need, and I will bring it myself."

"Oh, *Tita*. I would love to see you. Are you sure it's safe?"

Francesca waved away her question. "I will make it safe." She hesitated before continuing. "I know about Eduardo," she whispered.

Gabriela's silence belied the emotions likely raging within her niece.

Francesca quickly changed the subject. "We'll talk about it once I get there, all right?"

"All right."

DONAT AND ERWIN BOARDED THE TRAIN TO LUCCA, TAKING SEATS in the car next to the one Francesca Mancini was in. Not that she'd be able to identify them. She wasn't at the house the night they confronted Tomaso, but Donat didn't want to take any chances. The two-hour ride would give the brothers plenty of time to plan their surveillance. Luckily for them, Francesca had gone back to the restaurant for some files before she returned to the home where she was staying. Once her whereabouts were established, she was easy to follow.

"Are you sure she's going to see her niece? What if this is a giant waste of time?" Erwin hadn't been convinced when Donat insisted on buying train tickets, and complained about the effort wasted going back and forth.

"What if she is and we didn't go? It's only an afternoon. Besides, our orders are to follow her." They'd shadow her to Lucca and see what she did. If the trip turned out to be some sort of buying spree for the restaurant or a visit to a friend of Francesca's, then they'd catch the next train back to Scivoloso.

Erwin fell silent. The look on his face told Donat he'd go along but he wasn't happy about it.

Two hours later, the train pulled into the station and the passengers disembarked. Donat and Erwin followed Francesca at a discreet distance for the better part of an hour, past storefronts and through small crowds of late season tourists. The Mancini woman mainly window-shopped, occasionally ducking into a store, then reappearing empty-handed except for once, when she emerged with a large shopping bag.

Disappointed that Francesca appeared to have traveled to Lucca on a shopping spree, Donat concluded Erwin was correct —this time. He checked the train schedule on his phone, unwilling to listen to his brother complain one more minute about being stuck in Lucca. He was about to purchase tickets when Francesca stopped and glanced at her phone. She typed something and waited, then typed something again. After a brief moment, she slipped her phone into her purse and started walking with a determined stride.

Donat exchanged a glance with his brother. "The niece might have messaged her."

They followed Francesca along the cobblestone streets through the center of town, keeping far enough back so that if she looked, she'd only see tourists. A few blocks later, she turned left onto a feeder lane that led to the bike and walking path encircling the walled section of the city.

She moved at a steady pace along the gravel pathway and eventually stopped at one of the benches scattered along the top of the Renaissance-era wall. Donat and Erwin loitered several meters away, stopping behind a line of trees for cover.

They didn't have long to wait.

A young woman dressed in a light overcoat and blue scarf

appeared, heading toward Francesca. She resembled the picture of the woman on the screensaver of the phone Donat had found near the beach when they killed Eduardo.

"It's her." Donat slid his phone from his pocket and texted Lorik, telling him where they were and asking him if he wanted them to take care of both women. The reply was swift.

Be sure there are no witnesses.

Donat pocketed his phone. "He wants us to take care of them both. No witnesses."

Erwin nodded. "I'm sorry I doubted you, Donat."

"Don't worry about it. It was a fifty-fifty chance either way."

The two women embraced, then sat on the bench. Francesca reached into the large shopping bag and pulled out a package, which she handed to the younger woman. Gabriela smiled and gave her aunt another hug.

After several minutes of watching them interact, Erwin said, "We're going to be here a while, aren't we?"

Donat shrugged. "We can't do it here." He waved at the bicyclists and pedestrians passing them. "Too many witnesses. If we have to wait, we wait."

Over an hour went by, and their quarry still hadn't moved. Clearly, the two women had much to catch up on. Donat scrolled through his Instagram account on his phone, while Erwin played a game on his. No one would notice two men sitting on a bench immersed in their phones.

A group of several people walked past, and Donat scanned their faces. He recognized one of them and nudged Erwin. "It's the old man from the wine bar." He nodded at the silver-haired man on the outside of the group. "Does the guy he's talking to look familiar?"

Erwin glanced at him and nodded. "Yeah. I think he's the owner of the bakery in Scivoloso."

"What are they doing here?" Donat watched as the group

crowded around the Mancini women. "What the fuck?" Alarmed, he stood to get a better look and keep track of Gabriela and Francesca.

The group moved away from the bench with Gabriela and Francesca in the center. Donat and Erwin followed at a distance. The group turned off the main pathway and headed down a different feeder lane to the center of town. Donat and Erwin trailed them through town to a parking lot just outside the ancient wall, where they all squeezed into a full-sized van. The older man climbed into the drivers' seat. The engine rumbled to life and the group drove off, leaving Donat and Erwin staring after them.

"Dammit." Donat stopped himself from throwing his phone in a fit of pique. He took a deep breath and let it go.

"How did they know?" Erwin looked mystified.

"Obviously the Mancini woman texted someone to help her. She must have made us on the train."

"But how? She has never seen us."

"I don't know." He checked the time. "The drive from Scivoloso is a little over an hour."

"Then we should have taken a car instead of the train."

Donat narrowed his eyes at his brother. "How would I know she'd be able to just drive off? Normally that's not the case when a person takes the train."

Erwin shrugged. "Lorik says we always have to be a step ahead."

"Fuck Lorik." Donat spat in the dirt. "We'll have to watch her more closely."

"She's going to be suspicious, which will make her more careful."

"You think I'm stupid?" Donat cuffed his younger brother upside the head. Erwin gave him an annoyed look. "I'll figure something out."

"Sure, Donat." Erwin turned and started walking.

"Where are you going?"

"Back to Scivoloso."

Leine read the text from Francesca and breathed a sigh of relief. The plan worked. The group that had gone to Lucca to help Francesca and Gabriela were due back in an hour. Manny was keeping an eye out for anyone tailing them, but so far he hadn't seen anything suspicious. They dropped Gabriela off at her friend's house with her promise to go to Rome and lie low until someone let her know it was safe to return.

When Francesca noticed the two thugs from the surveillance video watching her and Gabriela from behind a line of trees, she'd texted Leine, and Leine called Manny. They quickly devised a plan to exfiltrate the two women, with Manny using his delivery van to haul the rescue group to Lucca. The plan hinged on the assumption that Lorik would be averse to witnesses after Eduardo. That assumption had paid off.

With that crisis averted, Leine went back to working on the bookstore's security. Funny how she felt less safe in a small town in Italy than in sprawling Los Angeles. But Scivoloso itself was perfect. The views, the people, the proximity to the Mediterranean and Tuscany, her historic bookstore with the funky apartments on the upper floor. She'd always dreamed of a slow-paced lifestyle, one that held just enough adventure to keep things fresh. She thought a small town would deliver that dream.

She'd been wrong.

She finished what she was doing and went upstairs. Now for the tricky part. She grabbed a canvas pack and a length of rope lying on the bed, then climbed through the attic and onto the roof, using an old access door someone had constructed decades before. Careful of the slick tiles, she tied herself off to the old brick chimney so a misstep wouldn't send her careening into the sea below.

Sunshine warmed her back as she worked, and the salty sea air helped clear her head. A slight breeze ruffled her hair. She stopped what she was doing and marveled at the view.

Maybe she'd have a rooftop terrace built once everything settled down. She went back to her work, testing her idea when she was finished. Satisfied her theory was sound, she gathered her tools, stuffed them into the pack, and untied herself from the chimney. Hopefully she wouldn't have to use her invention, but at least it was there if she did.

8

———

"Why haven't you burned that fucking restaurant down?" The gray sky outside the villa window matched Lorik's foul mood.

Donat kept his eyes down, unwilling to meet his boss's gaze. "It's been... challenging."

"Oh, really? Like what? Did Superman show up and blow out the flames?"

"No, but each time we tried, someone extinguished the fire."

Lorik rolled his eyes. "So they've posted a sentry or something. Put that shit on a delayed timer. No one will see if no one is there."

"We tried that."

"This is not rocket science, Donat. Use explosives if you have to."

"You want us to destroy the building?" That didn't make sense. Where would the tribute come from if there was no restaurant?

"Of course not, idiot." Lorik waved at the air. "Just...fuck with his inventory or something. Break his glassware, steal his wine.

Unless you'd rather break bones." He peered closely at Donat. "I didn't think so."

"He's an old man. What would that accomplish?"

"Old men can transmit fear. Fear will bring the others in line."

"Action can also invite loyalty." To Donat, taking advantage of an old man didn't show strength.

"Are you getting soft on me, too? You fucked up the hit on the Mancini women. What am I supposed to think?"

Donat shook his head, ignoring the jab regarding their failure in Lucca. "It's not soft to do things in a way that evokes fear but also keeps the town from a full mutiny."

"Oh? And how do you intend to do this?"

"Cut off the head of the snake." Donat leaned forward in his chair. "Jona's informant says everything changed when the American arrived."

"So he thinks she's the cause of the town banding together?"

"He does."

"Why? She's an American expat who moved to Italy for the romance of it. There are thousands like her."

"Because now they are refusing to pay. And because they were able to thwart our attack on the Mancinis. Before the woman arrived, did you have trouble collecting from them?"

"You have a point." Lorik studied Donat. "Have you contacted her yet? Get her to pay up and I guarantee the rest of them will fall into line."

"She hasn't opened her store yet. Jona's tried, but she's slippery, like an eel. She's never there."

"Bullshit," Lorik sneered. "She's hiding from him. Break in if you have to. Scare the hell out of her. Demand the money. If she doesn't pay, hurt her. Just enough. We make the rules."

Donat smiled. Foreigners were always fair game, even though she was a woman. Brutality visited upon an American who acted like a cowboy would create the desired results in the rest of the town. This ought to be fun.

"My thoughts, exactly."

LEINE SLID THE LAST BOOK FROM THE RECENT SHIPMENT INTO place on the bookshelf and glanced at her watch. Mid-morning. The feeds for the Mancinis' and Manny's restaurants had been quiet—for now. She had no doubt Lorik would try again. She just wasn't sure which method he'd use.

Thanks to the quick response team, or QRT, that Manny and Leine had put together, Lorik's attempts at burning down Manny's restaurant hadn't achieved the outcome Lorik anticipated. It stood to reason he would attempt some other kind of extortion.

The question was, what? She'd ensured every business owner in town had a direct line to Manny's mobile, which initiated cascading alerts to each member of the QRT. Within minutes, Lorik's intended victim would be joined by a dozen or more townspeople, all intent on repelling the attack, whether that meant extinguishing a fire or showing up in force to intimidate Jona.

So far, it had worked brilliantly. Just like it had in Lucca.

But criminals were like a virus—their approaches mutated. Leine had warned everyone there might be an escalation in Lorik's tactics.

Leine picked up the now-empty box. She turned toward the back room for another set of books when there was a knock at the door. A man she didn't recognize dressed in a bulky camouflage jacket motioned for her to open the door. His smile didn't put her at ease.

She set the box down and went to the door.

"We're not open," she said through the glass, pointing to the sign on the door.

"I have message for you," he answered in English.

"From who?"

"Open the door."

Leine shook her head. "Sorry. Come back when we're open."

The man's expression hardened. He opened his coat to reveal a holstered gun.

Apparently, his boss had figured out where the town organizing had originated.

Leine widened her eyes and stepped back, working the scared-as-shit angle. "I haven't done anything wrong," she protested, shaking her head.

"Open the door, now, or I shoot."

There was no way he'd risk the attention from a gunshot in broad daylight, but a typical American expat likely wouldn't know that. Still acting scared, Leine quickly unlocked the door and took several steps back as he entered.

"What do you want?"

The man closed the door and pulled the shade down. He drew his gun and said, "You have become—how do you say? A thorn in my boss's foot."

"Side." When he gave her a blank look, she added, "A thorn in your boss's side."

He waved his gun. "Whatever. You must pay. Now."

Leine shook her head. "I'm not open for business. There's no money."

"I don't care. And neither does my boss." He narrowed his eyes and moved closer.

Leine held up her hands and took another step back, feeling for the edge of the runner beneath her feet. "Look, maybe we can work something out."

"You will pay." He shrugged. "Or you will die. This is all we will 'work out.'" He stepped toward her, his feet firmly on the rug.

Perfect.

Lightning-fast, Leine seized his gun, aimed, and fired. The gunman's eyes rolled back as the bullet entered his brain and he collapsed to the floor.

Leine slid the weapon into her waistband and grabbed the edge of the rug, dragging it and the dead gunman into the back room.

She'd barely made it through the doorway when the bells over the front door jangled.

"Ava?"

Oh, for fuck's sake.

"I'm coming," Leine called.

Leine closed the door to the back room and walked to the front of the store. Her visitor was Nadia, the elderly woman who owned the gelateria next door.

"Hi, Nadia."

Wisps of white hair had escaped the confines of the bright green headband Nadia wore, giving her the look of an absent-minded professor. Perhaps an inch over five feet tall, she was breathing hard as she gripped the door frame. Concerned, Leine helped her inside and closed the door. Nadia pulled her into a surprisingly firm embrace.

"Ava! I'm so glad you're all right." She held Leine at arm's length. "I thought I heard... there was a loud bang and I—" Her words came out in a stream of excited Italian punctuated by little gasps as she attempted to catch her breath.

Leine gently extricated herself from the hug, and wiped her hand at the perspiration that had formed on her forehead from dragging a dead body several feet. "You're sweet to check on me. I must have had my music on too loud while I was cleaning. What did it sound like?"

"Like a gunshot." Nadia's normal coloring had returned, and her breathing was rapidly approaching normal.

Leine scanned the street through the bay window. "Could it have been a car backfiring?"

"Maybe." Nadia looked doubtful. She took a deep breath and let it go. "Ever since we began to fight back against the *criminales,* I've just been so nervous." She wrung her hands. "It's like the stories my parents told me of the war." She said the last in a whisper, as though afraid to stir up ghosts from the past.

"Thank you for your concern, Nadia." Leine wrapped her arm around her shoulders and led her to the door. "But I'm fine."

"Yes. Yes, I can see that. Thank God." She made a sign of the cross and kissed her fingers. She glanced around the bookstore. "Can I help with anything? I may be old, but I'm strong." Nadia raised her arm and flexed. Her bicep bulged a couple centimeters and she grinned.

"Thank you, but no," Leine replied with a smile, and gently herded her out the door. "It's just a little cleaning and some finishing touches."

"So you will open soon?"

"We'll see. That's the plan, though."

"Please don't hesitate to call if you need anything." Nadia gave Leine a meaningful look. "If it wasn't for you, I don't think the town would have had the balls to band together to fight the bastards. You've given us all courage."

"You've got it backwards. I draw my courage from all of you."

Nadia waved at her words. "Nonsense. Everyone here appreciates what you've done."

Leine's smile faded as Nadia left. She closed the door and made sure it was locked before returning to the back room and the dead gunman. Luckily, the blood hadn't quite soaked through the rug. Using leftover bricks from the remodel, she duct-taped several to the body and then taped the rug around the dead gunman for good measure. Then she got the package into position and opened the trap door.

With a pang of regret for the ruined floor covering, she heaved the body through the opening. For a moment, it hung up on a lip of limestone before it dislodged and landed with a splash in the sea. Leine made a mental note to chip away the rock in case she needed to use the trap door again.

Good thing it was high tide.

9
———

Lorik slammed his fist on the table. "Where's Jona?"

Donat cleared his throat. "We haven't heard from him since yesterday."

Erwin clasped his hands in front of him and took a step closer to his brother. A guarded look passed between them.

"I thought I told you to take care of the American." Lorik gestured in the general vicinity of his laptop. "I haven't been paid shit."

"Have you tried his mobile?" Erwin asked.

"Of course I tried it, you fucking moron." Lorik's expression darkened, giving Donat the impression that his boss was rethinking his brother's use of oxygen.

"Jona asked to be the one to shake her down."

"And did you back him up?"

Donat shook his head. "He didn't think it was necessary."

Lorik narrowed his eyes. "Why is that?"

"Because she's a woman," Erwin offered. Donat elbowed his brother, hard. *Don't bait the boss.*

"Really?" Lorik exclaimed. "My mother is 'just a woman.' She's a better shot than I am."

Erwin's nervous laugh told Donat he realized his mistake. "But she's an *American* woman. Not Albanian, like your mother."

Lorik frowned at the younger man, disbelief on his face. "You do know that America has more guns than people, right?"

Erwin muttered that he did.

Lorik gave Donat a warning look. "Go to the American, find out what happened to Jona. Use any means necessary."

"Any?"

"If she gives you trouble, kill her and dump the body somewhere she won't be found." Lorik shrugged. "She'll be just another expat who couldn't deal with the slow pace of village life."

LEINE CHECKED THE SECURITY FEEDS FOR THE MANCINIS' restaurant. Then she scanned Manny's. All appeared quiet. That wouldn't last. She doubted Lorik would give up easily. Especially now that his collections manager had disappeared. No doubt he'd pull out all the stops in an attempt at compliance. She'd told Manny that Jona would no longer be a problem, but warned that Lorik would be out for revenge. Manny had made sure everyone in town was on high alert.

She turned off the lamp next to the bed and closed her eyes, intending to catch some rest before Lorik's next salvo.

A short time later, the sound of glass breaking jolted her awake.

Someone was downstairs.

She glanced at the tablet on her nightstand displaying the feed covering her front door. Broken glass covered the entrance floor. Leine frowned in annoyance. She'd have to order a replacement.

Two shadowy figures with suppressed pistols could be seen

moving through the bookstore. They looked familiar, although they wore balaclavas. One was tall, the other short and stocky with sloped shoulders, like a bull.

With the security app open on her phone, Leine rose from the bed, grabbed her own suppressed semiauto from under her pillow, and slipped behind the door to wait.

Squeak.

One of the intruders had just hit the third step of the staircase.

Squeak.

Now the sixth.

It wouldn't be long.

The feed on her phone showed the stocky one moving through the bookstore, headed for the back room. She had a full magazine with a round in the chamber and the element of surprise. The guy coming up the stairs would be easy.

The one below, perhaps not so much. That depended on how hard the first fell.

The landing groaned softly, the weight of the prowler more than the old floorboards could bear. Leine raised her weapon and waited.

The man eased through the doorway, gun first, and turned toward the bed. Leine shot him in the head, stepping in to ease his fall onto the runner covering the floor. Though tall and thin, the man was solidly built. Blood coursed from the hole in his temple, and she sighed. There went another rug.

She shot him once more for insurance, then turned him over.

It was Erwin, Donat's younger brother.

Which meant Donat was likely in the shop below.

Leine headed downstairs, careful to step on the outside of the treads so they wouldn't creak and give up her position.

At the bottom she waited, listening to the other man moving through her back room, looking for what, she didn't know.

Easing around the doorway, Leine crept up behind him. He straightened, sensing her presence. Leine shot him twice, wincing as he sprawled forward onto her desk, then fell back, dragging everything on it with him to the floor.

She rolled him onto his back and confirmed the second gunman was indeed Donat. She hadn't seen a third gunman on the video feed, but that didn't mean there weren't more outside.

Leine stepped around Donat and moved quietly through the doorway into the bookstore. A cold breeze blew through the broken door glass—the privacy shade billowed with each gust. Glass shards crunched underfoot as she moved to the front door. A white van, similar to the one Donat and Erwin had used the night of Eduardo's murder as well as the night of the attempted shakedown at the Mancinis', was parked at the top of the street. The darkened interior made it difficult to see if someone else was inside.

Leine went to the back room to grab her coat and body armor, then walked outside into the street. She paused for a moment, giving any occupants time to see her, then strode toward the van, suppressed gun in her hand.

She'd gone several steps when the engine turned over and the headlights blinked on. She stopped as the van pulled a U-turn in the middle of the street and drove away.

So there had been a third gunman. Why hadn't he come inside with Donat and Erwin? Was he acting as a getaway driver? Leine headed back to her shop. Time to install additional insurance.

It was going to be a long night.

10

The clock read four-thirty by the time Leine managed to haul the first gunman down the stairs to the trap door. Thankfully, she still had the furniture mover disks she'd used on her couch and dresser. Combined with the floor runner, Erwin was surprisingly easy to move.

She took her time dragging him down the stairs, wincing each time his head hit. Since Nadia, the woman from the gelateria, didn't live above her own shop, there wasn't anyone nearby to hear. It took another forty-five minutes to weight both corpses with bricks, secure the rugs, and shove them through the hole in her floor.

She watched with satisfaction as both bodies dropped without hanging up on the rock chute and splashed into the Mediterranean. The time and effort involved in chiseling away at the lip of limestone had paid for itself. She closed the trap door and wiped at the perspiration on her forehead.

Half an hour later, Leine finished securing the nail-studded two-by-four to the ceiling of the stairwell and stowed the ladder back in the downstairs closet. She checked the trip wire for the correct amount of tension.

Perfect. She'd tackle the breakaway for the trap door tomorrow.

Now for the hard part.

Armed with a bucket, a wire brush, and a bottle of bleach, she tackled the blood stains on the floor. Forty-five minutes later, she stepped back to assess her work.

Although faint, the stains on the old wooden planks were there to stay. The bleach had helped, but a Rorschach remained, marring the caramel-colored oak. She could order another set of rugs to cover them, but what would Santa think? No stranger to blood spatter, the detective would likely guess it was fresh-ish. She'd have to think of an explanation.

As if on cue, her phone chimed, indicating a video call from Santa.

She checked her reflection in the tea kettle and wiped a splotch of blood from her cheek. Then she answered the call with a smile.

"Hey there."

"Hey." Santa smiled back at her.

Leine curled up in the chair near the desk, careful to keep the screen on her so he wouldn't see the cleaning supplies.

"You look healthy," Santa remarked. "Village life must agree with you."

She pushed her hair back from her sweaty face and nodded. "Yeah. I just finished a bit of a workout."

"Running on the beach?"

"Something like that." She eyed the bloodstain, estimating the size of the rug she'd need. She could always replace the floor.

Santa leaned in close. "You know, I've been fantasizing about you on a beach lately..."

"Do tell."

The conversation veered into risqué territory, giving Leine a much-needed reprieve. She never liked lying to Santa. Maybe she'd fess up when he got there. It's not like he didn't know about her past.

Maybe.

Evidently, you could take the girl out of the assassin, but you couldn't take the assassin out of the girl.

"Who the fuck is this woman?" Lorik sputtered as he paced the villa's living room.

Dark beams loomed overhead, scarring the ceiling, pressing down on Nestor Popov. Strangely, a feeling of claustrophobia hit him whenever he stood inside the massive room.

Lorik's face had flushed an alarming shade of crimson. "Why didn't you back up Donat and Erwin?"

Nestor's cheeks heated. "They told me to stay with the van, that they would take care of things. They wanted me to keep the van running, in case they needed to leave quickly."

"Obviously they were wrong." He glared at him. "What the fuck were you thinking?"

"I'm sorry, boss. I will make it up to you, I promise." Neither of the brothers' bodies had been recovered, so there was a tiny chance they were still alive. But Nestor didn't think so. Not after he caught sight of the American with the pistol heading toward the van. Memories flooded back from a night long ago, when he'd worked for a powerful arms trafficker by the name of Nikolai Abramov.

The Leopard.

He'd thought she was long dead. They all did. He'd actually tried to talk himself out of what he'd seen. Except he couldn't shake the shiver of fear he felt when he recognized her.

At the time, leaving with the van seemed the safest option.

"And just how are you going to make it up to me?" Lorik narrowed his eyes.

"I know who she is."

"You what?"

"Remember Nikolai Abramov? The London warehouse fire back in 2000?"

Lorik nodded, his annoyance obvious. "Yes. Of course."

"I was there when she killed Abramov's men."

"The Leopard is here? That can't be." Lorik scoffed. "She died years ago."

"I thought the same. It was a lie."

Lorik studied Nestor. "If this is true, then we have a larger problem than I thought."

"Let me make a phone call. There is someone who would be very interested in learning where she is."

"Who?"

"I can't tell you that."

"This person, how powerful is he? I can't take the chance of awakening a giant that may end up destroying my operation just to get revenge."

"Are you saying that you want to take care of this yourself?" Did Lorik understand what he was up against?

"That is exactly what I'm saying." Lorik waved his concerns away, obviously unconvinced of the threat the Leopard posed. "You work for me, yes?"

Nestor nodded.

"Then you must do as I say. If there is leverage to be had, it will be mine. You must tell me this person's name, and I will see how much they want the woman."

"Let me do some research. Find out where he is. I haven't spoken with him in years. He may not even be alive."

"As soon as you locate him, let me know." Lorik rubbed his hands together. "This disaster may well turn out to my advantage yet. In the meantime, set up a meeting with the woman. Here."

"She'll want to meet somewhere neutral."

"Fine," Lorik grunted. "Find a place that appears neutral but allows us to have the upper hand."

Nestor assured Lorik he'd do his best, then left the villa, relieved to be away from Lorik and the oppressive beams.

Fuck Lorik. Nestor knew exactly where the man was. And this man would definitely pay a high price to find out the Leopard's location. If Nestor handled things right, he'd be able to retire anywhere he liked, could leave behind all the killing and thuggery.

No longer an energetic, ambitious young man, Nestor was getting tired. He thought of the place he'd recently bought with his earnings—the one on the lake back home. He wanted to spend his days fishing and drinking. He'd earned that, surely.

But he was Lorik's man. Quitting was not an option. To quit such an organization meant death, either during a job, or by the hand of one of the boss's men.

Inside his car, he opened his console, selected one of the three burner phones inside, and placed the call.

11

T he crumbling walls of the small chapel still retained some of their earlier glory. The stained-glass windows had long been broken or removed, but vivid blues and yellows still graced the masonry. The arched, moss-covered ceilings testified to a grandeur long forgotten, as did the few niches where oil paintings or tapestries once hung. A spear of sunlight illuminated a stone tomb complete with a cast replica of some forgotten nobleman, greenery sprouting along its broken and dusty surface, becoming indistinguishable from the surrounding forest. A nuthatch scuttled headfirst down a vine leading from an empty window to the floor.

Lorik's man, Nestor, had delivered the request to meet with directions to the abandoned structure earlier that morning. Leine arrived early to recon the terrain.

A sunny but cool day, the brilliant blue sky belied the storms that had threatened the coastal town in previous days. The hike to the top of the wooded hill invigorated her. She'd never have known the chapel was there without directions. The current landowners had let nature claim the structure for her own.

Leine did a perimeter check, skirting the weeds and shrubs

growing near the building. She took note of several spots where Lorik's men could hide, working through exit strategies in case the meeting went sideways.

All in all, a decent meeting place. Although Lorik would have an advantage in numbers, Leine had the advantage of his miscalculation. He didn't know her background. Most likely he thought of her as some kind of anomaly—a silly American who believed she could stand up to him and his thugs.

Leine loved it when people underestimated her.

Lou's research had unearthed few details on Lorik and his operation. A small-time hustler, in 2016 Lorik Rrahmani had committed some kind of faux pas and been prevented from initiating larger plays by a boss higher up in the organizational chain. Still, a guy had to make a living. Thanks to his patron's connections to one of the Italian mafia families, as long as Lorik didn't bother the big boys, he was allowed to operate his little fiefdom in northern Italy.

She checked the time. Lorik and his men would arrive shortly. She set her pack down and selected a short-barrelled MP5K submachine gun, a 9mm pistol, and plenty of ammunition—weapons she hoped she wouldn't have to use—and hid them in the chapel.

A girl had to be prepared.

At the sound of a vehicle approaching, Leine walked outside. A black Suburban parked at the foot of the rise leading to the chapel. Lorik and three gunmen got out and headed toward her.

Leine waited as they huffed their way to the top. Lorik was the only one of the four who didn't look winded.

"You must be Lorik."

"And you must be Ava." He carried himself with studied nonchalance, but his body language told her he was primed for confrontation. He nodded to the man on his left. "Search her."

Leine held out her arms as Lorik's man patted her down. He finished and stepped back. "She's clean."

"Check inside."

Two of his men did as he asked. Several minutes later, they reappeared.

"Clear."

Leine let out a quiet breath. She'd hidden the hardware well, but one of them could've gotten lucky.

Lorik gestured toward the chapel. "Shall we?"

The three gunmen positioned themselves at different points near the open doorways, while Leine and Lorik walked to the center of the space, near the tomb. The nuthatch was long gone.

Lorik stopped and crossed his arms. "What happened to my men?"

"Right to the point. I like that." Leine crossed her arms, mirroring him. "I don't know where your men are." It was the truth. Once their bodies hit the Med, she had no idea where the current took them.

"Why don't I believe you?"

Leine shrugged. "Look. For whatever reason, they're gone. They shouldn't have broken into my store. By the way, you owe me a new door."

"You have balls, I'll give you that. I must admit, though, your judgment seems to be off."

"And what would lead you to conclude that?"

"Common sense would dictate that you bow to the superior force." He waved his hand at his men. "Four against one."

"Looks can be deceiving."

Doubt lit his face for a moment, then disappeared. "I'm going to quote one of your American movies. This here town ain't big enough for the both of us."

Leine stifled a smile at the Albanian's attempt at a Western accent. "I agree. I take it you'll be leaving soon?"

"I'm not interested in negotiating."

"I didn't say I wanted to negotiate. I'm here because you requested a meeting. Negotiation was never mentioned."

"Do you want me to destroy the town?" He leaned forward, his expression turning dark. "Because I will if you continue to obstruct my business."

"Now who's lacking common sense? If you destroy the town, you destroy your source of revenue."

"The town has banded together to fight against me. You're like a fucking union or something." He shook his head, his annoyance obvious. "There is nothing else I can do."

"They don't deserve to be robbed. Making a living is hard enough. What you're doing isn't sustainable. You're overstepping your bounds."

"This works in other places. How do you think I made it to where I am today?"

No points for the lame bluff. Time for a lesson in economics.

"Do you offer anything in return in those other places? The more you demand 'tribute' without anything in return, the less reward there is for someone to accept your terms. The workers will eventually revolt. Soon, the only thing left will be the buildings. Shops will close. People will leave. No one likes to be coerced." Time for the carrot. "You're a successful businessman. Surely you see that?"

Lorik waved at her words. "You don't know what you're talking about. This is how it's done."

"Your method is not sustainable. The only way to make taxation palatable is to give something in return. Even Don Corleone offered help and protection when people needed it." She studied him. By the look on his face her reference to the movie *The Godfather* had landed. "What can you give the people of Scivoloso that will make them happy to pay? If there's nothing, then there's nothing for you here. The town banding together against you is not your problem. It's a symptom of something far deeper. If you take without giving, you're a thief, not a patron. Wouldn't you rather people relied on you for something other than fear?"

"Fear works."

Leine gave him a look. "Not well. And not for long."

"Fine. Say you are right. What do you suggest?"

"I think we're past that, don't you? You've already shown them how far you'll go to bring them to heel. There's no coming back from that."

"My men contained the fire at the grocery. No one was hurt."

"I'm talking about Eduardo."

Lorik froze. "Who?"

"The man your thugs killed."

"Who told you this?" He narrowed his eyes.

"That's not important. Several in town are aware you resorted to murder. Why, no one knows. But you can see how that puts a damper on things."

"This is because of that bitch," Lorik muttered, his face flushing red.

"See, that kind of attitude isn't going to endear you to the townspeople." Leine edged closer to the tomb. "I'm not sure what 'bitch' you mean, but you see my point, yes?"

"Ah. It was you who disappeared the girlfriend." He nodded, the light dawning. "I wondered why we couldn't find her. You were also behind the rescue in Lucca."

Leine ignored his accusations. "Why have the kid killed? What could you possibly gain?"

"I didn't."

"Well, it sure wasn't the assassin fairy. C'mon, Lorik. Someone saw your men that night. Your excuse doesn't fly."

"The girlfriend, yes?"

"I didn't say that."

Lorik sighed. "My men were moonlighting."

"You hire them out? To whom?"

"I didn't say that."

"It was implied."

"Enough." Lorik turned to his men. "Kill her."

Leine dove behind the tomb. Rounds thudded against the stone, gouging and chipping at the masonry. She hit the floor and ripped the submachine gun from under the vines, then slid the switch to full auto, crawled to the far end, and came up shooting.

She caught them by surprise. The first gunman fell where he stood. She shot the second as he scrambled for cover. The third gunman dove behind the crumbling masonry walls. He grunted. She'd hit him.

Lorik had disappeared.

Leine moved low and fast behind a marble column with a better location and scanned the room. Everything had gone eerily quiet. No birds, no movement. She took a couple controlled breaths to calm the adrenaline coursing through her and waited.

Someone clapped.

"Impressive." Lorik's voice echoed through the space. "You have killed two of my men, and wounded another. So. Where do we go from here?"

"How about you move to another town?" Leine peered around the column. Lorik's shadow spilled across the floor from the arched doorway to her left.

"How about you join my organization?"

Leine chuckled. "Nice try."

"You obviously have superior skills. Your compensation would be generous."

"You're seriously trying to recruit me right now?" Leine shook her head. "How often does that work?"

"You'd be surprised."

"Tell you what. You leave town, leave the people alone, and I'll let you and your thug live."

"No."

"You should really take my offer," she warned. "I'm going to keep coming after you until you're either dead or you leave."

"I have invested a lot of money into my house. My vineyard is producing some of the best wine in the region."

"So sell it. The market's good. You'll make a mint."

"No."

"Are we going to do this? Really?" She checked her watch. "I don't have all day, and neither do you."

"Why do you say that?"

"Because moving your operation is going to take time, and you need to be gone in ten days." Before Santa arrived from L.A.

"You're giving me a deadline?" Lorik laughed. "I will call my powerful friends to help. You don't want to awaken a sleeping tiger."

"You don't have powerful friends, Lorik. If you did, you wouldn't be trying to carve out a living in a small town on the coast of Italy."

Silence. She'd hit a nerve.

"You don't know what you're talking about."

"Come on, Lorik. Leave the town alone. Surely there's something else you could do, somewhere else?" She needed to tread carefully. Although a tiny cog in a larger wheel, Lorik was still likely connected to someone powerful. No one conducted business in a vacuum. It wasn't the Eastern European way. If she didn't let him save face, that could bring unwanted attention to the town.

And to her.

"Let's make a deal."

"You're not really in a position to negotiate," Leine said, "but go ahead."

"I stay in my villa, but take my business to another town. You leave me alone, and I'll leave your precious Scivoloso alone."

"What kind of guarantee do I have that you'll uphold your end?"

"I am a man of my word."

Leine laughed. "Yeah, and I'm the President of the United States. Not gonna happen."

"You will just have to see. I will cease all operation in Scivoloso. But you must forget I exist."

Time to end the negotiation. "I may regret this, but let's give it a shot." Letting him get on with his life would be better than stirring up a nest of viperous oligarchs.

Maybe now she'd be able to get the damned bookstore open.

12

———

"Did you find the information?" Lorik paced his living room, growing more agitated with each step.

Ignoring the claustrophobic pressure of the heavy beams above him, Nestor shook his head. "The man is a ghost. I think perhaps he is dead." He wasn't about to give up information on the man who wanted to find the Leopard. Not with the finder's fee Nestor had been promised once she was dead.

Lorik stared through the expansive windows to the vineyard below. "We must get rid of her, but it can't be traced back to me. I don't know her connections. A woman like that must have powerful friends."

"I told you what her capabilities were." Nestor let the sentence hang in the air. Even with his warning, Lorik had underestimated her at the chapel.

Lorik stopped and turned on Nestor. "She killed my men." His breath came fast. "She has humiliated me."

"You said you agreed to a truce. Why not lull her into believing this fiction? Then eliminate her when she's not expecting it."

"Because I lose money every day that I don't collect."

Nestor shrugged. "What is more important? Money or revenge?" He had to delay Lorik from killing the American woman. If he did succeed in killing her, Nestor's anticipated payday would evaporate.

Lorik sighed. "You have a point. What is more important than honor?"

Nestor breathed a silent sigh of relief. He'd bought some time.

AFTER NESTOR LEFT, LORIK RETURNED TO HIS OFFICE. THE CHIEF of police was where he'd left him, in the chair opposite his desk.

"Shall we continue our conversation?" Tito De Luca asked. The scent of garlic and wine mingled with the heavyset man's overly sweet cologne—not a pleasant combination.

"Of course. Where were we?"

"You were about to explain why we shouldn't shut you down?"

Lorik nodded. "I understand your concerns, Tito, but you don't need to worry. Our agreement still stands. We've just encountered a small hiccup."

"You must take care of the American. Since she came to town things have deteriorated."

"I've got it under control."

"Do you really?" De Luca leaned forward. "My men are complaining. The cost of living is high."

"Haven't I taken care of your problems? That boy, what was his name?"

"Eduardo."

"Yes, Eduardo. Is he no longer a problem?"

"Yes, but there is still the issue with the Mancini girl."

Lorik waved his concern away. "She will be dealt with."

"And how is that? Do you even know where she is?"

"I am very close." He wasn't, but it would do no good to inform the chief of police. It was as though Gabriela Mancini had disappeared into thin air. She was no longer in Lucca. "I believe the American had something to do with her disappearance."

"Then you must get that information from the American, find the girl, and eliminate them both. She's a material witness. We don't know what Eduardo told her or if he gave her evidence."

"I have another idea."

De Luca held up his hand. "I don't want to hear it." He stood to leave. "Just get it done."

Lorik stood and offered his hand. After a moment's hesitation, De Luca extended his and they shook.

The chief left, and Lorik sat back at his computer. His revenge against the American woman would have to wait. First, he needed to find out what the Mancinis knew.

Then he would kill all three women.

13

Leine finished the last of her wine and slid some cash across the bar. There were few customers at Manny's that evening—a quiet weeknight. She loved the ambience—low lights combined with soft music playing over the speakers—classic and relaxing.

Santa would love it.

"Thanks for the wine."

Bruno smiled as he pushed the money back. "You're welcome. But your money is no good here."

"Please, keep it. Put it toward your college fund or something."

Manny appeared in the doorway to the back room. "You will never pay for anything in this restaurant as long as I am alive." He walked to the bar. "What you have done for this town will never be repaid."

"That's a lovely sentiment, Manny, and I appreciate your generosity. But I always pay. Besides, Lorik could still renege on the agreement."

Although things had been quiet for a few days, that didn't mean Lorik was going away that easily. Leine still checked the security feeds, and added cameras in several areas of town. According to Tomaso, the local police chief objected when he found one of them, but Leine went ahead and installed the cameras where the businesses wanted them. She'd let the owners deal with the police.

Ignoring both men's protests, she left the money on the counter and headed back to the bookshop. Condensation from her breath preceded her as she walked along the cobblestone street, and she burrowed into her coat for warmth. She loved Europe—especially Italy—which was why she kept coming back, usually after some epic shift in her life. The coast of Italy had been a favorite location for her and her first love, Carlos. She'd met Frank Basso there, too, when she'd escaped the horror of what Eric, her old boss, had tricked her into doing so long ago.

Now, she wanted to show it to Santa, wanted to live out the rest of their days together, doing nothing more dangerous than kayaking the Mediterranean or hiking through vineyards.

Which was why she had to make certain that Lorik and his kind weren't an issue.

She breathed in the mild evening air. The scent of garlic and onions from one of the many eateries that dotted the town's main thoroughfare reminded Leine she hadn't had dinner. A plate of walnut pesto ravioli sounded like just the ticket. Instead of heading back to her place, she turned left, taking a shortcut through the alley, headed for a small osteria that served fantastic pasta.

Leine walked along the dark back street, cataloging in her mind how much more she needed to do before she could open the bookshop. To her left, salt bush claimed what was left of a medieval brick wall. To her right were the rear entrances of several brick and stone structures built sometime in the nineteenth century.

As she calculated the remaining outlay, including the remodel of the two small bedrooms upstairs, the nerves along her spine tingled, bringing with it a familiar awareness. Senses immediately attuned to her surroundings, she nonchalantly reached inside her bag for her loaded semiauto. She slowed her breathing and listened as she threaded a suppressor onto the barrel.

Finely honed situational awareness was difficult to explain and took time to develop. Once cultivated, the ability to sense her surroundings, to detect small changes, often meant the difference between life and death.

There.

Between her footfalls, a sound. It was slight, but noticeable.

The way ahead had few opportunities for cover. Leine chastised herself for taking the shortcut, leaving her with no options for escape. Was she merely being tracked, or did her tail have more malicious intent?

Most likely the latter.

The dark street might thwart an imminent attack, although whoever was behind her could be using night vision gear. If her tracker wanted her dead, they would wait until she cleared the residential area before committing to the kill.

She kept her pace even and ducked into a recessed doorway, momentarily disappearing from view. The funnel-like alley worked both ways—her attacker had the same lack of options.

Leine waited, but didn't hear anything. She dropped to a crouch and checked the alley. The shadows behind her appeared static. Whoever was following her had found their own hide, either in another doorway or behind one of the large stone planters she'd passed.

She leaned back and sorted through her options. She could wait out the tail, but that could mean a long, cold night ahead.

Or she could confront the threat—possibly foolish depending on who she was up against.

There was one other option.

The tracker would be as attuned to small sounds as she was, anticipating her actions. She grabbed a handful of gravel and tossed it at the wall across from her.

A shadow behind one of the large planters moved, revealing the silhouette of a head. Leine squeezed off three rounds, rewarded by a grunt and the clatter of a gun on cobblestones. She emerged from the doorway, gun first, and moved toward the threat.

Thwwwttt.

The flash from a second suppressed weapon near the ground guided her aim. Leine buried two rounds in the man, ensuring he was dead. She moved to the body and kicked the backup weapon from his hand. The moon's blue glow illuminated his face—she didn't recognize him. She slid her phone out of her bag and snapped a photo. She'd send it to Lou for identification.

With the threat neutralized, her adrenaline receded. It was then she noticed the hot pain in her left side. She felt along her lower rib as she stooped to locate the first weapon. Her fingers came away wet. Gingerly, she peeled away the blood-soaked shirt to determine the extent of the damage.

"Dammit." Gripping her side to stem the flow of blood, she pulled out her phone and called the one person she could trust.

TEN MINUTES LATER, MANNY ARRIVED IN HIS VAN. HE HUSTLED TO the stoop where she sat and opened the first aid kit she'd asked him to bring. He used his phone's flashlight to illuminate the damage. A sharp intake of breath was his only acknowledgement of the gunshot wound.

"Don't worry, Manny," Leine said. "It was a through-and-through." She nodded at the cobblestone street. "I'm sure you'll find the spent casing somewhere over there."

"You should never walk alone in the dark." He handed her a bottle of water and a blister pack of antibiotics.

His worry touched her, confirming her decision to call him for help. She tried to smile. "It's just a flesh wound."

Technically correct. The round had chewed through tissue and likely shredded muscle. The wound would take time to heal, but she'd been lucky. The shooter was obviously a pro, having two suppressed weapons. She'd searched his pockets and came up empty—no wallet, no passport, no identifying information. He had no tats, and the bland features of someone who could melt into a crowd unnoticed. He'd sported a knife in an ankle sheath, in case of close combat.

"We should get you to hospital," Manny urged.

Leine shook her head. "Not a chance. Just help me wrap up. The more pressing concern is disposing of the body."

With a nod, he pulled a roll of gauze and a thick bandage from the first aid kit, which he handed to Leine. She placed the bandage on the wound, then he wrapped the gauze around her torso.

Satisfied with the dressing, Manny glanced at the dead gunman. "I think I can get him into the van. Getting him out will be easier."

"Let me help," Leine said. She stood and a wave of dizziness washed over her. She put her hand on the wall to steady herself.

Manny gave her a look. "You need to see a doctor."

"I lost some blood. I'll be fine after a little rest."

"Go, sit in the van. There's more water and an energy bar in the console. I'll take care of this."

Leine started to protest, but realized he was right. She would only be in the way. Manny was in good shape for a guy in his early seventies. He'd been climbing his family's terraced vineyards since he was a kid, and had the massive quadriceps to prove it. Instead, she picked up the spent brass, then made her way to the van and got in.

She finished the energy bar and half the water by the time Manny closed the back doors and climbed into the drivers' seat. Luckily, no one had seen or heard the attempted assassination. With a quick look in the rearview, he started the engine and pulled away from the scene.

"Was this Lorik's doing?" Manny asked.

Leine shrugged. "I don't know, but it certainly appears that way." She pulled up Manny's security feed on her phone and fast forwarded to the time she left the restaurant. The gunman appeared in several frames as he stalked her. She accessed another camera she'd passed a few blocks later and saw the same man. Unaware of the recently installed security device, he didn't attempt to hide his face.

Manny drove north of town to a pull off near a cliff overlooking the Mediterranean, and backed up to the edge.

"You sure you don't need my help?" Leine asked.

Manny gave her a grim smile. "It's been a while, but one doesn't forget how."

Leine cocked her head. "You've done this kind of thing before." It wasn't a question.

Without a word, Manny exited the van and went around to the back, where he opened both rear doors. A short while later, the dead gunman met his watery grave.

The old mafia term, "sleeping with the fishes" crossed her mind. Well, organized crime was organized crime. Conducting illicit business varied little from country to country. Different languages, different ways of doing things, but similar players with similar ambitions. She wondered what Manny's story was. She wouldn't pry. He'd tell her if and when he was ready.

Besides, she had more pressing concerns. Now that she and Manny had tied up this loose end, she needed to pay Lorik a visit.

14

The villa was quiet and dark. The crisp night air and silence of the surrounding vineyards matched Leine's cold determination. She waited for the perimeter guard to round the corner of the house and disappear before she made her way to the cellar door, picked the lock, and slipped inside.

Suppressed pistol in hand and ignoring the dull ache in her side, she moved down the hall to the grand staircase and paused. Guttural snorks emanated from the living room. She scanned the large space through her NVGs. The source was Lorik's body man, asleep in a chair. Leine left him there. No need to kill him—yet.

She dug inside her coat pocket for a small, square object and made her way to the foyer table—a marble-topped, Rococo piece set in the middle of the space, just off the living room. She secured the listening device to the underside of the table like so much chewed gum. Voice activated, the bug was sensitive enough to capture conversations in both the foyer and the sitting room, and would last several days.

The runner on the stairs muffled her approach to the upstairs landing.

Two rooms spoked off the landing with a hallway to her left and right. A quick scan of the rooms revealed a library and an office—neither of which were occupied.

Moving down the hallway to the right, she eased closed doors open. An opulent marble bathroom. A vacant guest room, its bed untouched.

She retraced her steps to recce the second hallway. The first door led to another guest room. The second, a large linen closet. The third was the master suite.

The double doors were unlocked. She slipped inside and quietly locked them behind her. Soft, even breathing filled the space. She stopped and listened for a moment as she scanned the room. The bed's occupant was alone.

Three strides brought her alongside her quarry.

She checked the brief spike of annoyance she had upon seeing Lorik's peaceful expression as she eased the drawer to the nightstand open and removed the .45 he'd stashed there.

She slid his gun into her vest, raised her pistol, and covered his mouth with her hand.

"Wakey, wakey," she cooed in a soft voice.

Lorik's eyes snapped open. The surprise was plain on his face as it dawned on him what was happening. His gaze flickered to the nightstand, but Leine tightened her grip. He sank back into the pillow.

"I thought we had a deal." Leine narrowed her eyes. "You leave me and the town alone, and I let you stay."

He tried to say something through the glove covering his mouth. She lifted her hand and put a finger to her lips.

"What are you talking about?" Lorik hissed. "I've done nothing."

"Then who paid me a visit tonight?"

Lorik looked genuinely surprised. "I don't know."

"I don't believe you."

"May I?" He indicated his desire to sit up.

Leine nodded. She kept the gun trained on him as he slid to a sitting position.

"You must believe me. I keep my word."

"Sure, Lorik." Leine slid her hand underneath his pillow. No weapon. "It had to be you. No one else has a reason to want me dead."

Doubt flitted across his features, then evaporated.

She raised the gun. "What?"

"It's nothing."

"It's not nothing. What do you know?"

"One of my men says he recognized you."

Well, that wasn't good. "From where?"

"Years ago. A warehouse fire in London."

"Uh-huh. And this has to do with my surprise guest tonight, how?"

"He said you killed several men and burned down the warehouse. He worked for the man who ran the operation."

"What was his boss's name?"

"Niko Abramov."

Leine tensed. She hadn't heard that name in a long time. "Go on."

"Nestor mentioned he knew someone who wanted you dead. I told him not to contact this person. That he should find out where he is and give me the information."

"Nestor is mistaken. I never burned down a warehouse in London." Technically true. The fire hadn't been her fault.

Lorik shrugged. "Then this person is chasing a ghost. But I would be careful."

"Do you have a name?"

"No. Nestor said he would try to contact this person and

report back to me, but he did not supply a name." He frowned, obviously annoyed. "It appears that Nestor is playing both sides."

"Both sides? So you tasked him with finding this person who wants to kill me so you could cash in?" She shook her head. "That's a dick move, Lorik."

"No, no, no. I wanted the information to give to you."

"Somehow, I don't think so." She curled her finger around the trigger. "Time's up."

He raised his hands. "Wait. I have an idea."

Leine waited.

"According to Nestor, this person is well connected. I don't know the details, but neither of us wants him here, yes? You would like to stay alive, and I would like to remain in my villa and continue to run my business."

"Yeah. You see how it's going to be difficult for me to trust you, right? You asked Nestor to find information on this person because you wanted in on a payday that could get me killed."

Lorik nodded, looking chagrined. "Yes. But that was before I knew Nestor was playing me. Now, our interests are aligned." He pointed at her, then himself. "This is a true bond between us. We both want the same thing but for different reasons."

"What's your idea?"

"We combine forces. There is strength in numbers."

"But I don't trust you."

Lorik nodded. "As a good faith offer, I will give you Nestor."

"He betrayed you, so you want to foist him off on me? Hard pass."

"He knows who this person is, yes?" Lorik studied her. "I believe that you would have no trouble getting this information from him. When we know who we're up against, we can plan an effective counteroffensive."

"Why don't you do it? Save us both a lot of trouble. You know him."

"Ah, yes, but he thinks you killed many powerful men. He fears you much more than he does me, which I will undoubtedly have to fix."

Leine sighed. It was likely the best deal she'd get with Lorik. Much as she wanted to, killing him now wouldn't help her find out her enemy's identity.

"Fine. Set it up."

"You have somewhere to conduct the interrogation?"

"That won't be a problem." Keeping the gun trained on him, she took a step back. "This is your last chance, Lorik. If you double-cross me, I will find you. You won't like the outcome. Are we clear?"

Lorik nodded. "We're clear."

Leine pulled the .45 from her vest and held it up. "I'll leave this on the table downstairs." She walked to the door, unlocked it, and turned. "You might want to have a word with your security guy. If I were you, I'd use someone else."

15

Roan Kadare stubbed out his cigarette on the cracked concrete floor, then dropped the butt into a metal box underneath his cot and closed the cover. Although smokes weren't usually hard to come by in prison, especially for someone who had an outside man like Kadare, occasionally the guards choked the supply chain when they needed a raise.

Fucking prison.

The rat fuck responsible for Kadare's enforced stay in the Albanian prison system was currently a gelatinous mass at the bottom of the Black Sea. Kadare had ensured the man understood who was responsible for the degradations the man was made to endure before being dismembered and stuffed into a barrel filled with sulfuric acid.

For Kadare, revenge was less a criminal act than an art form.

The burner mobile in his pocket buzzed. He fished it out and flipped open the old-school clam shell. "What?"

"There's a problem." The voice belonged to Aron, his link to the outside world.

Kadare closed his eyes and stifled a groan. "Tell me."

"The present we sent to Italy never made it." Aron paused. "You want me to send a replacement?"

Even though the mobile was likely clean, Kadare was nothing if not paranoid and required all communication to be in code. The guards were certainly able to intercept wireless communication, and the one who'd smuggled the burner in wasn't especially trustworthy.

"You sent the gift I suggested?" The specialist he'd told Aron to hire had cost him a small fortune.

"Yes, of course."

"How do you know the gift didn't get to the recipient?"

"It was lost in transit. No one knows where it is. She's still there, though, so a replacement would work."

Interesting. When Nestor sent the Leopard's location to him via Aron, Kadare's spirits soared. Nothing got his juices flowing more than exacting revenge on his and his late brother's enemies. The Leopard was top of that list.

Especially since everyone thought she was dead. He'd kill her before anyone found out, then let certain people know with a texted photograph of her mangled body.

He'd be a legend.

Roan Kadare had been a young man when the woman assassin had killed both his brother, Fatos, and the man who had taken over his brother's operations, Nikolai Abramov. Roan Kadare hadn't been prepared to assume the responsibilities of the extensive trafficking network, but he'd been a quick study, narrowly escaping with his life as others plotted to overthrow the inexperienced younger brother.

He'd been ruthless, hitting back hard when challenged, and harder when attacked. His enemies soon thought twice before opposing him.

"Then we'll have to send a replacement." Kadare fell silent as he thought. Who could he use? But more to the point, how many should he send? It was one woman, for fuck's sake.

"Do you have instructions?" Aron asked.

"Wait for my call." He closed the clamshell and returned the phone to his pocket.

His revenge would take a bit more planning than he'd anticipated.

16

———

Leine spread the new rug over the bloodstained floorboards with a sigh. It would have to do until she could get an installer to give her a bid on a new floor. She poured herself a cup of coffee, her mind returning to what Lorik had said about someone wanting her dead. She'd racked her brain, but couldn't come up with anyone in particular. She'd pissed off a lot of people in her day, but with her previous line of work that was inevitable.

Besides, she'd killed most of them.

Could it have something to do with the Association? That was unlikely. As far as she knew they thought she was dead. After Leine and her team exposed their Libyan prison and mining scheme, they'd scattered to wherever the ultra-rich went to lick their wounds. There'd been no evidence of them regrouping.

Of course, they'd been operating under the radar for years, so there was that.

Still, the attack didn't read like the Association. They tended to be more strategic. The attacker from the other night acted like a hired gun. The Association had their own assassins. They wouldn't use outsiders, and they'd most likely send at least two, since they knew her.

That left a number of her past target's peripherals—family members bent on revenge, or associates who had a bone to pick, for whatever reason. Abramov's people were a possibility—Nestor had worked for Abramov when he was alive, so it was possible he knew someone who might be interested in a revenge killing. But she'd been out of the hit-for-hire game for close to two decades. That was a long time in assassin years. Most of the actors from that era would likely be dead or in prison. A few may have gone legit, although that was a stretch.

Once a criminal...

She had to stop thinking about who and start dealing with what. Someone was after her. That couldn't be denied. What could she do about it? Leaving Scivoloso was a non-starter. Whoever wanted her dead would likely follow her wherever she went. It was better to deal with the situation here and now, although she surely didn't want the folks in town to bear the brunt of her past.

Leine closed her eyes, took a deep breath, and let it go. She'd just dealt with Lorik and his goons. For good or ill, the town depended on her to keep them safe. Add in scheduling the floor install, getting the door repaired, Santa arriving in a little over a week, and the bookshop's grand opening.

No pressure.

She'd have to take Lorik up on his offer to give up his guy, Nestor. He was the key.

Leine slid her phone from her back pocket and hit speed-dial. Lou Stokes picked up on the second ring.

"Hey, Lou. I need a favor."

"You sound tense. Something to do with our Albanian friend?"

Good old stable Lou. Someone she could always count on. "Not sure. Someone sent a hitman after me."

"Well, *that's* not good. The Association?"

"That was my first thought, but they think I'm dead, so I doubt it. A one-man hitter isn't really their style."

"Russian?"

"No idea. We didn't chat. There weren't any identifying tattoos."

"I assume he's no longer a problem."

"You would be correct in that assumption. Looks like I'm going to need a few weapons."

"Let me check around, see if I can scare up some intel, maybe find a way in. Give me a day or two. I got a guy in Florence who can get you any hardware you need."

"Thanks, Lou."

"You gonna be all right? Want me to send reinforcements?"

"That shouldn't be necessary. I've got a line on someone who may have more information. I'll contact you if the situation changes."

"You do that."

Leine ended the call and sighed. Los Angeles was beginning to look awfully good.

17

Nestor glanced at the armed guard in the tower and tried to swallow. His throat was dry as the Sahara. The guard stopped pacing and studied Nestor as he hurried past on his way into the prison.

Prisons made Nestor nervous—and not just for the obvious reasons. When he was a kid, his mother insisted on bringing him and his brother to visit their father. His father didn't take well to being incarcerated, had defied the guards so often that they named the prison's version of solitary confinement after him.

Animals in cages. That was the impression Nestor had taken home each time they visited. He'd come to dread visiting day, had fought his mother to be left at home, but to no avail. She dragged the two boys to the prison to see their father every week to show them what happened to criminals. The experience only served to instill a deep aversion to getting caught.

Nestor emptied his pockets into the shallow dish. He'd made sure he carried nothing of value that could be confiscated. With a disappointed look at the slim pickings, the guard waved him through.

Nestor sat on one of the dirty plastic chairs in the waiting room, prepared for a long wait to see Roan Kadare. He'd been surprised to be granted an audience with the infamous crime boss. Normally, this kind of access required a substantial amount of cash.

He assumed Kadare himself had bribed the guards to allow this meeting, which indicated Kadare's interest in what Nestor had to tell him. If he was satisfied with the information, Nestor's bank balance would be nominally richer. He'd be paid a more substantial sum when Kadare acted on the information and successfully eliminated the Leopard.

It was telling that Kadare didn't use his middleman this time. Prison would not be an easy place to plan an assassination without the guards getting wind of it and demanding hush money. Nestor assumed they monitored communications into and out of the prison. Kadare's man, Aron, had told him to use oblique language when discussing the particulars, in case the room was bugged or a guard was nearby.

Nestor's knee started bouncing of its own volition. He pressed his hand against his thigh to stop the involuntary tell. Showing the waiting room guard how nervous he was wouldn't earn him any points with Kadare. And Kadare would be sure to hear about it.

Fifteen minutes later, the guard called his name. Another guard showed Nestor through two locked doors to an empty room with a lone metal table and several grungy plastic chairs. The guard left, closing the door behind him. Nestor's heart thudded alarmingly fast at the finality of the click.

He sat on one of the chairs and stared at the wall in front of him. The peeling yellow paint revealed a green-tinted cinderblock wall. An older model camera had been mounted in a corner near the ceiling. Perhaps it didn't work and was only being used as a deterrent, but Nestor would follow Kadare's instructions no matter what.

Was this his future? He closed his eyes, thinking about his father dying in his grimy cell, all but forgotten by his wife and family. His mother had eventually stopped going to the prison, especially once her boys grew old enough to resist her efforts to get them to visit. When Nestor had asked her why she'd stopped, she replied that she'd failed. She'd only gone so that he and his brother wouldn't travel the same road. By that time, both brothers had drifted into fencing stolen goods and drug dealing. Nestor's brother eventually died from a gunshot wound during a raid on one of the warehouses, and it looked like Nestor was on his way to the same fate, although he kept his dealings secret from his mother.

Then he met Fatos Kadare, Roan's older brother.

Getting hired on with Kadare's crew gave him something he'd never had before—status. His association with the notorious crime boss also showed him another side of criminal life he'd never known: the benefit of loyalty. No matter where he went, his connection to Kadare protected him and opened doors.

When Nestor found out the Leopard had killed Fatos Kadare, he'd vowed vengeance and willingly jumped to Abramov's crew, thinking he'd be able to take part in hunting her down. The Leopard killed Abramov soon afterward, and reportedly died in the warehouse fire Nestor himself had set. Nestor never told anyone he'd set the fire. Giddy at the assassin's death, Nestor closed the book on his need for vengeance. Or so he thought. With the big boss dead, he drifted for the better part of a year before hiring on with Lorik's crew. He'd never dreamed Kadare's younger brother would survive and thrive like he did.

No one had.

All of which brought him to this prison, on this day, with

information about the Leopard to give to his ex-boss's younger brother, Roan. Nestor wasn't one to believe in Providence, but it seemed like the universe was directing him to this point in time, to exact his vengeance on the Leopard in the name of both Fatos Kadare and Nikolai Abramov.

After the Leopard's death and the younger Kadare's payday, Nestor swore to himself he'd change his name and leave for parts unknown, getting as far from Lorik and Roan Kadare as humanly possible. Perhaps his place on the lake wasn't far enough.

The door opened and a guard led Kadare into the room. The crime boss was gaunt and wiry and dressed in a red jumpsuit. A lurid skull tattoo adorned his shaved head, giving him a menacing look. The chain from his cuffed wrists to his ankles clanked as he walked.

The guard seated him across from Nestor, attached the chain to the table, then stepped back to stand near the door.

Kadare's face split into a grin. "Little brother. How nice to see you."

Nestor smiled back. They'd decided before his visit that Kadare would refer to Nestor as his little brother. "I'm sorry I didn't come sooner."

The crime boss chuckled at his concern. "I understand. I'm just happy you're here." He turned to the guard and scowled. "Some privacy?"

The guard hesitated, then exited the room. As Kadare turned back, his scowl changed to a deadly serious look.

Nestor stifled the urge to squirm as Kadare studied him. His cold stare reminded Nestor that not all men had souls.

"You are Nestor." It wasn't a question.

"Yes." Nestor sat forward, eager to have the audience over. "I have the information you requested—"

Kadare gave him a warning look. Nestor fell silent.

"You have information on our brother?"

Nestor nodded. Brother was code for the assassin Kadare had dispatched to kill the Leopard. Nestor had rehearsed his answer on the flight to Albania.

"He's on holiday in the Mediterranean."

Kadare tensed. He reminded Nestor of a venomous snake, coiled and ready to strike.

"And you are certain he hasn't returned home?"

Nestor nodded again.

"And you believe our sister knows where he is?"

Interestingly, Kadare had chosen "sister" as code for the Leopard.

"I do."

"And you're sure it was she."

"I'm positive. Not only that, but I believe she bought his ticket."

Kadare's eyes glittered in the harsh glow of the ceiling light. "She must have used an intermediary."

"I believe she did this on her own."

"Impossible. This gift was to be a surprise."

"Remember London?"

"Of course I remember. She had help then, too. She worked for the travel agency."

Another code—this one for the Central Intelligence Agency. "Not long ago she sent two of my boss's men on holiday. Maybe even a third."

"And how do you know this?"

"I was there for two."

Kadare studied him for a moment. "How is it that you didn't take the same trip?"

Cold dread shot up Nestor's spine. That he'd escaped twice from the Leopard wouldn't instill confidence in his loyalty. "Perhaps she wanted a witness." A lame answer, but Nestor couldn't think of something better.

Thankfully, Kadare let it slide. "She runs a bookstore now."

"Yes. It's not yet open, though."

"Do you have the drawing?"

Nestor rummaged in his pocket and pulled out a piece of paper, which he unfolded and slid across the table to Kadare.

Kadare studied the map of Scivoloso. He pointed to a large X crudely drawn over one of the buildings on the bluff overlooking the Mediterranean. "This is hers?"

"Yes."

"Your boss knows nothing about your visit here?"

"As far as I know. I told him I was coming to visit my mother. I have told him I would try to locate the person who wants this woman dea—" Nestor self-corrected. "The person who wants to surprise our sister with the gift. He wants to be apprised of events going forward."

"You haven't told him where I am." The implied threat in Kadare's cold, dead eyes brought chills to Nestor's spine. He resisted the urge to shudder.

"Of course not. No. He doesn't even know your name."

"Hmm." Kadare refolded the paper and slid it into his pocket. "How loyal would you say your boss is?"

Nestor glanced nervously at the camera in the corner.

"The camera's only for show."

"Ah. Okay." At least the guards wouldn't see that part of their meeting. "His loyalty depends on how much money is involved," he replied, his voice low.

Kadare nodded. "We'll keep our meeting secret, for now. But I might have a use for your boss in the future."

"I'm sure he'll be happy to provide whatever assistance you need."

"We're done here." Kadare called for the guard.

Nestor stood to leave. He couldn't wait to get out of the oppressive room.

"Remember, should this information be wrong or in any way compromise me, you will be held accountable."

The guard opened the door as Nestor bobbed his head, indicating he understood the threat.

Nestor stumbled out of the prison, sprinted to a nearby trash can, and vomited.

18

Leine kept the engine running as she waited for Nestor to exit the bakery. The sun glinted off the stone of the seventeenth century building, bathing the sidewalk outside the store with a subtle glow. The light of the Italian coast wasn't like anything she'd experienced in other places. Both soothing and beautiful, she wanted nothing more than to sit in a hammock and read all afternoon.

Yeah. That'll happen.

She checked her messages. Thankfully, Santa hadn't called. There wasn't a lot of time before he arrived. She needed to resolve this question of who wanted her dead before he got there. She didn't want to put him in danger. Could she ask him to delay? What excuse would she use? With a sigh, she realized delay tactics would only draw out the inevitable. She needed to come clean with him, let him know what was happening.

Maybe later.

Five minutes ticked by before Nestor walked out holding a white paper bag and a lidded cup. Lorik had called earlier that morning, letting her know where and when he'd send Nestor to get lunch. She'd already wasted two days waiting for Nestor to get back from visiting his mother.

Nestor got into the car and started the engine, then pulled away from the curb, headed for the villa. Leine followed at a distance, waiting for him to turn onto the less-traveled road leading to Lorik's. When he reached the gated entrance, she pulled up behind him at an angle to block his escape and leapt from the car.

He jabbed the button on the call box repeatedly as she advanced, but the gate remained closed.

At least Lorik was cooperating by not letting him in.

He glanced in his side mirror as he locked the doors and fumbled to raise his window. Too late and too slow. Leine shoved the barrel of her pistol through the opening, the muzzle coming to rest against his temple.

His eyes cut to the console beside him.

"Hands on the steering wheel. Now."

Nestor's breathing increased as he complied. "What are you doing? Who are you?"

"You know exactly who I am. Turn off the engine and hand me the keys."

His hesitation did him no favors. Leine dug the muzzle into his temple and growled, "Do. It. Now."

He did.

Leine scanned the car's interior for easily accessible weapons. Finding none in plain sight, she pressed unlock on the key fob and opened the drivers' side door. She stepped back, her gun aimed at his head. "Get out of the car or you're dead. Keep your hands where I can see them."

Hands in the air, Nestor did what she asked. "I don't understand—"

"Put this on." She handed him a black hood.

"Do you know who you're—"

"Just do what I tell you and you'll stay alive."

Once he'd done as she said, Leine pulled a pair of plastic cuffs from her pocket. She yanked his arms behind him and cinched them around his wrists.

She tossed the keys into the front seat of Nestor's car, then pushed him toward hers.

He dug in his heels and shifted into belligerent mode. "You can't do this to me. I work for a powerful man."

"Yeah? Who's that?"

"Lorik Rrahmani."

"Oh. Well, in that case..." She popped the trunk open and shoved him inside.

"You're a dead woman." The hood muffled his voice somewhat, but his fear came through loud and clear.

She slammed the trunk closed and climbed behind the wheel. Several loud thuds against the trunk's interior were accompanied by imaginative insults in Albanian and Russian, one or two of which Leine hadn't heard before.

She followed a circuitous route to the warehouse, designed to confuse him. She pulled in through the open bay and cut the engine before she got out and rolled the door closed. A few stray boxes of wine and glassware had been stacked to one side, next to a sheet of clear plastic duct taped to the floor. A metal folding chair stood in the center of the plastic. Normally, she would have two or three armed associates to intimidate the person to be interrogated, but she figured Nestor knew he was being questioned by the Leopard, which would be enough to fuck with his mind. Besides, she didn't really have anyone who could fill the role other than Manny, and she didn't want to involve him if she didn't have to. Using his warehouse was enough to put a target on his back.

She walked to the car and popped the trunk, staying well

clear in case Nestor tried anything. The black hood bobbed as he sat up and tried to see through the fabric.

"Take this thing off me," he said in a panicked voice. "I can't breathe."

She hauled him out of the trunk and removed the hood. He bent over and took several greedy breaths. At least he wasn't asthmatic. Once his breathing returned to semi-normal, she guided him onto the plastic sheeting toward the chair. His body went rigid.

"I see you're familiar with this situation." Even better. Leine had learned from experience that physical intimidation was less effective than its psychological counterpart. Give anyone enough time and the right circumstances and their imagination would terrify them far more than reality ever could.

Besides, multiple studies on physical pain during interrogation showed a high percentage of false positives. Meaning the person questioned would say anything to make the pain stop. Psychological manipulation proved to be much better at gleaning actionable intelligence. Leine was a fan of both positive and negative reinforcement but found each effective in different circumstances.

She pushed Nestor across the plastic. Before he sat down, she cut his cuffs and shoved him into the chair. Holding the gun on him, she pulled out two more plastic cuffs and handed him one.

"Cuff your ankles."

Nestor looked around at the empty warehouse. "We are alone?"

"Not exactly."

Surprised by the voice, Leine turned as Manny walked toward them. He carried a tool belt in one hand and a white folding table in the other, which he proceeded to set up a couple meters from where Nestor sat. From the tool belt he selected a hammer, a vise grip, and several framing nails, and laid them on the table.

"What's he doing here?" Nestor scoffed. "You need help from an old man?"

Not skipping a beat, Leine repeated, "Put on the cuff. Now."

Manny picked up the hammer and took a step toward him.

Nestor glanced from Leine's gun to Manny's hammer. The bravado disappeared from his face. "Fine." He bent over and cuffed his ankles together. Manny put the hammer back on the table and held out his hand for the second cuff. Leine gave it to him and he re-cuffed Nestor's hands to the chair behind him.

When he was finished, Leine took him aside and whispered, "Who *are* you?"

Manny replied, "When I was here earlier to pick up wine for the shop, I noticed the plastic and the chair." He shrugged. "I thought I could help."

"We really need to talk about your past," Leine said. "But thank you."

Eyes sparkling, Manny executed a short bow. "Of course."

Manny went over to the table and picked up the hammer and a handful of nails, which he shoved into his pocket. He held up one of the nails so that Nestor could see it. Nestor eyed him warily.

"Did you know that a *Spetsnaz* soldier will hammer a nail—just like this one—into the skull of a captive when they wish to extract information?"

Nestor swallowed. "And what would an old man like you know of *Spetsnaz*?" he said, lacing his voice with manufactured contempt.

Leine watched Manny. She originally thought he'd been a member of the Italian mafia, but he could have been military; one didn't necessarily preclude the other.

Manny leaned over and parted his hair, revealing a divot in his scalp.

Nestor scoffed. "You expect me to believe you survived being interrogated by the Russians?"

Manny shrugged. "Believe what you will. I'd be delighted to show you how it feels." He took another step toward him.

"Wait." Nestor turned his attention to Leine. "What do you want? I'll tell you anything you need to know."

"Why don't I believe you?" Leine cocked her head. "Tell you what. Let's try a question. If you answer it truthfully, we can continue without any"—she glanced at Manny— "assistance."

Nestor nodded. "Ask me anything."

"You know who I am."

He nodded again. "I recognized you the night you killed Donat and Erwin."

Leine made a buzzing noise. "Wrong answer. How do you know I killed anyone?"

Nestor gave her a strange look. "Because you are the Leopard."

"Flattery will get you nowhere, Nestor." Leine rolled her eyes. "And just to be clear, I'm *not* the Leopard, or whatever apex predator you believe me to be."

"You have an uncanny resemblance to her."

"Oh? How would you even know what this Leopard looks like?"

"I was there when you killed those men at the warehouse in London. I was driving the van." The last was said with bravado, as though he was proud to have been a lowly driver for Abramov.

"You're still operating under the assumption that I am who you think I am. I'm not." She stared at him. "I'm worse."

Obviously uncomfortable, he lowered his gaze. "How do you know this if you don't know who I'm talking about?"

"I never said I didn't know who the Leopard was. I only said I wasn't her." She snapped her fingers, and he raised his head, a defiant look on his face. "From what I understand, she died in that warehouse. At night. Lots of dark at night, wouldn't you say?"

Nestor shook his head. "That is a lie. She's alive and standing in front of me now."

"I suspect it was you who pushed the fiction that whoever killed the guards that night in London was the infamous Leopard." Leine nodded at Nestor. "Who set the fire? Did they find a body?"

"She—you—set the fire to cover her tracks, then escaped. Her colleagues picked her up later, but she died of her injuries."

"Wow. Really? That's the story?" Leine shook her head in disbelief. "I guess if someone wants to believe something badly enough, they'll accept whatever fiction they're given."

"The only fiction is that you died."

"Enough. Last chance to show me you're serious about avoiding the next phase of this little get-together." She moved behind him.

He twisted in his chair, trying to see her.

"Obviously I can't dissuade you from your misidentification, which has put me in a very trying situation." She continued around the side of the chair and stopped directly in front of him. "And by that, I mean someone is trying to kill me, and it's because of you." She raised her gun and aimed it at his face. Manny advanced closer, still holding the hammer and nails.

Nestor's face drained white. The penny dropped. He was about to die.

"No, no, no. You are mistaken. I have done nothing like what you are saying."

Leine and Manny exchanged looks. The panic in his voice told them a confession was imminent.

Leine squinted at him. "I think you're trying to save your ass." She gestured to Manny. "Go ahead, Manny. Do your worst. We'll see if he changes his story." *Good God. I sound like a character in an old gangster movie.*

The ploy worked.

Nestor's eyes saucered as Manny stepped closer.

"Stop. Please. I cannot tell you this. He will kill me," Nestor said, his voice cracking. Manny paused, waiting for him to continue. Nestor's breathing had become shallow and erratic, little explosive puffs of air, signaling his fear. "I—when I saw you that night, I was certain you were the Leopard. I told my boss, Lorik, I thought it was you and that I knew of someone who would pay for that information." He looked at the floor.

"And? Who did you tell?" Leine asked.

"Please don't make me tell you." The guy was close to tears.

"If you don't, you'll die. And I have to say," she nodded at the hammer and nail in Manny's hands, "it looks like you're going to be in a world of hurt."

Nestor raised his head. Resignation and fear filled his eyes.

"Roan Kadare."

19

———

R oan Kadare.

A name from the past, and not a welcome one. Manny looked a question at her, but she shook her head.

"Who is Roan Kadare?" She wouldn't know the name if she wasn't the Leopard.

"The younger brother of a man you—I mean, the Leopard— killed. His name was Fatos Kadare." Nestor's expression revealed what could only be described as devotion when he said the Albanian trafficker's name.

"And this younger brother sent an assassin to kill me?"

Nestor nodded. "I believe he did."

"Where is Roan Kadare now?"

"In prison."

"Where?"

"Albania, near the border with Kosovo."

"Have you spoken directly with him?" Manny asked.

"No. Only with his associate, Aron."

"What information have you given him?" Obviously, Nestor had told him she lived in Scivoloso. What else did he know?

"Only that you live in Scivoloso."

"Did you tell him I own the old bookstore?"

Nestor shook his head. Leine studied him closely. She couldn't tell if he was lying.

Most likely he was. She'd have to prepare in any case.

She sighed. "What's his next move?"

"I don't know. He doesn't tell me anything."

"Then what good are you?" Nail held high, Manny took another step closer.

Nestor squeezed his eyes closed.

"Wait a minute." Leine gave Manny a look. He lowered the hammer. *Who was this guy?*

People were a mystery.

"Look, Nestor. I don't want to kill you. But I'm not comfortable setting you free. You could go to Kadare and tell him I interrogated you, and that I know who's coming after me. That just doesn't work for me."

Nestor's eyes widened at the prospect of not being killed. "I promise, I won't tell him anything."

"That's right. You won't. Because you love your mother, right?"

"What about my mother?" Worry skated across Nestor's face.

Lorik had offered Nestor's mother's location to Leine to assure his employee's silence once she finished questioning him. They'd both agreed that if Nestor disappeared, Kadare would become suspicious and more difficult to anticipate, so killing or detaining him for very long was off the table.

"Let's just say I know where she lives. I also know where your extended family members are." Not that Leine was interested in hurting innocent bystanders, but if the threat of doing so would keep Nestor from giving a heads up to Kadare, she wasn't above using the ploy.

Misery joined the fear in Nestor's eyes. He nodded. "I understand."

"And I will know if you warn her," Leine added.

"What do I tell my boss? He's got security cameras near the gate. He'll know you picked me up at gunpoint."

"Security camera, singular. Tell him. I don't care if he knows. In fact, I prefer that he wonders what you told me."

"I didn't tell you anything about Lorik or his operation."

"He won't know that."

MANNY TIDIED THE WAREHOUSE WHILE LEINE SLID THE HOOD OVER Nestor's head and tucked him back inside the trunk. He'd pissed himself during questioning, and Leine was loath to let him in the car.

Elongated shadows bled across Lorik's vineyard by the time Leine dropped Nestor at the foot of the driveway. Someone had moved Nestor's car, so he made his way up to the villa on foot.

He'd most likely keep his promise not to tell Kadare that he'd given him up to Leine. Kadare would not be pleased with what he'd done and was not a person who took betrayal in stride. From what she'd heard, he was a special kind of crazy that couldn't be reasoned with. If he found out Nestor had caved to his interrogators, especially a woman and an older man, he'd kill Nestor with no regrets.

Now that she knew who the threat was, she needed to find out as much as she could about him. Her contacts from the old days might be of some help. First, though, she'd see if there were any rumblings on the Agency grapevine. She texted Lou to verify what Nestor had told her about Roan Kadare, then headed home.

LOU CALLED HER BACK THE NEXT MORNING. LEINE TOOK HER PHONE into the bookshop to give the estimator from the flooring company space to take his measurements and to keep the conversation private. To his credit, he hadn't mentioned the bloodstains.

"So I found out a little more about your friend, Roan," Lou said.

"Okay?"

"Your source was right—Roan Kadare is in prison in north-eastern Albania. He'd originally been assigned to Rezina." A prison in Moldova, Rezina was notorious for human rights violations and inhumane conditions.

"Rezina to a prison in his home country? That's quite a transfer."

"Turns out he had an ace up his sleeve. With help from his patron in Albania, he appealed his conviction and found a simpatico judge."

Leine snorted. "More like bribable." She moved further out of earshot of the floor guy. "Anything else?"

"Word is he's making a move on an old enemy. Albania isn't known for its incorruptible prisons, so ordering a hit from his cell wouldn't be difficult, just expensive. How the hell did he find you?"

"One of Lorik's guys recognized me from the warehouse fire in London back in 2000. He told Lorik he'd try to track the guy down."

"And assumed Kadare would send a team to take you out. This guy's your source for the name?"

"Yep." Leine leaned against a bookshelf and sighed. "He goes by Nestor. Lorik assumes Nestor's working both him and Kadare, but I can't see an underling taking on both bosses.

Nestor said he didn't contact Kadare directly. He dealt with someone named Aron. We need to find out who he is."

"I got a guy willing to intercept calls in and out of the prison, so we'll know more soon enough."

"Great. Charge the account whatever it takes."

"I've got half a mind to submit this to the suits at the Agency. It happened on their watch."

Leine smiled. "I didn't exactly follow protocol."

"No, but you did what you were supposed to do. You just got a little carried away."

"Understatement of the year, Lou." A little carried away included eliminating Fatos Kadare's entire hunting party. It seemed like a good idea at the time. The young girls Kadare had trafficked for the men's entertainment and the endangered Amur leopards he wanted to kill probably thought so, too. "So what do you suggest? Leaving isn't an option. He'll only track me down."

"Want some backup?"

Leine stared out the picture window into the street. A few late season tourists strolled by, picking their way along the narrow cobblestone street, snapping selfies in front of the picturesque buildings.

"Don't pull the trigger yet. I'd like to keep this contained, if possible." She had to fix this, and soon. "Too many innocent bystanders."

"I don't think you have much choice, Leine. But I'll do whatever you think's best."

"Thanks, Lou. I'll keep you posted."

Leine ended the call and slid the phone into her back pocket. She plastered a smile on her face as the estimator handed her his clipboard detailing the bid.

Not too bad. "How soon can you have this done?"

"Within the month."

Still smiling, Leine shook her head. "Is there any way to move this job to the front of the line?"

The floor guy smiled back. "Of course." He took the clipboard, scribbled something, then handed it back to her. "A small surcharge."

Leine stifled the sarcastic reply that sprang to her lips. Small would not be the word she'd use to describe what he'd written. She handed the clipboard back to him.

"When can you start?"

20

———

Two nights later, Leine made her way along the dark sidewalk, headed back to the bookstore after a delicious dinner at Tomaso and Francesca's restaurant. Eager to see how far the installers had gotten on the new floor in the back room, she quickened her pace. The installer had been good to his expensive word and moved her job to the front of the line, had even engaged more workers to get the floor finished on her timeline. From what she'd seen earlier, they'd done a good job matching the rest of the wood.

Half a block from her building, Leine stopped to check the security feed on her phone. She advanced the feed from the time she'd left, then paused it as someone appeared at the entrance to the bookshop. She rewound the feed and hit Play. Their face obscured by a hoodie, the person left a package to the right of the door, then moved out of the picture. She fast forwarded, but there was no other activity.

A bomb? Or something else, like ricin, or some other poison? Maybe it was an actual delivery for the store, and she was being paranoid. But a delivery this late?

Nah.

The bug she'd placed in Lorik's foyer hadn't picked up any conversations about an attack, although he could have done the planning somewhere other than the sitting room or the foyer. She slid her gun from her bag and keyed in a code on her phone that unlocked the electronic keypad she'd recently installed on the door. Harder for someone to pick, with the added feature of not having to mess with a key. When she got to the door, she gave the package a wide berth and reached for the handle.

Thwack!

The round hit just above her head, splintering the door frame.

Leine turned the handle and crashed through the doorway, slamming the door shut as she did. Rounds chewed through the plywood covering the missing door glass. She low-crawled to the back room, where she hauled up the trap door, revealing a canvas bag attached to the metal rungs of the ladder.

Ignoring the pain in her side from the other night's gunshot wound, she ripped the waterproof bag from its quick-release carabiner and unzipped the top to reveal an MP5, three semiautos, night vision gear, a flashbang, a frag grenade, several full mags, and body armor. She pocketed the flashbang and one of the pistols, then grabbed the ballistic vest, submachine gun, NVGs, and extra ammo. She closed the hatch and kicked the rug back in place, then returned to the shop. The images on her security app showed three gunmen in balaclavas stacked outside the front door. All wore tactical gear and carried assault rifles. It wouldn't be long before they breached the entrance.

She backed up to the stairwell, then turned and took two and three stairs at a time to the upper floor, careful to avoid the tripwire. When she reached the top, she secured the vest.

Then she waited.

The front door smashed open, and the sound of footsteps pounded the floor. She glanced at the feed—the three combatants swarmed in formation into the bookshop, reinforcing her initial observation that these men weren't garden-variety criminals.

She swiped to the stairwell feed. One of the gunmen was heading up, his rifle leading the way.

Just another couple of steps.

The intruder climbed two more stairs and froze. He didn't have time to look down at the tripped wire as the weighted, nail-studded two-by-four swung from its perch near the ceiling and slammed into his face. He screamed.

Leine moved from behind the doorway and fired a three-round burst, hitting him in the head and neck. He tumbled down the stairs and she dropped behind the door to wait for the other gunmen's next move.

The security feed showed both near the stairwell—one signaled to the other to go outside, most likely to find another way in.

Good luck with that.

The remaining gunman stepped over the body of his fallen comrade and headed toward the upper floor.

Cold.

Professional.

His gun held at high-ready, he wasn't as gung-ho as his predecessor. He studied the nail-tipped booby trap hanging in the middle of the stairwell before he eased slowly up the last several steps.

Leine pulled the pin on the flashbang and rolled it across the landing. She closed her eyes, opened her mouth, and plugged her ears as it detonated. The blinding flash and loud bang in the confined space would disorient anybody.

She stepped from her hide and fired. The two bullets ripped through the other gunman's face, and he toppled down the stairs.

Footsteps overhead told her the third gunman had avoided the tripwire she'd installed on the roof. The access from the attic was well camouflaged, so the only way into the old building would be through the upper floor windows, one of which sported a rusty iron shelf meant for a flower box. The other window looked out over a sheer drop into the Med and would take some serious climbing skills.

Her trap was simple—in addition to booby trapping several roof tiles so they'd slide free when stepped on, she'd loosened the screws securing the shelf to the wall so that any amount of weight would cause it to separate from the building. As an added deterrent, she'd puttied glass shards into the recessed window frames.

Alternatively, he could try going through the roof, although she'd camouflaged and secured the access. She doubted he'd come prepared with the equipment required to cut through tile and thick wood joists.

Listening intently, she followed the gunman's progress from the front of the building where the window and the flower box were located, to the opposite side at the back of the house.

Where most of the quick-release tiles lived.

Something clattered across the roof like rocks skittering, followed by what could only have been panicked scrabbling for purchase on the shifting tiles.

There was a loud *thud* and a truncated yelp, more rolling and scrambling, then—silence. Leine moved to the window overlooking the sea and peered down. She could just make out the dark, lifeless form of the gunman being tossed by the frothy white waves.

At least now she'd only have to dispose of two bodies.

Apparently, Kadare had decided to escalate. It was time to call in reinforcements. She pressed her hand to the wound in her side and winced as she climbed over the bodies and down the stairs. A perfunctory inspection revealed large pools of blood had leaked from both, undoubtedly staining the stairs. Leine grimaced.

"I just cannot get a fucking break." The words echoed in the small space.

At this rate, she'd have to put the floor guy on speed-dial.

21

R oan Kadare closed his eyes and pulled in deep breaths, searching for calm. The second crew he'd sent to eliminate the American had never checked in. They hadn't provided photographic proof or requested their final payment, which meant something was wrong. He'd used a hit squad from his days employing hardened fighters from Kosovo, warriors who'd taught him effective ways of obtaining information from unwilling partners, as well as tactics for revenge he'd never have thought of himself. These men had worked as a team for years and carried out the occasional hit for Kadare, no questions asked. No muss, no fuss, as his mother had liked to say.

The walls of his cell loomed closer, suffocating him. He swiped at the sweat forming on his forehead, threatening to dribble into his eyes. Even though the guards were corrupt and easily bought, his power was too limited in prison. Obviously, he needed to do this himself. The personal touch was the only way to get things right.

Aron had cultivated one of the guards on the night shift,

rooting out his weaknesses, learning where his family lived. In a stroke of luck, he'd found a new hire and a new father—one whose cynicism hadn't yet wormed its way through his psyche, and who would likely do anything to save his wife and baby daughter from harm.

After checking to make sure no guards were nearby, Kadare knelt by his bed and removed a loose brick covering the space where he kept the flip phone. Aron answered on the second ring.

"Have you heard from our friends yet?" Kadare asked.

"No, nothing."

Kadare nodded to himself. "It's time, then. Is your new friend ready?"

Aron paused before answering. "I believe he is, yes."

"Keep me informed."

Kadare snapped the phone closed and shoved it back inside its hiding place before covering the space with the brick. Elvis Sadiki, the head of the family in Albania to which Kadare belonged, would not be pleased that Kadare broke out of prison before completing his sentence. Sadiki had pulled strings to transfer Kadare from the hellhole that was Rezina. He'd likely view Kadare's escape as an insult. Kadare would not be able to return to Albania. A small price to pay. His need for revenge blazed deep inside him, urging him to reduce the Leopard to a mewling kitten before he severed her head from her body.

That would be a day for celebration.

Leine ended the call and slid her phone into her back pocket. After requesting "another small surcharge" for the additional work, the floor guy promised to come that afternoon.

Thankfully, a roofer from the next town over had a cancellation and had already repaired the missing tiles. She'd hate to have to weather one of the coast's infamous storms with a damaged roof.

The floor guy would likely insist she pay him even more to keep his mouth shut—although the additional bloodstains on the stairs and soon-to-be-repaired bullet holes might be enough of a deterrent. She'd be sure to steer his imagination in a dark direction, capitalizing on his fear of retaliation.

With a sigh, Leine positioned the new throw rug over the stain from the previous night's attack, idly wondering if there was a way to write the rugs and repairs off on her U.S. taxes. She hoped the hitmen hadn't been on Lorik's payroll, but part of her refused to trust anything he said. He could have been in league with Kadare. A healthy dose of skepticism never hurt, especially when dealing with a criminal.

She'd just finished inputting the inventory for the store into her software program when her phone rang. It was Lou.

"Hey, Lou. What've you got?"

"My comms guy at the prison just called with something interesting. Apparently Kadare connected with one of his outside guys, the guy named Aron, and mentioned that 'it was time.' For what, we don't know, but I'd be extra careful if I were you."

"Duly noted. He tried again a couple nights ago."

"And you're just telling me this now?" Lou's voice held an edge. "What happened?"

Leine gave him a brief synopsis.

"Any clue who they were?"

"Again, no tats, no identifying information."

"What kind of weapons?"

"AKs. The lead had an HK416."

"Could be anyone. Did you catch an accent?"

"They used hand signals. They were professional, compared to Lorik's guys; a well-trained unit."

"Former military?"

"Most likely."

"You sure you don't want help? Art and his guys are a plane ride away. They could be in Scivoloso in a few hours."

"Yeah, probably. If Kadare's escalating, and it sure sounds like it, that's going to put the town in danger." Which was the last thing she wanted. "I thought I could contain things."

"Don't beat yourself up. How could you have known the dust up with Lorik would extend to Kadare?"

"In my experience, this kind of altercation usually ends badly. Give Art a call. If he's available, let me know when and where to pick him and his crew up."

"Will do. And Leine?"

"Yeah?"

"Be careful."

"You know I will."

Leine ended the call and stared out the window. White, puffy clouds danced along the horizon, belying the tumultuous emotions racing through her. There was no escaping her past. She ought to know by now that any attempt at a normal life was destined to fail. She'd killed too many people. Yes, the majority of them were scum-of-the-earth, which was being unkind to scum, but still, she'd ended lives and made enemies. And not just when she was with the Agency. Afterward, too.

She thought back to several of her freelance kills, remembering how low she'd flown—the kill wall she'd deleted from her laptop attested to her mental health at the time, or lack thereof. If she could have done things differently, would she have?

Stop second-guessing yourself, Leine.

She shook her head to clear the guilt and stuffed it deep. Compartmentalizing she could do.

Perhaps Lorik would actually be willing to help. Not out of any altruistic tendency, but to stave off someone larger and more connected from taking his place. Before she secured his support, she needed to let the town know what was coming.

22

———

O mar pushed the garbage cart down the empty corridor as he scanned the hallway for other guards. The stench was nauseating. He squeezed his eyes closed and muttered a prayer for forgiveness for what he was about to do.

He was scared. Not only was his new job at the prison in jeopardy, but now his family was in danger. The thought of what Aron had threatened to do to his wife and precious daughter ripped his soul from his body. There was no way he could be responsible for the defiling and murder of the two most important people in his life. He had to submit to Aron's demands. If anyone discovered the escape was his fault he'd be fired. But losing his job was preferable to losing his family by an order of magnitude.

The video Aron had sent of his wife and child playing at the park near their apartment chilled Omar to the bone.

Omar checked the time—1:51 a.m. He stopped at cell six and hoisted the bag of garbage collected by the swing shift onto the cart, then into the large bin. He'd volunteered when the guard who normally collected trash called in after being brutally attacked near his home.

Omar wasn't naïve. He knew Aron had ordered the attack. Aron's resolve to break his boss out of prison terrified Omar. Aron hadn't killed the other guard but came awfully close.

Message received.

Would Aron make good on his promise not to hurt his wife and daughter? Omar had no recourse but to trust him.

Three more cells, three more bags of rotting garbage. He kept two in reserve on the cart. The last one had broken loose, spilling its contents onto the floor. Omar hastily scooped up as much as he could and dumped it into the larger bin, holding his breath so as not to breathe in the stink.

The next cell was Kadare's.

He pulled the cart alongside the cell door before scanning the hall.

Still empty.

He tapped gently on the door, then pulled the keyring from his front pocket and selected the correct key. He winced at the *snick* of the lock and opened the door, alert for squeaky hinges. Kadare peered out. Seeing no one in the hallway, he slipped past Omar and climbed onto the cart and inside the bin. Omar quickly covered him with the two bags of garbage, shut and locked the cell door, and continued down the hall.

Ten minutes later, Omar finished his rounds. The larger bin was piled high with garbage, some of it overflowing onto the cart itself. He started for the loading dock at the back of the prison, nodding at the night shift guards he passed.

"Quite a haul tonight, eh, Omar?" The night duty supervisor walked up to him and whistled. "Not hard to believe that much rubbish comes from the trash we guard, right?"

Omar smiled and wiped at the perspiration on his forehead. "You know what they say, trash is as trash does."

The boss gave him an odd look. "Do they, now?"

Omar cleared his throat, the smile frozen on his lips. His supervisor moved closer to the cart and scanned the night's haul as though he was going to go through the bin. Omar's heart stuttered.

Instead, the supervisor grimaced and stepped back, waving at his nose. "Get that garbage out of here before you stink the place up."

"Right away, boss."

Omar's knees went weak as he steered the cart past empty bins and through the double doors leading to the loading docks and the garbage truck idling there.

"Last one," he said to the man working the controls. The other man nodded and waited for Omar to position the cart. He tensed as the truck's mechanical arm lifted the bin off the cart and upended the trash into the gaping maw of the truck. There was no sign of Kadare.

So far, so good.

The mechanical arm returned the empty bin and Omar maneuvered it out of the way, placing it with the others at the back of the loading dock. The garbage truck's engine turned over and it rumbled away from the dock. Omar ducked behind a column and pulled out his phone to text Aron and typed the number 12, signifying a successful escape.

Omar had held up his part of the bargain—his wife and daughter would be safe as soon as Aron received confirmation that Kadare had escaped the garbage truck and was on his way to Italy.

Omar breathed a sigh of relief and slid his phone into his pocket.

ROAN KADARE GRIMACED AT THE STENCH EMANATING FROM HIS clothes as he waited in the bushes on the side of the road. Hands shoved into his pockets, he stamped his feet to bring his circulation back from the biting cold. Puffs of condensation formed in the air as he breathed. Aron would be there any minute to pick him up.

A hot shower and a warm meal first, then vengeance.

The only part of the escape they could have planned better was the transfer into the truck. Thankfully, he'd had the presence of mind to cling to the garbage when the mechanical arm lifted the bin and he tumbled into the truck, using the trash as camouflage. Getting out was easy when the truck slowed to take a turn. Aron assured him he'd find him along the regular route to the dump. Traffic was nonexistent that early in the morning.

A pair of headlights appeared in the distance. Kadare moved from his hiding place and scrambled up the side of the ditch, remaining hidden in case the car wasn't Aron.

The SUV drove slowly. Kadare recognized the make and dark color of the vehicle—Aron had texted him the information hours before the escape—and emerged from the shadows.

"It's good to see you, boss." Aron smiled as Kadare climbed into the passenger seat.

Kadare rubbed his hands together, glad for the heater's warmth. "Where's the gun?"

Aron nodded at the console beside him.

Kadare found the 9mm in the console, checked the magazine, and racked the slide. "Did you take care of the guard?"

"I did…"

Kadare gave Aron a sharp glance. "What?"

Aron hesitated. "It's nothing."

"The fuck are you on about? Tell me."

"What about his widow? And his child? Now they have nothing."

Kadare rolled his eyes. "And? What would you have me do?"

"Why not give them a little money? You can afford it."

"Give them a little money," Kadare repeated. He stared at Aron.

"It's only right." Aron shrugged.

"Right." Kadare raised the 9mm and pulled the trigger. Aron's blood and brains exploded onto the driver's side window. Luckily, his skull had likely deflected the bullet, leaving the glass intact.

That'll make the trip easier. He wouldn't have to freeze his ass off with an open window.

He got out of the vehicle and walked to the drivers' side, where he hauled Aron out and left him on the road. Kadare glanced down at the body and shook his head.

"You're too soft, Aron."

He climbed into the SUV, made a U-turn, and headed west.

23

Manny stood at the bar, poring over lunch receipts as Leine walked into the empty restaurant. He saw her and smiled.

"Ava. To what do I owe the pleasure?"

Leine climbed onto a stool and slid her bag from her shoulder. "We've got a slight problem."

"That doesn't sound good. Tell me."

"Roan Kadare escaped from prison."

Manny peered at her over his reading glasses. His intelligent gray eyes registered no surprise. "I see."

"I'm taking care of things, but I feel a duty to warn the town. Things could get rough."

"Then we should devise a plan. Tell me what we're up against."

"I don't know what kind of resources he has. I assume he'll try to raise a crew."

"Will he ask Lorik?"

"Perhaps."

"This man is Albanian, right?"

"The same as Lorik."

"Uh-huh."

Leine narrowed her eyes. "What?"

Manny's prodigious brows drew together. "Albanians are family oriented. Their need for vengeance is equal only to La Cosa Nostra. In fact, the Albanian mafia is one of the only criminal organizations the Italian mob likes to work with. They feel —how do you say?—at home with them."

"I've heard that LCN doesn't enjoy dealing with the Russians, given their aversion to rules."

"The Russians have no code." Manny's distaste was obvious.

Leine gave him a look. "Sounds like you have some experience there."

"No comment."

"Yeah, we still need to talk."

"I'm an open book."

Leine rolled her eyes. "I think it's possible that Roan Kadare is still connected."

"Even after being in prison for so long?" Manny studied her. "He is the man who sent the assassin after you?"

Leine nodded. "And three more the other night."

"Why didn't you tell me? I could have helped. Although I see you are still in one piece." He leaned over the bar, and, looking from one side to the other whispered, "Where did you hide the bodies?"

"That's a story for another time. Right now, I have to warn the town. I need a plan."

Manny smiled, his eyes lighting up. "This sounds fun."

"Seriously? The man is dangerous."

"Before you came to town, life was the same, every day. Now," he snapped his fingers, "we have excitement like I haven't had in years." He spread his arms. "I feel alive."

"And I'd like you to stay that way." Leine shook her head. Clearly, Manny was a bit touched. "I have a few friends coming to town to help. I was also thinking about enlisting Lorik and his men."

"In case he prefers not to have an overlord?"

"Exactly."

"I will be sure to tell everyone to be on the lookout."

"I'd prefer you ask them to go to ground."

"What about their businesses? They have to make a living."

"Tell them to use a skeleton crew. It would be better if they closed, but I realize that's not always feasible."

Manny waved away her concerns. "Bah. The least you can do is allow them to participate. You've done much good for this town by getting Lorik off our backs. They will want to help you in whatever way they can."

Leine nodded. "Point taken. With the number of people involved, we'll need a cohesive plan. We've already got security cameras, which will help with early warning."

"I'll station lookouts along the two routes into town."

"Excellent. I may need a distraction or two."

Manny nodded. "Done."

"Do you know how many and what kind of weapons are available? Kadare won't be shy about using guns and explosives."

"I have a pretty good idea. Many of us have hunting rifles. The odd explosive."

"That works. I have a contact that can provide whatever else we need."

It was Manny's turn to give Leine a look. "Of course you do." He went into the back of the restaurant and returned with a blank sheet of paper and two pencils. They bent their heads together and started to devise a plan.

By the time Leine left the restaurant, she felt marginally better about bringing a shit storm to Scivoloso.

She just hoped they could stop Kadare before he did any real damage.

24

L eine pulled up to the villa gate and waited while whoever was monitoring the security feed identified her. The brilliant afternoon sun warmed her face, and she leaned her head back. Throughout her life she'd learned to steal moments of tranquility, even in the midst of high-tension operations. Moments that helped restore sanity and calm. She had a feeling this would be the last time for a while—at least until she dealt with Roan Kadare.

The gate yawned open, and she drove up the driveway.

A slightly different entrance than my previous visits.

Earlier that morning, when she called and requested a meeting, Lorik had sounded surprised, but responsive to her request. She had to make the case that it was in his best interest to help protect the town from Kadare. That, or she'd have to fight both Lorik and Kadare.

Not a pleasant prospect.

Lorik's villa appeared deserted. No smoke wafted from the chimneys, and the perimeter guard was nowhere to be found. She parked and followed the walkway to the front doors. As she approached, the door opened, and one of Lorik's men walked out. He wore a shoulder holster with a gun snugged inside, and the blank look of a professional bodyguard. Apparently, Lorik had acted on her suggestion to replace his body man.

"Please spread your arms," he said in English. His British accent surprised her. Most of Lorik's men sounded like they were from the Balkans.

She complied and the man used a wand to check for weapons. He asked her to turn, which she did, and he repeated the process. Satisfied she wasn't armed, he said, "He's waiting for you in the library."

Leine walked through the high-ceilinged foyer and into the library. Lorik sat at a black baby grand at the far end of the room, plunking at the keys. An ashtray with a lit cigarette sat on the top corner, along with a highball glass half full of something amber. Scotch, if she were to guess.

Lorik stopped playing and looked up as she approached. He picked up the cigarette and took a long drag, then stubbed it out as he exhaled.

"Right on time." He stood, taking his drink with him, and gestured toward a brass and glass drink cart, circa 1950s, filled with liquor bottles, glasses, and stainless bar accoutrements. "Help yourself."

"Maybe a glass of wine?"

In response, Lorik took out his phone and typed something. A moment later, the bodyguard appeared with a bottle of red and a wine glass. He opened the bottle and poured the wine, then left the room.

"I see you took my advice on your bodyguard."

"He came highly recommended."

Leine picked up the drink and breathed in the aroma. Cherries, a hint of chocolate, and a light oaky scent. She studied the label. "From your vineyard?"

Lorik smiled. "Yes. I hope you enjoy it."

"Skol."

She held up her glass in a toast and took a sip. He did the same with his drink.

"It's lovely. You aren't having any?"

"I've been in Italy too long and consumed too many bottles. At this point I prefer a good Scotch."

"Understood. I'm normally a tequila kind of girl. But I do love a good red now and then."

"Now that we have the niceties out of the way, what is it that you want? I assume this has something to do with Nestor's interrogation?"

"I found out who wants me dead, and he tried again."

"Obviously he failed. Who is it?"

"Roan Kadare."

It took a minute before recognition flickered across Lorik's face. "Fatos's younger brother?"

"The one and only."

"And how is this my problem?"

"Nestor told him I was still alive. He's your guy. You owe me, especially if you want to keep Kadare from taking over Scivoloso."

"But he's in prison."

"He's decided he'd rather not be."

"I was under the impression that Elvis Sadiki coordinated his transfer from Rezina. Unless Kadare's time is up, he must remain in prison until he has worked off whatever Sadiki paid for the move."

"Yeah, well, looks like he prefers vengeance."

Lorik narrowed his eyes. "You killed Fatos?"

"So they say."

"Nestor didn't tell this to me."

"Nestor is probably hoping for a big, fat payday from Kadare."

"Why shouldn't I sabotage his end run, as you Americans say, and collect this big payday?" He gestured at Leine. "You have no weapons. It would be easy for me to detain you."

"If you say so."

Doubt lit his eyes for a brief moment, then disappeared. "Say I agree to help you. What's in it for me? I assume you want me to stop him from carrying out his vengeance."

"If you don't, you do realize he's not going to stop there? You think you can just go back to your life once he accomplishes his plan? When he sees what you've built for yourself, he won't want to leave." She didn't know that, of course, but she could play on Lorik's fear of losing the villa.

Lorik took another sip of his drink. "You make a good point. Tell me what you want, and I will tell you whether I will do it."

"If Kadare comes to you, and I believe he will, I would like you to tell him whatever he wants to hear, then not do what he asks."

"That will put me and my operation in danger."

"Sabotage can be invisible if done right."

"You think he will come to me for reinforcements?"

Leine shrugged. "He might. He got the information from your guy. How much do you want to bet Nestor gave him the lowdown on your business?"

By the look on Lorik's face, she'd hit a nerve.

"I also need you to back me and the town if it comes to that."

Lorik raised his chin. "Ah. Now we get to what you really want."

"I really want you to kill Kadare if he shows up here, but I'm a realist. Even you might have a hard time doing that to one of your countrymen—especially one with his connections. Perhaps you could alert me when and if he shows up?"

Lorik's expression told her that was a nonstarter.

"At the very least, I want you to trick Kadare into thinking you'll help him. But it would be good to know I have backup if I need it."

And hopefully keep Lorik from taking Kadare's side if things get squirrelly.

Lorik studied her for a moment. "What else do I get for this assistance? If a man like Kadare finds out I double-crossed him, he'll stop at nothing to kill me."

"I'll take care of Kadare. Then we can go back to our original agreement—you keep the villa and vineyard, and I won't kill you."

"You still haven't convinced me. If Nestor is waiting for a big payday as you say, why wouldn't Kadare pay me for killing you?"

"Because I believe that Roan Kadare wants to kill me himself. If you take that away from him, he may become enraged enough that he comes after you. You've heard of his temper?"

"Another good point." Lorik held out his hand. "I believe we have a deal."

Leine bit her tongue and shook his hand. Using sarcasm at this juncture wasn't worth it—besides, what she wanted to say might not translate well in Albanian.

"I'll need to know your strategy so that I can develop my own."

"Sorry, Lorik. You're on a need-to-know basis."

"You still don't trust me." His words were a statement, not a question.

"Show me that I can. Then we'll talk."

Roan Kadare slammed his phone on the table and scowled at the wall of his hotel room. Apparently, his time in prison had depleted the loyal base he'd built over the years. He would need to rely on paid mercenaries, which wasn't at all how he envisioned his plan.

What the hell did you think? That everyone would just wait until you returned? People have to make a living.

Still, their disloyalty pissed him off.

He had plenty of funds after accessing his offshore accounts in Cyprus. But hired guns were far less desirable than loyal soldiers.

His anger bubbling beneath the surface, he leaned his head back and closed his eyes to think. Who else could he call? He'd run out of names, and using Elvis Sadiki's crew was no longer an option. He doubted any of them would cross that line to help him.

Nestor.

Didn't the underling's boss live near the target? Lorik something? From what Nestor mentioned, the man was low-level Albanian mafia who was persona non grata with his patron back in the old country. Kadare and Lorik's shared homeland would go a long way toward securing the man's loyalty and make it all the easier to talk him into lending Kadare his forces. Not only that, but Nestor believed the Leopard had killed at least three of his crew, which would also help bring his boss around to Kadare's plan.

And Kadare could be very persuasive.

His mood soaring, Kadare opened his eyes and picked up his phone. Nestor answered on the third ring.

25

Leine waved at the small group standing on the sidewalk outside Pisa International. Art Kowalski waved back and headed toward her, his crew in tow. She recognized the shorter of the men who had a shaved head and tattoo of the rod of Asclepius, and another, much taller man, who sported long, black hair and an earring: Jorge, the medic, and Zarko, the smartass. Both were excellent operators she'd worked with before. The other three she didn't recognize.

Art's crew stashed their carry-ons in the back of Manny's van, while Art walked over and gave her a big hug.

"Good to see you, Leine. Remember me?"

"It's great to see you, Art," Leine replied. "And yes, I remember you. And Jorge and Zarko."

"Yeah. Just checking. Last time we spoke, you weren't exactly yourself."

Art and his crew had helped Leine, Lou, and Santa fight back against the Association at a time when she'd been experiencing chemically induced retrograde amnesia. She'd only just begun to piece together her life with help from a hypnotherapist when he and his team returned to their home base in Greece.

"Let me introduce the rest of this motley crew."

Jorge and Zarko gave Leine a quick hug. She turned to the other three.

"This is Pierre," Art said, indicating a tall, dark-haired man who looked to be in his late twenties. "Our comms guru."

Pierre smiled, revealing deep dimples in an unlined face. The youngest of the group, his accent suggested a Haitian background. "I'm also really good at Parkour."

"That could come in handy." Leine shook his hand. "Am I correct in assuming you've spent time in Haiti?"

Pierre nodded. "Born and raised. Been working on infrastructure for the last few years, trying to get hospitals and schools back online."

"I imagine that's been difficult."

"Challenging, yes. Gangs run Port-au-Prince. They're hard to work with, you know?"

"Is that why you're here?"

He nodded. "I needed a break."

Art gestured toward the lone female of the group. "This is Gina. She's amazing with any weapon you hand her—especially knives. Her other strength is strategy."

Gina smiled and shook Leine's hand. Wavy, chestnut brown hair framed a heart-shaped face with full lips and brown eyes. A curvy, athletic physique completed the picture. She oozed confidence. "It is so good to meet another woman in this business." She rolled her eyes at the men behind her. "I grow weary of their childish jokes."

Leine grinned at Zarko and Pierre, who both clutched their hearts in mock pain. "I understand completely." She shifted her attention back to Gina. "Your accent, Italian?"

"*Si.* Art thought it would be a good idea to have a native speaker. Although he tells me that you are quite proficient?"

"I am, yes. But it's always good to have someone who understands nuance."

"It don't sound like there's gonna be a lotta nuance in this operation." The last crewmember shouldered his way forward to shake Leine's hand. His blond hair, serene blue eyes, and Fu Manchu goatee gave the impression of a warrior monk. His accent screamed south Texas. The way he held himself and his assertive manner suggested a healthy ego paired with military training.

"This is Sam," Art continued. "He's an artist when it comes to explosives. Pretty good in hand-to-hand, too."

Sam smiled and looked at the ground in what could have been construed as humility. His "aw-shucks" attitude and easy-going smile didn't mesh with Leine's initial assessment.

She returned the handshake. "We should get going. It's an hour and some change to Scivoloso. We can talk about the op on the way there."

"Sounds good to me." Art had everyone load into the van. Sam took off in another direction.

Leine looked at Art. "He's got his own ride," Art replied as he climbed in the front passenger seat. Leine started the engine and pulled into traffic, headed for the A12.

"So, what's the skinny?" Art asked. "Who'd you piss off this time?"

Leine sighed. "No good deed goes unpunished. Isn't that what they say?"

Art snorted. "What happened?"

"I helped the residents in Scivoloso get out from under an extortion scheme run by a local thug. Turns out one of his crew worked for a target I neutralized over twenty years ago. He recognized me and put the word out."

"A hit from the Agency days?"

Leine nodded. "Albanian mafia—Fatos Kadare. The aggrieved party is the younger brother of the target, Roan."

"Ouch. Albanian *and* family revenge? That's a one-two punch. Why did it take him this long?"

"I was supposed to be dead."

"Damn you for living," Art quipped. "What about this small-time criminal you bested in town? He gonna be a problem?"

"I'm not sure. We have a deal, in theory. If Roan Kadare enlists Lorik to help kill me, which is a fairly sure bet, he's supposed to go along to make Kadare think he's onboard. But if things go sideways, he says he'll back me up."

"Let me guess—you persuaded him that Kadare wouldn't be satisfied with just killing you?"

Leine nodded. "Lorik's especially fond of his villa and vineyard. Kadare just escaped from prison. He's going to need a way to make a living."

"Interesting. So we need to take out Kadare. How much does he know about you?"

"Where I live, what I look like. He's already tried to kill me from prison. Twice. The failures of which are likely the reason he decided to escape. Lorik's guy, Nestor, is his contact in Lorik's organization."

"Any way to get to Nestor?"

"Already done. Lorik offered him to me for questioning. That's how I found out it was Kadare."

"How organized is Lorik?"

"From what I've seen, it's loose. He's got maybe a dozen soldiers left."

"Left?"

"I burned through five of them." Jona, Donat, Erwin, and the two gunmen at the abandoned church. Lorik's cooperation had been surprising, to say the least.

Art whistled. "Yeah, I wouldn't rely on ol' Lorik to come through for ya. Not if you neutralized that many of his guys."

"Maybe. But it also sent a message. His men tried to kill me. I defended myself. When Lorik asked how supporting me would benefit him, I told him if he helped me I wouldn't kill him."

Art chuckled. "Vintage Leine." He fell silent for a moment.

"What d'ya think, Art? Shock and awe?" Zarko asked from the backseat.

Art shrugged. "Maybe. Let's get to the safe house. I want everyone's input. If that's all right with you, Leine?"

"Perfect."

At that moment, an electric blue Ducati motorcycle screamed past, the helmeted driver hunched behind the windscreen.

Leine whistled. "Nice bike."

Art nodded at the fast-disappearing rider. "That would be Sam."

26

———————

A little under two hours later, they pulled into the courtyard of a picturesque farmhouse on a hill overlooking the valley. Just outside of Scivoloso, the two-story brick building and surrounding property was far enough from the main road into town to be discreet, yet close enough for quick mobilization. Sam was standing next to the Ducati, waiting for them.

Art exited the van and took in his surroundings. The afternoon sun glinted off a small grove of olive trees to his left. Bright fuchsia bougainvillea curved over the front door as the scent of roses mixed with lavender perfumed the air. The blue tiles of a pool could be seen through a second arch of bougainvillea.

"How'd you find this gem?"

Leine helped the crew with their bags. "One of those online vacation rental sites." She'd had Lou make the booking under a false identity.

"If only that was available back in the day, huh? Would've made going to ground a whole lot easier."

"And more comfortable."

Art nodded. "One of the worst hideouts I ever used was in

Poland. A rusty old shipping container inside a junkyard in the middle of winter. No heat, no water. I'd never been so damn cold. Originally used as a *Spetsnaz* safe house. The rats outnumbered the cockroaches five to one."

"You got me beat." Leine handed the last bag to Zarko. "My worst was a cave in Yemen. Cold, dirty, no running water, toilet was a spot on the ground, as far from my bivvy bag as possible. Lots of bats, but at least there weren't any rodents."

"That you could see."

"Good point."

Art and Leine followed the rest of the group into the farmhouse.

"Put your things away, clean up a little, and then meet back down here in twenty," Art told everyone. "We're going to do some planning."

"There should be enough rooms to have your own. First come, first served." Leine smiled as Pierre and Zarko tried to beat each other up the stairs. Pierre easily bypassed Zarko by scaling the banister. Jorge and Sam just shook their heads.

Gina rolled her eyes at Leine. "See what I have to put up with?"

"Ladies first, guys," Art said.

"So much for feminism," Zarko grumbled good-naturedly.

Leine turned to Art. "You want a drink?"

"Don't mind if I do."

She led him to the kitchen. Leine grabbed a couple of cold beers from the fridge and handed one to Art.

He took a sip and sat down at the square table occupying the middle of the room. Leine remained standing.

"You doin' all right?" Art asked. "You seem a bit tense, if I may be so bold."

Leine sighed as she pulled out the chair across from him and sat down. "That obvious?"

Art snorted.

"This couldn't have come at a worse time." She shook her head. "I thought this would be a cake walk. Move to some little Italian town, open a bookstore, hide from the world with Santa once he retires." She sipped her beer and set the bottle on the table. "He's going to be here in a week."

Art's eyebrows arched in surprise. "He doesn't know what's going on?"

Leine shook her head. "I don't want him to worry. And I *don't* want him to think moving to Italy was a mistake."

"Was it?"

"Maybe." She blew out a sigh. "Los Angeles is looking pretty good right now. I miss the anonymity."

"So what if it was a mistake? You're entitled. It's not like you could've anticipated Roan Kadare."

"I know. I just wanted this to be...perfect."

Art scoffed. "Shit, Leine. You know perfection is the enemy, right? Ain't no way you can get everything perfect. Try giving yourself a break." He leaned over and touched his bottle to hers. "Let's take care of Kadare and this Lorik guy, if we need to. Then, you can get on with your life –whether it's here or somewhere else." He leaned back. "Easy, yeah?"

Leine smiled. "You always did make sense, Art. Thanks."

"Thank me when this is over. My first thought is to set a trap, depending on the town's layout and where Kadare lands."

"I want to keep civilian casualties to a minimum. None, if possible."

"That'll depend on whether we use them or not. How amenable are they to helping out?"

"Manny—you'll meet him later this afternoon—says a majority are onboard." She frowned. "I'd prefer not to use any."

"You're a softy, Leine. If Manny says they're good to go, we gotta use 'em. There's no telling how many soldiers Kadare's gonna rustle up. Right now, we're sitting with my crew, and you. That's seven. Not that we can't do a lot of damage with seven well-trained operators, but I'd feel a whole lot better if we had some lookouts and diversions in our toolkit."

"Yeah, I know. It'd be so much easier if we could take the fight to the enemy. I hate waiting for the first strike."

"You don't believe Lorik's gonna give you a heads-up?"

"I'd be surprised."

"Then we need somebody on surveillance." He grinned. "I've got just the person."

27

H is throat uncharacteristically tight, Lorik stood in the villa's doorway as the gleaming black Yukon made its way up the winding drive.

Through the windshield it appeared that Roan Kadare had come alone. No bodyguard, no driver, not even a woman.

Odd, although he had just broken out of an Albanian prison where he'd been serving a decades-long sentence. Employees didn't always stick around until the boss got back, especially if they hadn't been provided for in the interim.

A man has to eat.

Nestor walked out to greet their visitor. The traitor had returned from his interrogation by the American subdued. Lorik could tell he'd been through some things, although the Basso woman hadn't inflicted any visible damage. Lorik asked him why he'd abandoned his car at the bottom of the drive, allowing the lunch to grow cold. Nestor said the American had picked him up, but that he hadn't answered any of her questions. Lorik let it slide. He'd half-hoped she'd eliminate the little fucker, taking the decision off his plate. But she'd obviously controlled herself.

Lorik put a smile on his face. *Might as well be pleasant.* The Basso woman's words flitted through his head. Kadare was here to enlist his help, of course. But if what she predicted turned out to be true, then all that Lorik had built—the remodeled villa, his small but flourishing vineyard, the tributes he managed to eke out from neighboring towns—was at stake. If Kadare successfully eliminated his enemy, what would stop him from trying to take over Lorik's little slice of the pie? Defying Elvis Sadiki was not a great professional move, and likely the reason Kadare was here for Lorik's help. Without the largesse of his patron, Kadare would have to build a new business from the ground up.

Lorik's own patron wouldn't help him if it came to that. Hell, he didn't even like Lorik. The only reason his patron allowed him to run his crew in Scivoloso was because he was family. Otherwise, he'd likely be at the bottom of the Mediterranean.

Kadare exited the SUV and largely ignored Nestor, his shrewd gaze falling upon the man whose help he'd come to request. Lorik resisted the urge to put out his hand in friendship, preferring to see how Kadare wanted to play it.

Kadare grinned and held out his hand, which Lorik took in his own. He had a firm palm, and the man's energy oozed from his pores. But it was Kadare's eyes that were most striking. Lorik had met all kinds of men in his illustrious career, but none had the unnerving indication of psychosis that now met his gaze.

This was not a man to cross.

In that instant, Lorik realized he wouldn't be able to fulfill the deal he'd made with the Basso woman. He'd have to help Kadare kill his enemy, unless Lorik killed Kadare first. Eliminating Kadare would likely attract the attention of Sadiki, which would be lethal for Lorik—Sadiki might not be happy with Roan Kadare, but he was still his patron. Sadiki would contact Lorik's boss, and things would escalate.

No, he needed to assist Kadare in his quest for vengeance.

Then, when the wild dog least expected it, Lorik would euthanize the threat now standing before him. An accident, of course.

At least he made good on his original promise of allowing Ava Basso to interrogate Nestor. The greedy little traitor had no idea Lorik gave him up. Hopefully, because of this, she would view Lorik's decision not to hold up his end of their bargain as less of a betrayal. Obviously, the Basso woman was dangerous. But in playing the long game, Lorik figured crossing Kadare was the more lethal choice.

Although, there might still be a way to play both sides.

"Good to finally meet, Lorik. Nestor's told me much about you."

Lorik glanced at his soon-to-be-ex-employee. "All of it good, I hope."

Kadare didn't respond. Instead, he took in the villa, the vineyard, and the territorial view. "Spectacular place you have here." He shook his finger in Lorik's face. "If you're not careful, someone may try to sweep this out from under you."

"They can try."

By the look on Kadare's face, the veiled threat did not go unnoticed.

He nodded toward the front door. "Are you going to invite me inside this magnificent villa? I'm curious to see what you've done. Nestor tells me you've been remodeling for two years now?"

Lorik narrowed his eyes at Nestor. "Has he?" His mood plummeted as he led the way into the villa. All the work and sweat he'd expended to get the villa and vineyards into shape, not to mention the small fortune he'd spent, was going to go up in smoke. He had no doubt Kadare would devise a way to take over the estate, likely by assassinating Lorik. He'd probably order Nestor to do it. To lessen that possibility, Lorik needed to neutralize the little prick.

They entered the grand foyer and Kadare whistled. "Very nice. Understated, but elegant." He nodded in approval. "I like it." He walked into the sitting room. "I'm impressed, Lorik. You've done well."

Lorik waved dismissively at his home. "It's an old building with a lot of problems. It's taken me years to create decent living conditions."

"Show me the rest. Then we can talk of eliminating our enemy."

Once the tour was over, the two men retired to the sitting room. Lorik fixed them each a Scotch and handed one to Kadare.

"Your empire has good bones," Kadare remarked. "But it could be so much more."

"Meaning?"

Kadare sat forward in his chair. "You and I—we should go into business together."

Lorik hadn't seen that coming. "What are you proposing?" He wasn't about to tell him the pickings in the area were slim, hardly enough to sustain even a midsized criminal enterprise.

"Look at the big picture." Kadare spread his arms wide. "We could own every small town in Italy."

"What about 'Ndrangheta and the Cosa Nostra? They've already got a stake in the larger cities like Florence and Pisa."

Kadare waved at the air. "Leave them their cities. There is real opportunity here."

Lorik nodded. He had a point. Lorik hadn't been successful in securing much business outside of Scivoloso, but he hadn't tried that hard. Ever since the Basso woman arrived and issued her ultimatum, he'd been rethinking his trajectory. He enjoyed everything that went with having a vineyard. The wine it produced was some of the best in the area. True, his acreage was small, but he could always buy more. Even so,

Kadare's suggestion intrigued him enough to continue the conversation.

Leine ended the call and slid her phone into her back pocket.

"Who was that?" Art asked. Planning over, Art's crew had dispersed, some to the pool to catch the last of the sunshine, some to their rooms to rest up for the next day. Gina left to recce the villa.

"Lorik. He wanted to see if I was going to stay at the apartment above the bookstore."

"Ah. So an attack is imminent." The listening device Leine planted under the table in Lorik's foyer had picked up Roan Kadare's arrival.

Leine nodded. "Lorik was clipped on the phone, like he was in a hurry to finish the call. When I asked him if he'd heard anything about Kadare, he said something vague and changed the subject."

"Looks like you'll be spending the night."

"Lorik also said he wanted to meet. This afternoon."

"Did he tell you why?"

"Again, he was vague, but insisted that it would be worth my while. He also said I'd know where."

"Which means?"

"An abandoned church not far from here, where I met him the first time."

"Think it's a trap?"

"Maybe. Odds are good since Kadare's here."

"How many men you think Lorik will use?"

"Last time he brought three. I killed two and wounded one,

so I'd say at least that many. If it's a trap with Kadare, I'd say a whole lot more."

"Describe the area. I'll mobilize the crew."

———

LEINE PARKED AT THE BOTTOM OF THE RISE AND KILLED THE ENGINE. The church ruins had a malevolent appearance at dusk. A chill skittered up her spine. Was Kadare waiting for her? She keyed her mic.

"I'm here."

"We're in position," Art answered. "No activity yet. Gina just texted me that there hasn't been any movement at the villa, either."

"Any sign of Lorik or Kadare at either place?"

"One sighting of Lorik through a window at the villa. Nothing of Kadare."

Leine adjusted the Velcro on her vest and exited the vehicle. She drew her gun and climbed the path leading to the church. If Kadare was there, he was waiting to pick her off. Why?

She reached the church and walked inside, gun first.

A bat swooped past, and she raised her weapon. The interior appeared empty. She moved through, clearing the space.

No Lorik.

She was about to leave when something about the tomb caught her eye. The lid had been moved, leaving a slim gap between it and the tomb.

"Found something." She attempted to slide the heavy stone, but it wouldn't budge.

"What is it?" Art asked over the earpiece.

"I'm going to need a hand."

"I got it," Zarko replied. A minute later, he slipped into the church.

"The lid's been moved."

"Zombies?" Zarko arched his eyebrows.

"Probably not."

Between the two of them, they moved the lid far enough to shine Leine's penlight into the space.

Zarko whistled. "That's quite the stash."

"What d'ya got?" Art's voice came over her mic.

"There's a cache of AK-47s"—she swept her light around the interior of the tomb—"an SVD Dragunov sniper rifle, five or six TT-33s, and a whole lot of ammo."

"That's pretty neighborly of Lorik, don't you think?"

"Yeah, but why?"

"I assume he doesn't know you already have a stash from Lou's guy in Florence."

"Not unless he's got a pro tracking me." Leine had made sure no one had followed her to Florence when she picked up the guns.

"He's trying to even the scales," Sam offered. "Maybe he feels guilty because he isn't gonna help you like he said."

"Or he wants to make sure you're armed so Kadare doesn't win," Pierre offered. "You mentioned he was worried about Kadare taking over his stuff."

"Either of those could be true. And at the same time."

"Might want to watch out for explosives," Art warned.

"Copy that." She leaned in further, shining her light underneath the lid. Zarko checked the other end with his mini-Maglite.

"Anything?" she asked. He shook his head. "Not seeing anything here."

"You check for pressure plates?" Art asked.

"Affirmative. There don't appear to be any."

Art let out a long sigh. "Okay. Pierre, you help them with the weapons. Sam and Jorge cover the church."

"Copy."

"Looks like we'll be able to arm the citizenry," Art said.

"Yeah, but at what cost?"

"C'mon, Leine. You can't fight both Kadare and Lorik and keep your friends in town safe. They'll have a better chance if they're armed."

"We don't have time to train them."

"Pray and spray, baby."

"Seriously, Art?" Granted, using an AK-47 didn't require precision—one of the reasons for its popularity around the world—but the idea of Francesca or Tomaso fighting a hardened criminal like Kadare didn't sit well with her. "Why would Lorik want me and the town well-armed? Kadare's likely going to demand that Lorik use his guys, right? That would put them in danger. It doesn't make sense."

"I'm gonna go with him not wanting Kadare to win, and hoping the weapons stash buys him and his men some good will," Art said. "Look. Either way, once we make sure the firearms do what they're supposed to, we've got more to work with, right?"

"Yeah." Leine had to agree. Why look a gift horse in the mouth?

They transported the guns and ammo to the farmhouse with Manny's van, then retired for the night.

28

The next morning, Leine and Zarko made breakfast for the crew, then brewed coffee and set out pastries and chairs in the living room for the folks from town as they started to trickle in. Leine had borrowed a white board and some dry erase markers from the school and set up near the fireplace at the far end of the living room. While they waited, Gina gave the group a lesson in knife throwing in the forecourt. She was good, hitting each target dead-center with a set of wicked twelve-inch knives.

Francesca and Tomaso arrived first, followed by Nadia from the gelateria, and Angelo, the grocer. Several other business owners and their handpicked employees came, as well. Manny and Bruno arrived with a case of wine.

"For later, when the hard work is finished," Manny explained.

Leine counted eighteen, not including Art and his crew. A good showing. Every one of them willing to put their lives on the line for their town.

She introduced Art and his team, giving a brief introduction of each. Then Art and Manny presented the team's plan, with Art explaining that everything could change in an instant depending on what kind of attack Lorik and Kadare decided to execute.

"How will we know if something changes?" asked Eppie, an employee from a gift store near Old Town.

"Good question." Art wrote two cellphone numbers on the white board in blue marker. "Put these numbers in your contacts list on your mobile phones." Several of the attendees pulled out their phones and entered the numbers.

"Keep your phones with you at all times," Manny added. "Text either number if you run into problems or something changes at your end that you think we need to know. The first one is Ava's, the second is Art's. Either will work. One of them will figure out what to do."

Leine took up the thread. "I appreciate the bravery you've shown by being here. There aren't that many people who would risk their lives to fight for their community."

"We're not just fighting for the town, Ava," Francesca said. "We're fighting for you. You made Lorik stop extorting our businesses. You also saved my niece's life. I can't thank you enough." Murmurs of support came from the rest of the group.

"And don't forget," Tomaso added, "Ava saved you both from being murdered that day in Lucca."

Francesca nodded. "Like I said, I will never be able to repay you."

Leine wasn't sure how to respond. Usually her actions stoked anger. She targeted bad actors, and bad actors didn't usually appreciate her efforts. She rarely had time to check up on the people she'd helped before another crisis demanded her time.

"Thank you, Francesca. And thank all of you." She gestured to the group. "You've welcomed me and made me feel at home in

Scivoloso. That is a priceless gift. I'm sorry things have escalated to this point. Roan Kadare is not a man to be underestimated. To that point, I would like to offer an additional level of defense." She searched the faces of the group. Who would survive this senseless war of revenge? If only she could fight Kadare and Lorik on her own.

Well, they were here now. "We recently came into a cache of weapons."

A few attendees shifted uncomfortably in their chairs.

"If you'd rather not use a gun or any of the other weapons we have at our disposal, you don't have to. There is still a lot you can do."

"Like what?" The question came from a pretty young woman with dark purple hair sitting in the front row. Leine remembered her from a restaurant in town.

"We'll likely need a diversion when Kadare's men show up. You can block their progress, especially if they're in a vehicle, by causing a traffic jam or placing an obstacle in the street they can't drive over, that kind of thing.

"You can also text us their position. We've suggested several places to hide along the route through town that we anticipate them taking. But don't be a hero. If it feels or looks too danger-ous, stand down. We don't want anyone hurt or worse."

"What about casualties?" Angelo asked.

"I'll let the expert take this one." Leine gestured to Jorge.

The meeting continued for another hour and a half. By the end, everyone knew what was expected of them. Six opted for a weapon. Four men had access to a shotgun or a hunting rifle. The other eight would observe and report. Several broke off from the larger group to work on diversionary tactics.

"We don't know exactly when they're going to make their move, but it won't be long," Art said. "Gina has visually confirmed Roan Kadare is at the villa, and that a group of men has assembled there, so we assume the attack will take place in the next twenty-four hours."

Manny cracked open the wine. "Then we must toast to a successful conclusion to this war against our town."

Leine raised her glass but didn't drink. She hoped he was right.

Lorik finished loading a high-capacity magazine and set it on the pile before he picked up another. "Nestor, go with Aleksander into town, do some reconnaissance."

Nestor zipped his hoodie against the damp chill of the crowded wine cellar. Even though it was late morning, a layer of frost coated the roofs.

Kadare had insisted on using the smaller, unheated space as a staging area for the attack on the American. Lorik had agreed, which surprised Nestor. The room was large enough for only four or five men and the weapons, with the rest of the crew spilling out the cellar door into the courtyard. The men were abuzz with the excitement always prevalent at the start of an operation.

Why not use the larger sitting room at the front of the villa? There would be space to spread out and not bump into each other like they were doing now.

The immediate plan was for Lorik's men to locate the Basso woman and isolate her. He assumed then Kadare would swoop in to deliver the coup de grâce. Besides Nestor, Lorik, and Kadare, there were nine additional gunmen for a total of twelve.

Everyone wore body armor and carried radios, giving the impression of a military-style operation. None of the gunmen were actually ex-military, most having gained their bona fides fighting with other gangs like Nestor had. Three were on loan from an acquaintance of Lorik's who ran an operation several kilometers to the east.

Twelve didn't seem like nearly enough.

"What's eating you, Nestor?" Kadare asked. "You look as though you lost your best friend."

Should he say something? If he didn't and the op failed, he'd never forgive himself. Nestor steeled his courage. "Are you sure we have enough men?"

Lorik and Kadare both chuckled. Kadare finished seating the last round in a magazine before he looked at Nestor. "I could do this alone, but Lorik insists on finding and detaining the Leopard for me." He shrugged, seemingly unconcerned. "Why wouldn't I take his offer? The only objective I'm concerned with is that I kill her myself. Anything else is logistics."

"I only mention this because of her ability to evade capture."

"She has nine lives, yes?" Kadare grinned and held up an assault rifle. "We have twelve men. She will not have enough lives."

There was a murmur of agreement from the rest of the contingent. Nestor backed off. There was no reasoning with Kadare, and Lorik seemed content to do as he wished.

"Of course." Nestor grabbed two loaded AKs with extra magazines and headed for the courtyard. Aleksander, Lorik's body man, stood in the doorway. Nestor nodded to him. "Let's go."

As the two men walked to one of three white Hiluxes parked outside, Lorik appeared at the door of the cellar. Nestor glanced up in time to see Aleksander and Lorik exchange looks.

Nestor stowed the AKs on the floor behind the seat and

climbed in. Aleksander got behind the wheel and started the engine.

"What was that about?" Nestor asked.

"What?"

"That look Lorik gave you."

"I don't know what you're talking about." Aleksander pulled away from the villa and headed down the drive. The man's clipped British accent had always bothered Nestor. He couldn't put his finger on why, but the man rankled him.

Nestor let it drop, although a spark of insecurity nibbled his gut. He tried to relax, but not knowing what kind of shit storm they were headed into, plus the look between his boss and Aleksander, put him on edge. Had Lorik been upset that Nestor contacted Kadare in prison and then ordered his body man to watch him? Nestor had no idea that Kadare would escape and come to the villa. Surely Lorik understood that.

Maybe he was being paranoid.

Aleksander reached the bottom of the drive and took a right.

Turning left would have brought them into Scivoloso. Why had he turned right? The possibility that Lorik might be gunning for him turned the tiny spark of insecurity into cold dread. Did Lorik know the Leopard had interrogated him? If so, he could have mentioned it to Kadare. If Kadare thought he'd been betrayed, he would order Nestor's execution.

Who better to do this than Lorik's bodyguard?

"Where are we going?" Nestor inched his hand closer to his gun, the weight of the weapon in his holster reassuring.

"I've got something I need to do first," Aleksander replied.

They drove through the countryside, passing farms and villas that rented rooms to rich Europeans and Americans under the guise of *agroturismo*. Places for city dwellers to brag to their friends of being farmers.

Nestor supposed the money from the tourists helped the economy. He just didn't like tourists. Or rich Americans.

A few kilometers later Aleksander turned up a little-used gravel road that led back into the hills. There weren't any homes or other structures in sight.

At this point, Nestor was positive Lorik had told Aleksander to kill him and leave his body somewhere it wouldn't be found. There'd be no evidence except his bones after the wolves consumed his flesh.

His mood dark, Nestor stared out the window, his hand now firmly gripping the butt of his gun. The only question that remained was one of timing. Aleksander glanced at him.

"What's wrong?" he asked.

"What do you mean?" Nestor injected as much sarcasm as he could into his words.

"You've been acting weird since we left the villa." Aleksander shifted into a lower gear to compensate for the steep incline. "Are you that upset Lorik and Kadare wouldn't listen to you?"

"That isn't it." He pulled his gun and leveled it at Aleksander. Sweat poured down the sides of his face. "I know you're supposed to kill me."

"What the fuck, Nestor?" Aleksander slammed on the brakes and the pickup skidded to a stop. Nestor braced himself against the door and managed to keep the pistol aimed at the other man's head.

His foot still firmly on the brake, Aleksander slowly raised his hands. "I swear, brother, I'm not going to kill you."

"Then what was that look between you and Lorik, huh?" Nestor waved the gun at him, his anger and fear ratcheting higher.

"You really want to kill me?" Aleksander gave him a resigned look. "I thought we were on the same side."

Nestor shook his head, his thoughts muddled.

"I need air."

He opened the door and half-fell, half-climbed from the pickup. Slamming the door closed, he took a deep breath and exhaled, watching the condensation form in the air. The breeze sliced through him, reminding him of the inadequacy of his sweatshirt against the cold. Aleksander got out, careful to keep the truck between them.

Smart, Nestor thought. The engine block was good cover.

"What the fuck is wrong with you?" Aleksander asked, switching to Nestor's mother tongue. "Who do you think wants to kill you? Lorik?" When Nestor didn't say anything, he shook his head. "Why? He needs all the men he can get." He studied Nestor. "Kadare? Possibly," he conceded. "He is one crazy motherfucker. But again, he needs all of us. If he wants somebody dead, he's going to wait until this is over."

Nestor let the other man's words sink in. Aleksander was right. He lowered his pistol and shrugged to loosen the tension in his shoulders.

Aleksander studied Nestor. "Are we good? You aren't going to pop me while I'm driving, right?"

Nestor smiled. "Nah. I'll wait until we stop."

Aleksander cracked a smile. "Good. As long as we're on the same page." He climbed back into the pickup.

Nestor holstered his gun and did the same. What *was* he thinking? He couldn't tell anyone about the interrogation, or about the American woman's threat to his family. The guilt of giving up Kadare to the Leopard was eating at him. All of Lorik's men—men who were like family—were in danger, and it was his fault.

As they drove further back into the hills, Nestor glimpsed a small stone structure through the trees. "What are we doing here?"

Aleksander slowed to a stop and shifted into Park. "More weapons."

They exited the pickup and walked to the structure, which turned out to be a shepherd's summer cabin. Wooden shutters with padlocks had been installed from the outside, likely to deter squatters.

Aleksander retrieved a key from under a nearby rock and unlocked the door.

As Nestor's eyes adjusted, the interior resolved into spare but serviceable quarters. Cupboards and a small sink serviced by a pump handle took up one wall, with a stone-topped table and chair against another. A single cot made up with sheets and blankets had been shoved underneath one of the shuttered windows. Another shuttered window took up a portion of another wall.

"Tidy little place. This yours?"

Aleksander ignored his question and opened a small closet near the sink, from which he pulled a duffel bag, three rifles, and a shotgun. Boxes of shotgun shells and ammunition for the rifles followed. "Put the guns in the truck."

Nestor did as he requested and walked back inside the cabin. Aleksander stood near the bed, in the process of zipping the duffel bag closed.

"Is the cabin Lorik's?" Nestor asked. "He never mentioned it."

Aleksander turned. He had a gun, which he aimed at Nestor's head. Nestor raised his hands and began to back up.

"Stop."

Heart thudding, Nestor stopped. He could make a run for it —freedom was only a few feet behind him. By the look in Aleksander's eyes, he'd be dead before he made it to the door. Resigned, Nestor remained where he was.

"Remove your gun and slide it to me."

Why hadn't Aleksander shot him? Nestor glanced at the

floor. Probably didn't want his blood soaking into the stone. He removed his best chance at escape, placed it on the floor, and kicked it to him.

"I knew there was something about you that didn't fit." Nestor scoffed, covering his fear.

"You know nothing." Aleksander gestured to the cot behind him. "Sit on the cot and remove your shoes."

Nestor walked to the bed and sat as Aleksander retrieved Nestor's gun and moved in front of the door. Nestor took off his shoes.

"Throw them toward the door."

"The fuck is this—you're going to kill me and steal my shoes?"

"Just do what I tell you."

With a shake of his head, Nestor threw his shoes toward the door.

"There are supplies in the cupboard—water, granola bars." Aleksander nodded toward the stove. "There's enough wood for a few days. I'd be sparing with building a fire. Just in case."

"You're not killing me, then?"

"Lorik wants you dead. But I'm not going to kill you, no."

Nestor's shoulders inched down as relief replaced fear. "So you're going to leave me here?" His spirits plummeted. He wouldn't be a witness to the Leopard's end. "What happens if I just leave?"

"You can try. Once I lock the door, there's no easy way out." He glanced around the structure. "Strike that. There's no way out, period."

Nestor made to stand, but Aleksander shook his head. He sat back down on the cot. "No one knows I'm here, right? What happens if you're killed?" Even though it was twelve against one woman, a massacre was a real possibility.

"Don't worry. There are contingencies in place." He turned to leave.

"Wait."

Aleksander paused near the door.

"Where do I, you know?" He pretended to hold his ass cheeks together.

Aleksander pointed to a scuffed white paint bucket in the corner. A roll of paper towels rested on the floor nearby.

"Seriously? That's going to stink."

"Enjoy your stay." Aleksander picked up Nestor's shoes and walked out, closing the door behind him. The scratch of a key in the lock told Nestor he was now a prisoner.

But why had Aleksander spared him? It couldn't be because they were close—they had barely exchanged ten words since he'd been brought on as Lorik's man.

Then an idea struck him. What if he was a plant? He thought back to when Aleksander had been hired. It was just before the Leopard kidnapped him for questioning. That had to be how she knew where to find him.

He had to warn Lorik and Kadare.

Nestor tried to open the window above the cot, but it had been nailed shut. Using his elbow, he smashed the glass panes so he could get at the shutters. They wouldn't budge. He found a butter knife in a drawer in the kitchen to use as a lever, but the dull blade bent, making it unusable.

He had to escape. Kadare and Lorik needed to know Aleksander was a traitor.

A rt's phone buzzed, indicating a text. "It's Gina. Lorik's guys are headed into town. Lorik and Kadare are staying put, for now."

Gina had counted a dozen gunmen, including Lorik and Kadare, although Lorik's bodyguard and Nestor had taken off in a white pickup and headed in the opposite direction from town.

"Everything's in place?" Leine asked.

"Yep."

She imagined the cascading text tree, with the message broadcasting simultaneously from Gina to everyone in the text group, alerting them to the impending attack. Just then her phone vibrated. It was the text from Gina. Manny and the rest of the volunteers would now be moving into position.

Leine checked the time. Two hours until sunset. Even though they didn't know what Kadare and Lorik were planning, Art and their group had the tactical advantage of knowing the enemy was coming and the size of his forces.

Art and Leine joined Zarko in the forecourt of the farmhouse. Elongated shadows from a nearby stand of cypress trees stretched across the gravel. The pool lights flickered on, as though expecting a late season soirée.

Leine's phone vibrated, and she glanced at the screen. It was Lou.

"Glad I caught you," Lou began. "Art told me what you're planning and that some people from town are involved."

"Against my better judgement."

"Help from other people is not a bad thing, Leine."

"It is if there are casualties."

"Their choice. You explained the risks and they still wanted to help."

"They did. But I would prefer they didn't take up arms."

"Art says there are a couple of hunters in the mix."

"Hunters, yes, but not of men." Leine sighed. "Was there something in particular you needed to tell me?"

"Nestor has been contained."

"Oh? How do you know that?"

"A little bird told me."

"No, really. How do you know?" *Don't play with me, Lou.*

"Lorik's bodyguard."

"The guy with the British accent?"

"That would be him."

"Where—how?"

"When you told me about the assassination attempt, I called in a favor."

"How did you manage to infiltrate Lorik's inner circle?" Leine asked. "Not that I'm complaining."

"His name is Aleksander—Alek for short. The friend who granted the favor has contacts in certain circles. Someone who knows someone who knows Lorik vouched for him. Lorik did a little research, and boom. He's hired."

"But I didn't mention anything to you about Lorik needing a new bodyguard."

"That was just good timing. I'd have been happy with inserting him into the rank and file."

"And you didn't tell me this because…?"

"I wanted to wait and see if he had longevity. You know how fast some of these guys go through bodyguards."

"Obviously Lorik's happy with him."

"The only wrinkle is that Lorik told him to finish Nestor, which I discouraged. We might have a use for him down the line."

"Interesting. Lorik was quick to give him up for interrogation."

"Nestor went to Kadare behind his back," Lou said. "Maybe Lorik expected you to kill him."

"We both decided that wouldn't be prudent. Nestor's death could make Kadare suspicious."

"Well, whatever the reason, he's on ice for now. I told Alek to contact you and Art via encrypted messages from now on."

"One less soldier for Kadare, and Lorik's bodyguard is on our side. Works for me. What's stopping Alek from taking out Kadare?"

"He can't get close to him. The guy's more paranoid than Adolf Hitler. Barricades his room. Wears body armor and sleeps with an AK—if he sleeps. He even has Lorik taste his food."

"Then it's up to us to put him out of his misery," Leine said. "Set Nestor free once we take out Kadare. If Lorik's still breathing, we can let nature take its course."

"Why didn't I think of that?"

Leine smiled. Lou was always a step ahead. "You don't have to keep impressing me with your preplanning. I'm already a fan."

Lou snorted. "Keep it up, Leine. I may have to pay you for ego strokes."

"Did Alek find out what Kadare is planning?"

"Negative. He's likely keeping everyone in the dark until it's their turn to do his bidding."

"And Lorik hasn't said anything to your guy."

"According to Alek, Kadare doesn't trust Lorik either."

"Kind of difficult to pull off an operation without telling the players what their role is."

"Agreed. Just be careful out there. Kadare's a snake. His drawing power might be weaker than it was, but he's a survivor."

"Copy that."

"Keep me posted on how things shake out."

"Will do." Leine ended the call. "Lorik's bodyguard's a plant."

"Nice," Art said. Zarko nodded in agreement.

"Lou always was a strategic thinker," Leine said. "He saved my ass on more occasions than I can count. I should have thought of planting someone with Lorik myself."

Art snorted. "Along with fighting off assassins, saving the folks in town from an extortion scheme, and getting the bookstore ready for a grand opening—piece of cake."

"Don't forget Santa coming to visit." To stay focused on the op, Leine compartmentalized everything except the counteroffensive. Thinking about Santa wouldn't help. She'd have plenty of time later.

Hopefully.

They climbed into an up-armored Range Rover with tinted windows—compliments of a friend in Rome who owed Art a favor. Zarko moved the Rover's tactical first aid pack to the side so he could fit his lanky frame in the back seat. A cache of weapons and ammo rode in the cargo area.

Jorge and Pierre had gone ahead to the rally point in Manny's van, which Pierre outfitted with a comms console capable of transmitting and receiving within a ten-kilometer radius. Jorge had brought enough supplies for a portable field hospital. Sam spent the previous afternoon and evening working on diversionary tactics. He and Gina would meet everyone at the rally point. All were connected via radio and text.

The remaining AKs from the abandoned church had been distributed among the van, the Rover, and Gina's pickup, a blue Hilux, along with the weapons stash Leine picked up from Lou's guy in Florence. Sam carried grenades and a pair of 9mm pistols. The vehicles could be used to transport casualties and personnel and would work as both roadblock and cover.

"Sitrep," Art said into his mic.

"Delta up." Jorge's voice came over Leine's earpiece, letting them know the field hospital was in place.

"Bravo up." Sam's drawl gave the impression he didn't have a care in the world, which went a long way toward calming jittery nerves.

"Foxtrot up, and I mean up," chimed in Pierre.

"Say again?" Art asked.

"The view from here is amazing," Pierre replied. "That's all I'm going to say."

Leine gave Zarko a look. Zarko shrugged. "He likes heights."

"Echo up. ETA in fifteen," Gina replied.

Art took the back way into town—a minute or two longer than the main road, but less possibility of being spotted. He turned down a side street and parked.

Leine scanned the quiet neighborhood, lined with trees that looked like they'd been there since the pirates attacked. Three blocks away, the bookstore stood on the cliff, overlooking the sea. Kadare would likely have Lorik's men start a search for her there.

Leine shrugged on a puffy coat, camouflaging her tactical vest, and walked to the corner to check the area. No pedestrians were visible, and the shops facing the cobblestones all had signs on their doors or windows indicating they were closed. Thankfully, it was mid-week and there weren't many tourists.

A sense of calm descended over her. They'd prepared as much as they could. The opposition had a finite number of combatants, and assumed Leine was unprepared for a large, coordinated attack.

"Showtime." Leine made her way back to the Rover to grab another loaded magazine. She would act as a decoy to draw out Lorik's men and didn't want to run short.

"Kadare and Lorik are still back at the villa," Art said. "Alek's there, too. There's no sign of Nestor."

"Lorik told Alek to take Nestor out."

Art's eyebrows shot up. "Alek did Nestor? Does Lou know?"

Leine shook her head. "Lou told Alek to hold off killing him—that he might have a use for him. He didn't tell me what Alek did, but I'm assuming Nestor's tied to a chair somewhere unpleasant."

Art's phone buzzed, indicating a text. "Got something from Gina." He handed the mobile to Leine. "Video."

She clicked on one of the files, which showed nine armed men climbing into three late-model pickups. The vehicles kicked up gravel as they drove away from the villa. Lorik and Kadare remained near the front door. A white pickup waited at the foot of the drive for the others to pass, then proceeded to the villa and parked in the forecourt. Lou's man, Alek, exited the vehicle.

Lorik, Kadare, and Alek had words. Frowning, Kadare gestured toward the pickup. The bodyguard responded to something Lorik said, and Kadare appeared to relax.

"Looks like Kadare was in on smoking Nestor," Leine remarked. "He doesn't seem too upset by Nestor's disappearance. Either that, or Alek and Lorik lied to him."

Zarko shook his head. "You think Lorik would have waited to have him killed until the op was over."

"Not if Kadare and Lorik believe Leine isn't prepared for an attack," Art said. "They probably think nine extra shooters is overkill. Especially with Lorik and Lorik's body man as backup."

Zarko gave Leine a look. "Didn't you neutralize a three-man kill team?"

"Don't forget the first assassination attempt," Art added.

Leine shrugged. "What matters is that we're ready for them."

Art and Zarko stayed with the Rover, while Leine headed on foot to the bookstore.

The sun had sunk behind the buildings, casting the area in deep shadow. The reproduction streetlights flickered on, spreading pools of light on the sidewalk, although there was still enough daylight to carry out the plan. Leine scanned the street, searching for signs of Lorik's men. Her cellphone vibrated, and she checked the screen.

It was a text from Francesca. She'd spotted all three of Lorik's pickups in Old Town, headed her way. Leine quickened her pace, clearing an iron gate in a stone wall covered in vegetation —a shortcut to the bookstore, and a good place to disappear if she had to.

Minutes later, she neared her building. The sound of vehicles headed her way echoed in the distance. Leine tensed as a pair of headlights bounced against the stone buildings, broadcasting the pickups' approach. She waited until the first pickup rounded the corner, then turned and walked in the opposite direction.

The sound of revving engines told her they'd seen her.

She ran.

31

"They found her!" Brandishing his cellphone, Kadare turned the screen toward Lorik, who was sitting in the back seat of the Suburban. Aleksander was behind the wheel.

Lorik read the missive from his man, Joel. "Do they actually have her? The text doesn't mention it." He couldn't imagine it had been that easy to roll up the American.

Kadare shook his head. "Not yet, but they're following her now. It's only a matter of time." He leaned back in the passenger seat with a contented chuckle. "Soon, I will destroy the woman who killed my brother and Nikolai Abramov. We'll have a celebration."

"If you say so," muttered Lorik.

Kadare glanced back at him. "What did you say?"

"I said, it will be so."

Kadare appeared satisfied with Lorik's answer. He tapped his phone and turned back to Aleksander to show him the screen. "See where they are? Follow them. I don't want to waste a moment." Aleksander nodded as he sped up.

Lorik wasn't happy with Kadare's plan. At least what he

knew of it. Sending all of his men to subdue Ava Basso seemed ill-advised. Why not keep back a contingent in case she slipped from their grasp? Kadare had scoffed at the suggestion. The only contingency plan they needed was the three of them, he'd said. Nine gunmen in three vehicles would be more than enough to subdue her.

Lorik didn't think brute force was the answer. But it was Kadare's plan, so Lorik remained quiet.

They'd just arrived in downtown Scivoloso when Kadare made a disgusted sound.

"Dammit."

Lorik leaned forward. "What happened?"

Kadare squinted at his phone and shook his head in disbelief. "She disappeared." His thumbs flew as he texted a reply. "Then find her. Fools." He spit the word.

Keeping his expression passive, Lorik leaned back in his seat. He wasn't surprised. The Basso woman was competent—and slippery. Served Kadare right for taking control of Lorik's men. Arrogant prick. True, the two men had discussed compensation, but Lorik still hadn't seen anything transferred to his bank account.

Lorik had allowed Kadare to take control of the kill. What else could he do? Lorik's men still thought of him as their boss, but for how long? He'd have to be careful how much power he relinquished.

It had been easy to get Kadare to agree to Nestor's execution, which dovetailed nicely with Lorik's own ambition of keeping control of his tiny empire. When Lorik told Kadare Nestor had betrayed him, Kadare demanded his execution. Lorik persuaded him that he should be the one to give Aleksander the order. Lorik would look strong to his bodyguard and to Kadare, and he'd rid himself of the pesky little problem.

His attempt at manipulating the American hadn't worked as

well. When he suggested she interrogate Nestor, he bet on her losing her temper and killing Nestor for him. Unfortunately, she'd shown considerable restraint.

Then she revealed Nestor gave up Roan Kadare as the man who wanted her dead. That act proved Nestor was a weak-willed traitor who wouldn't balk at saving his own skin. One issue remained clear: Nestor had betrayed Kadare—how long until he did the same to Lorik?

He needed to be disposed of.

"Yes!" Kadare shouted, jarring Lorik from his musings. He held up his phone. "They found her."

32

Riding shotgun, Leine kept an eye on their pursuers, giving Art a play by play. The lead pickup driver had some skill—something that couldn't be said for the other two. The drivers of pickups two and three appeared to have difficulty keeping up.

Twelve kilometers outside town, Art turned right onto a dirt road that wound through a remote wooded area.

"ETA two minutes," Art said into his mic. "Pierre, you have a visual?"

"Affirmative. All three are coming in behind you."

Art drove like a man possessed around corners and floored the accelerator on straightaways. The dirt road quickly transformed into the barest suggestion of a trail. Branches whipped the side of the Rover as they bounced along faint grooves in the earth.

Leine held fast to the armrest, checking the side mirror for a glimpse of the lead pickup chasing them. A forest of trees reflected back at her. "Looks like we have a window."

"One hundred meters," Pierre confirmed.

"Get ready, guys and gals." Art stomped on the accelerator, and the Rover rocketed forward.

Zarko handed two MP5s with extra mags over the seat back and armed himself.

The trees parted to reveal a clearing with a crumbling Roman wall at one end, its relevance long lost to history. Art steered the Rover behind the ruin and slammed on the brakes. The van stood a short distance away. The side door slid open. Jorge jumped out, carrying an MP5, and moved to a predetermined area to their left. Leine exited the Rover and sprinted to one end of the wall. Zarko took the other, with Art covering center.

Seconds later, the first white pickup screamed into the clearing, followed closely by the other two.

They were sitting ducks.

Leine and Zarko fired first, aiming for the tires. Gina, Sam, Jorge, and Art joined in, peppering the vehicles with gunfire. The driver of the first pickup opened his door and returned fire. The gunmen in the other trucks did the same, but were ineffective against a stone wall and hidden adversaries.

Leine dropped to her belly and fired underneath the lead pickup, aiming at the gunmen's exposed feet and lower legs. Their cries and lack of return fire told her she'd succeeded in taking down two. She continued to fire, finishing them off as they fell. She succeeded in hitting one more under the second pickup, before the rest realized what she'd done and blocked her shots by taking cover behind the wheels.

A gunman stepped clear of the third pickup and let loose with a barrage of automatic gunfire. A second later, a throwing knife hurtled through the air, embedding itself in his eye socket. He dropped his AK and crumpled to the ground. Gina melted back into the trees.

Another gunman apparently decided escape was his only option and took off running.

"We got a squirter," Art bellowed.

"On it," Sam said. "Cover me."

To Leine's right, an engine revved. Seconds later, Sam burst through the foliage on the Ducati and rocketed after him. Leine and the group blanketed the last four gunmen with suppressive fire. Two met their deaths, leaving alive the driver of the first pickup and a gunman from the third, who remained behind the vehicle's engine block.

"Had enough?" Art yelled from behind the wall as he reloaded.

"We surrender," shouted the driver of the first pickup.

Leine peeked over the wall. Arms raised, the driver stepped away from the first pickup. The other gunman remained behind the other vehicle.

"You are a coward," he shouted at the driver, his head momentarily bobbing above the hood.

That was all Pierre needed.

The report from the SVD sniper rifle echoed through the clearing. The gunman's head exploded and he collapsed to the ground.

"Put your hands behind your head, walk forward ten paces, and drop to your knees," Art ordered the driver. He did as instructed.

Sam returned to the clearing and parked the bike. He gathered the enemy's guns, while Leine and Zarko zip-tied the survivor.

"Get him?" Art asked.

Sam nodded. "All good."

The driver's radio chirped.

"Check in," a disembodied voice barked. "What's happening?"

"It's Kadare." Leine took the radio and turned it toward the last survivor. "Tell him you have me."

The gunman shook his head. "They won't come."

"Why?"

"We have strict orders. Only Joel is to report to Kadare."

Leine nodded. "And Joel is dead. Which will tell him you've been compromised."

The gunman didn't say anything.

The radio crackled. "Is anyone there?"

Leine raised the radio and pressed the transmit button. "Roan Kadare. This is the Leopard."

t the sound of the Basso woman's voice, Kadare straightened in his seat and pressed the radio to his ear.

Lorik hid his shock. His men had actually captured her? Relief swept through him. He'd chosen correctly. Now, all he had to do was kill Kadare after Kadare eliminated Basso.

"How does it feel to be on the losing end of an operation?" Kadare's voice oozed venom.

"So much losing," she oozed back. "For you."

Kadare's triumphant smile faltered. He swiveled, searching Lorik's eyes for an answer. Lorik shook his head. He had no idea what she meant.

"All of your men—or should I say, Lorik's men—are dead," she explained. "Except one. Please offer my condolences."

Shock spooled through Lorik as Kadare glared at him.

"Did you hear that?" Kadare hissed, his face flushing crimson. "Your men are dead." His breathing shallow, he pulled his gun and leveled it at Lorik. "She killed eight of your men. *Eight.* How did this happen?"

His throat dry, Lorik licked his lips as he stared down the

barrel of the gun. Would Kadare actually kill him? What was stopping him? If he killed Lorik, then he could take over Lorik's villa, try to muscle into whatever businesses he could. Lorik doubted Aleksander was loyal enough to fight for him.

So much for their business plan.

Kadare would continue to hunt Basso, try to cobble together an army to take her down. Beads of sweat formed on Lorik's forehead. Everything he'd worked for, gone. A spark of anger flickered inside him.

He'd be damned if he'd let this lunatic win.

"She's bluffing."

Indecision clouded Kadare's face. He pressed the transmit button on his radio. "Prove it."

There was a pause before someone answered. It wasn't the woman.

"She's telling the truth, boss. They're all dead."

Kadare looked at Lorik for confirmation. He nodded. The voice belonged to Zef, a loyal soldier who'd been with Lorik for years. Lorik closed his eyes. His earlier relief boomeranged to anger and resignation. This is what happened when he didn't honor his word. He should have stood up to Kadare when he first arrived. If he had, his men would still be alive. But he'd been blinded by Kadare's reputation, by his promise of wealth.

Kadare slammed his fist into the console. His chest rose and fell as he struggled for control. Combined with the color of his face, Lorik wondered if a stroke might be imminent.

Kadare let loose with a string of Albanian curse words. "That fucking American bitch." Spittle flew from his mouth. "She will pay."

Lorik nodded, an attempt at solidarity. He clenched his fists, allowing his anger at the death of his men to rise to the surface. If she could kill eight men, how many more would they need?

"We'll have to raise an army."

"Not an army." Kadare narrowed his eyes. "A specialized unit. This time, we go after what she values most."

THE INTERROGATION DIDN'T PROCEED AS SMOOTHLY AS LEINE HAD hoped. Lorik's man was loyal to the core. Psychological manipulation didn't work. He lost three fingernails before he told them Kadare had arrived with no hope of support from his patron in Albania. Leine and Art had already assumed that was true, but his confirmation helped solidify their theory.

Leine took Art outside Manny's warehouse to talk in private. "What's your take? Think Kadare bails?"

Art shook his head. "I think he escalates."

"You don't think taking out Lorik's guys is any kind of deterrent?"

"With Kadare?" He gave her a grim smile. "Not a chance. I know his type. He's got something to prove. His Albanian buddies didn't back him when he got out of prison. They're likely watching to see how he does. If he succeeds, he has a good chance of winning their respect. If he doesn't, well..." Art shrugged. "We'll see what happens."

"You're probably right." Leine stared into the distance. "We need to take the fight to Kadare. No one's safe unless and until we take him down."

"What are you thinking?"

"If we go with your assumption, then Kadare's already looking to hire muscle. He'll harden security around the villa first. We use bodyguard Alek to get him away from the villa."

"I like where you're going with this. Turn Alek into Kadare's body man."

"Exactly. Even though Kadare's paying the bills, he won't trust the hired men. Alek's been tested, and Lorik trusts him."

"The perfect opportunity."

Leine nodded. She slid her phone from her pocket and called Lou.

"Happy to hear your voice, Leine. How we doin'?"

"We survived Kadare's first attempt but stirred up a hornet's nest."

"I take it Kadare's still breathing."

"We took out Lorik's contingent, but none of the principals. We believe Kadare's going to escalate."

"He's hiring, you mean."

"Good probability. Could you put out feelers, see if anything comes up? I'd like to know what we're up against."

"Will do. Alek should be a good source for that, too."

"About Alek." She exchanged looks with Art. "Tell him to get on Kadare's good side. Kadare's not going to trust the help. Alek's already vetted."

"No problem. I'll call you back when I have something."

Leine ended the call and slid the phone into her back pocket. Now they just had to hope their plan would keep the town safe.

34

The bell tinkled above the door to the gelateria, indicating a late customer. About to close for the evening, Nadia put down the partially filled container of limoncello gelato, a favorite of her regulars, and wiped her hands on her apron before walking out of the back room to greet them.

Her breath caught and she froze in the doorway.

The man had his back to her, looking at the street through the large store window—but something was wrong. His attire didn't resemble any tourist or local she'd ever seen. Stocky and of medium height, he wore a dark knit cap, and a camouflage vest and pants. The barrel of some kind of rifle jutted out from the crook of his arm.

Heart pounding, Nadia locked eyes on him and took two steps back, her hand searching for and finding the AK-47 she kept leaned up against the wall. Scarcely breathing, she gripped the stock and eased the gun from its hiding place. Even though she'd practiced shooting the same model with the rest of the residents who'd opted to take a gun, she didn't remember it being so heavy.

Be brave, Nadia. He won't hesitate to kill you. Think of your parents and how they fought the Fascists.

Hardening her resolve, she raised the rifle and aimed. The man must have caught her reflection in the store window, because he spun in place, bringing the barrel of his gun up at the same time.

Nadia closed her eyes and squeezed the trigger, emptying the 30-round magazine in a matter of deafening, terror-fueled seconds. Glass shattered as the gun took on a life of its own.

He didn't stand a chance.

Seconds passed before Nadia realized she wasn't dead. She opened her eyes and stared at the carnage. Bullet holes peppered the lower half of the front wall and marched upward. The huge front window had shattered—glass shards jutted from the frame as though reaching for the missing pieces. Nadia shivered at a sudden gust of cool air.

On the floor at the foot of a dark red smear, the gunman lay slumped against a pink metal chair, his head cocked forward, chin to his chest. Blood and gore pooled on the black-and-white tile beneath him.

Shaking uncontrollably, Nadia fumbled in her apron pocket for her phone. It took three tries before she successfully brought up the group text, and three more before she was able to type a coherent message.

They're here.

***

Nestor glared at the cracked and blunted piece of wood he'd been able to pry from the bed frame. The still-intact shutter mocked him. Damn whoever built the seemingly indestructible cabin.

Damn Aleksander for leaving him there alive.

And damn Roan Kadare for wanting him dead.

The nauseating stench from the plastic bucket on the other side of the room wafted toward him, turning his stomach. He'd covered the opening and slid the putrid pail as far away from the bed as possible, but it didn't help. The granola bars Aleksander left him weren't exactly aiding his digestion.

He had to get free. Warning them about Aleksander and killing the Leopard would prove his loyalty to both Lorik and Kadare.

If they were still alive.

Nestor paced the room, holding his breath as he passed the bucket. The cold from the stone floor leached through his socks, and he shivered. He'd tried to break through shutters on both windows, but neither had budged.

He leaned his head back, thinking. Rough wood planks covered the high ceiling—likely an attempt at trapping warm air in the attic. Using the blunted section of bed frame, he tried to hit the planks, but couldn't reach them. Throwing it was even less effective. He scanned the room for something to stand on, but he'd already destroyed the bedframe. The table?

Nestor went to the stone-topped table and attempted to drag it across the floor. The thing barely budged. Well, then he'd try to break through where the table stood. He climbed onto the tabletop and raised the piece of frame.

He was still too low.

He glared at the pile of sticks that used to be the one chair in the cabin—he'd hoped to break through the shutters using one of the legs, but he'd overestimated the strength of the wood. It had splintered on the first try.

He scanned the room, his gaze settling on the plastic bucket holding his waste. Bile rose in his throat as he contemplated upending the pail so he could stand on the bottom. Would it be tall enough?

Holding his breath, he climbed off the table and walked to the bucket. Once he had a good idea how tall that was, he returned to the table and let out his breath. He eyeballed the distance to the ceiling—and sighed. It was close.

With his shirt over his nose, he carried the bucket to the sink and dumped the contents. The shirt did little to cover the eye-watering stench. The liquids drained, but the solids did not. Nestor pumped the handle for water, hoping to force the shit down, but none came.

Abandoning the effort, he climbed back onto the table, upended the bucket, and climbed on top of that. He raised the battered piece of frame and slammed it into the ceiling. The wood plank made a hollow sound. Had it moved?

Nestor tried again, harder this time. The plank jumped, then seated itself back in place.

Heartened, he slammed the wood into the ceiling again and again, slowly loosening the plank above the table. Finally, he broke through. The plank tilted to one side, showering him with decades of dust and dirt, and revealing empty space.

He battered away at the planks surrounding the first, enlarging the hole so he could fit through. Once he'd managed that, he dropped the piece of frame and lunged at the opening.

His first attempt failed spectacularly. The bucket shot out from under him, and he ended up half on the table, half off. He was bruised, but nothing felt broken.

His second try was better, but his stocking feet slid out from under him, and he landed hard on his ass.

He removed his socks tend tried again. This time, he was able to grip the edges of the ceiling with both hands, but fell a second later, the splintered wood ripping through his skin.

He tore a kitchen towel he found in one of the drawers in half, then wrapped his hands.

He was successful on his fourth try. He pulled himself up and into the attic, careful of the rusty nails and jagged wood.

The space wasn't as dark as he thought it would be. Strips of watery light shone through gaps in the slate tiles used for the roof. Nestor crawled to the nearest rafter and kicked at one of the tiles. The slate broke with minimal effort.

He was free.

35

Back at the farmhouse, Leine handed Jorge another semiauto to clean when her phone buzzed. Jorge's vibrated a moment later and he set the weapon down on the table. She pulled out her mobile and glanced at the screen. Jorge did the same.

It was Nadia. Leine read the text and replied: *Stay out of sight. We'll be right there.* She strapped on her tac vest and loaded up on ammo, while Jorge did the same. They raced through the hallway and headed for the van. Art and the rest of his crew were right behind them.

"What the hell happened?" Jorge climbed into the drivers' seat and started the engine.

"I don't know." Leine texted Gina, who was watching Lorik's villa. *Someone attacked the gelateria. Nadia's ok. For now. What's happening there?* They'd eliminated Lorik's men. Who the hell were attacking now?

Gina quickly replied. *No activity. Lorik and Kadare are inside. What do you want me to do?*

Stay where you are. Report anything new.

A second later, Leine's phone started to vibrate and didn't stop:

Francesca: *Gunfire at the restaurant. We're trapped. Tomaso and Tony left to fight. Send help!*

Manny: *Two gunmen outside. Bruno and I are barricaded in the back room with guns. We'll hold out as long as we can.*

Several more businesses sent texts pleading for help. Leine's gut twisted as she answered each one, working with Art on speaker phone to coordinate the crew and deliver help where it was needed most. Leine pulled Gina off recon and sent her to the Mancinis'. Zarko, Sam, Pierre, and Art headed toward other immediate threats. Jorge would pick up Nadia and stay with the van to monitor comms and treat casualties. Leine had Jorge drop her off near the back of Manny's wine bar. She carried an MP5 submachine gun, a 9mm pistol, and a backpack with a first aid kit and ammunition for both the SMG and AKs.

The sound of sporadic gunfire erupted from inside the bar as Leine sprinted to the rear entrance, taking cover behind a large garbage bin. The smell of rotting food mixed with the briny sea was not a good combination, and she kept her breathing shallow. She sent a text to Manny to let him know she was outside.

The reply came quickly: *A key is under the last wine crate to the right. Two gunmen are inside. Manny's holding them off ~ Bruno*

Leine found the key, unlocked the rear door, and slipped inside. Bruno was at the other end of the room, hunched over a stack of wine boxes furiously reloading the magazine for an AK-47.

"Situation?" she asked.

"Two gunmen shot their way in." Bruno nodded toward the front of the bar as he grabbed several rounds from a half-empty box of ammunition. "Manny's been holding them off, but we're running low on bullets."

Leine set her pack on the floor and pulled out three full

magazines for the AK, along with three for the SMG. She handed Bruno her 9mm and two extra mags. "You remember your training?" she asked, keeping her voice low.

He nodded. Even though some chose not to use an AK, several people from town opted to take a brief training session on weapons handling and firing, in case they found themselves in need. Bruno had excelled with a handgun.

She picked up the backpack and moved to the door leading into the bar. Bruno grabbed the three mags for the AK and joined her.

Leine cracked the door. Manny had his back to her, crouched behind the bar. The gunmen had upended the restaurant's thick mahogany tables to use for cover at each end of the restaurant.

"Go in low," she whispered. "I'll distract them by going high to draw them out. Take the gunman behind the table on your left. They won't expect being shot at from a low angle."

Bruno nodded. Leine opened the door enough to let him pass. Manny turned as Bruno slid the magazines across the floor toward him and headed for the corner of the bar. Leine burst through the door, MP5 on auto, chewing up the back wall with rounds. Leine dropped to a crouch and ran the length of the bar as the two gunmen in tac vests popped up from behind the table and returned fire, spraying the thick wooden bar with rounds. Glassware shattered and wine bottles exploded above Leine's head, spewing their contents and showering her and Manny.

Pop! Pop! Pop! Bruno fired at the gunman on the left. Waiting for a lull, Leine locked the bolt on the MP5 and ejected the spent mag, then inserted a fresh one and released the cocking lever.

The shooting paused. Bruno peered out from behind the bar, then fell back. "Behind the tables," he mouthed.

She turned to Manny. "Ready?" He nodded. She held up three fingers and counted down: *three, two, one.*

Manny and Leine broke cover at the same time and came up firing. The gunman closest to Bruno fired back. Bruno emptied his gun and hit the man in the neck. The gunman slapped his hand over the wound and dove behind the table. Bruno's eyes widened in surprise. Leine gave him a thumbs up and reloaded.

This ends now.

Leine gestured to Bruno and Manny to cover her. They nodded and moved into position, one at each end of the bar. At the count of three, they stood and started shooting. She leapt onto the bar and opened fire, pinning the two gunmen with a barrage of rounds.

Seconds later, their lifeless, bloody heaps littered the bar floor.

Heart thudding from the adrenaline, Leine climbed off the bar and picked her way over spent brass to one of the gunmen. Not surprisingly, he didn't carry identification. The edge of a tattoo peeked from his collar. She ripped open his shirt. A trio of swords accompanied by an ornate cross and an Italian blessing decorated his chest. More ink suggested he was military.

She checked the second gunman, who had no ID and similar ink on his arms and torso. Mafia?

Gesturing at the gunmen she said to Bruno, "Pull their weapons. And make sure they're dead."

"Manny's hurt," Bruno said, his voice panicked.

Leine moved behind the bar to check on Manny. Alarmed by his shallow breathing and gray pallor, she raced to him. "You hit?"

Manny shook his head. "I'm fine."

Leine looked him over. At first she didn't find anything, but when she tried to lift the rifle from his grasp, he moaned in pain. "Where?"

Manny grimaced. "Right side, under my arm." A string of

Italian expletives followed. "I'll be all right. Leave me. Others need your help."

Leine retrieved her pack near the doorway. She returned, her mind clear and focused as she tore open a packet of combat gauze from the first aid kit and applied it to the wound.

Manny winced. The remaining color drained from his face.

"Sorry," Leine said, wrapping the gauze tight to stop the bleeding. "The gunmen had tattoos with Italian imagery. One had an Italian blessing. Looked like these two might have been military."

"Mercenaries."

"Not mafia?"

He shook his head. "Unless Lorik or Kadare have a direct contact. The families won't want the attention that comes from a war."

She guided his free hand to apply pressure. "Three minutes."

"Leave me. I'm fine—"

"Dammit, Manny," Leine said through gritted teeth. "Stop arguing with me and apply the damn pressure." He did as he was told.

She keyed her mic and said, "Alpha to Delta, do you read?"

No answer. The radios were still in range, unless Jorge had set up outside town. She tried again, but no one answered. She found her phone and texted Jorge about Manny's gunshot wound.

Still no answer.

"Bruno, what's your Wi-Fi password?" He told her and she connected, then texted Jorge again. He replied a moment later:

Can he travel? We're knee deep. He added the street where he'd parked the van. It was two blocks away, near a park.

How many casualties? she texted back.

Jorge didn't reply. She checked her screen. *No connection.*

How had Kadare found so many gunmen so quickly? The

attack was too soon after they eliminated Lorik's group. And why were their comms down?

She assessed Manny. He appeared to have stabilized, although his coloring still looked like shit. "Can you walk?"

"Yes, yes. I can walk." He grasped the edge of the bar with his free hand and tried to hoist himself off the floor. Bruno ran to his side. With Leine's help, the two of them were able to get him to his feet.

Hopefully, Manny would survive the trip.

36

Leine, Manny, and Bruno reached the ersatz field hospital fifteen minutes later. The park resembled a war zone. Several people who had attended the meeting at the farmhouse sat on the grass and on benches, some wrapped in silver survival blankets, while others lay on the ground in sleeping bags. At first glance most looked all right, although two of the sleeping bag people appeared either sedated or deceased. Leine's stomach knotted.

This is my fault.

Art and Zarko patrolled the perimeter, along with two townspeople with hunting rifles. Nadia had joined Jorge at the van and was working triage while he attended to casualties. Leine and Bruno helped Manny over. He'd lost a lot of blood but was still coherent.

The field hospital filled the back half of the van. Jorge had everything laid out to ensure easy access: nitrile gloves, compressed gauze, QuikClot, tourniquets, splints, arterial forceps, titanium scissors, Israeli compression bandages, chest seal kits, and a cooler filled with bags of O-negative. Jorge was currently working to stabilize a man whose clothing was soaked in blood.

Pierre was inside the van, working feverishly to re-establish their comms. He'd set up a backup power source and a mobile receiver and transmitter for the radios at the front of the van's cargo area, extending their radio range a few kilometers. The radios wouldn't cover the entire town, but they were supposed to work in the immediate area.

Nadia checked Manny's bandage. Blood covered her coat.

"Are you hurt?" Leine asked.

The older woman shook her head. "Just shaken up. I've never killed anyone before. The blood isn't mine." She appraised Manny. "And you? You should be basking in the warmth of your family and grandchildren, not coming to a field hospital for a gunshot wound."

Manny managed a weak smile. "I have no family, and no grandchildren."

"Then you can share mine. I have enough for ten of us." Nadia checked his bandage. "It looks like the bleeding stopped." She handed Bruno a space blanket, two bottles of water, a handful of antibiotics, and a blister pack of painkillers, and pointed to a bench underneath a nearby pine. "Take Manny over there. Jorge will get to him as soon as he can." Bruno did as she asked.

"How many wounded?" Leine asked.

"Twelve so far." She glanced at Leine, her eyes growing moist. "We lost two, though."

"I'm so sorry." Leine put her hand on her arm.

Nodding, Nadia patted her hand. "We did what we could, poor souls."

"What have you heard regarding Kadare's crew?"

"The last report was nine down, but there are at least that many still active."

"Add two to the list." Leine leaned inside the van to talk to Pierre. "What happened?"

"They're using jammers," Pierre said, holding up a piece of tech about the size of a handheld cash point. "I've found two locations, but I've only got the one detector. I need to manually place it somewhere that will counteract both signals."

"What about using another frequency? The phones are quad band, right?"

"They're using fairly sophisticated jammers that can block a range of frequencies."

"What can I do?"

Pierre gathered up equipment to put inside a backpack, which he slung over his shoulder. "Cover me."

Leine let Nadia know they were leaving.

"Why don't you set it up in my store?" Nadia suggested. "It's one of the taller buildings on the bluff."

Pierre nodded. "That might work. Do you have the key to the front door?"

Nadia gave him a wistful smile. "I'm afraid you won't need one."

Leine and Pierre took back alleys and paused at each street corner to check for hostiles until they reached the gelateria.

"She wasn't kidding," Pierre said, looking at the broken windows. Someone had shot out the streetlights along the entire block, casting everything in shadow. The glass from the reproduction period lamps littered the sidewalk.

They dashed across the street and slipped inside the store. A pink neon sign with the name of Nadia's shop glowed on the back wall. Glass crunched underfoot as they passed the dead gunman slumped on the floor. They climbed several flights of stairs to the upper floor, but Pierre was still only able to block one of the jammers from that elevation. Leine searched for an access point to the roof and found a trap door to the attic, but they were unable to break through the solid wood panel.

Pierre nodded at the room they'd just left. "I can use the window."

They walked back to check the viability. Leine glanced at the roiling whitecaps below. "Are you sure? That's a long way down."

Pierre smiled. "It's what I do, remember?"

"Oh yeah. Parkour, right?"

"Right." He shrugged off his pack and started to remove the items he'd need.

Leine took a position near the door, listening intently for intruders. The window screeched, and she winced. Pierre had created a gap of several inches, but it wasn't wide enough.

"I'm going to need some help."

Leine slung the MP5 over her shoulder and joined him at the window. They both heaved on the frame, budging it a few more inches. Pierre tried to climb through, but it still wasn't enough.

"More."

"One. Two. Three."

They worked it open another couple inches.

"That should do it." Pierre bent over and started to wriggle headfirst through the opening. The floor behind them creaked. Leine spun in place and raised her weapon. At the same time, a gunman in a tactical vest and carrying an AK-47 mounted the last stair. Leine fired, hitting him in the shoulder, and his shot went wide. He grunted and dove for cover behind the wall. She continued to fire, chewing up the plaster wall, estimating where he landed.

She reloaded but there was no return fire. Leine moved to the door in a crouch, and glanced around the corner. The gunman lay sprawled in a heap on the hallway floor. She relieved him of his AK and shot him twice more to ensure his compliance. After a quick scan of the stairwell for more threats, she went back into the room. Pierre was sitting at the base of the window, gripping his leg.

"Shit." Leine ran to him. Blood saturated his thigh. She pulled the tactical knife from her ankle sheath and cut through the material to expose the gunshot wound. Then she cut a length of cord from the window blind and applied an ersatz tourniquet, using the knife to increase the pressure. Next, she pulled a compression bandage from her pack and wrapped his thigh.

He grimaced at her ministrations. "Don't think I'm going to be able to do much climbing."

"No kidding? I thought all you Parkour enthusiasts were oblivious to pain." She checked to make sure the tightness of both the bandage and the tourniquet was good. "That should hold you until we can get you back to Jorge." She nodded toward the detector. "Now, what do I need to do to set the device?"

Pierre gave her a sidelong glance. "No way, man. Scaling the building's too dangerous. We've got to find another route."

Leine returned the look. "Seriously? You think you're the only person who can climb a wall?"

"I didn't mean anything by it, but—"

"But what?"

He shrugged. "Aren't you a little, you know, old-ish to be climbing up the side of buildings? I mean, you're what, late thirties?"

Leine rolled her eyes. "A little older than that. And no, I'm not too old, as you so charmingly put it." She shook her head in mock amazement. "I just can't understand why you're single. Such a sweet talker."

"Hey, now, who said I'm single?" His lips twitched with a suppressed grin.

She smiled and picked up the tech. "Tell me what I need to do."

Ten minutes later, her pack cinched tight to her body, Leine pressed herself flat to the outside of the building, her fingertips gripping the edge of the roof, toes barely supported by a depression in the salt-eroded brick. The waves crashed ominously below her.

What the hell was she thinking?

Ignoring the suicide drop to the sea below, she pulled herself up and over onto the roof, sprawling across the tiles to catch her breath, grateful for the time spent strength training at the gym. She moved to all fours and crawled to the apex of the roof. A crisp wind cut through her, ruffling her hair.

She shrugged off her pack and pulled out the detector, which she turned on. The screen displayed icons indicating the locations of both jammers. She attached the device to the tile roof with 100-mile-an-hour tape and turned the dial to the frequency Pierre told her would jam the jammers. She checked her phone. Full bars. Leine texted Art to see if she was successful.

Testing.

Art wrote back. 5X. *Loud and clear.*

Pierre's been hurt. I'll bring him back to the park.

Gina's pinned down at Mancinis', Art replied. *Need you there. I'll send someone to help Pierre.*

Copy, Leine typed. *OTW.*

THE POLICE CHIEF SLAMMED HIS FIST ON THE TABLE. LORIK HAD never seen Tito De Luca so angry. He kept his hand close to his holster, not sure whether he'd have to shoot anyone.

"No—you listen to me, *faccia de merda,*" De Luca bellowed. "I call the shots here. Not you." He glared at Kadare. His face had taken on a shade of red reminiscent of marinara.

"You need to watch your tongue," growled Kadare. Lorik gave the chief a warning glance, but it went unnoticed. He moved further away from the two men.

"Watch my tongue? *Watch my tongue?*" De Luca looked at Kadare like he was insane.

Which, to be fair, was not far from the truth. If Lorik was going to bet, he'd put his money on the mad dog, Kadare. The man had no qualms about killing.

Lorik had tried to steer Kadare away from De Luca, but once he'd let it slip that the chief of police was tight with a major Italian crime family, he'd insisted Lorik set up a meet. The meeting went as well as could be expected between two alpha males trying to out-piss one another. In the end, De Luca had been satisfied with the money Kadare brought to the table, and Kadare had gotten his army. A win-win.

Until tonight.

De Luca turned his wrath on Lorik. "And who the hell armed our citizens?" He took a threatening step closer. The stench of garlic and bad gums proved powerful—shallow breathing didn't help as Lorik fought back a wave of nausea.

"I have no idea, Tito," Lorik answered, averting his eyes. Neither Kadare nor De Luca could know he'd told Ava Basso about the stash of weapons at the church. What was done was done. He couldn't take back his actions, much as he'd like to. He'd allowed guilt to guide his decision to help the American— he wouldn't now.

De Luca narrowed his eyes at Lorik. "I don't believe you."

"Why would I do something so stupid? You know me, Tito. I would never work against my own interests, much less yours or Roan's."

De Luca glared at him, but seemed to accept his explanation.

He turned back to Kadare. "You've gotten half of the men you hired killed. The Don will not be happy. You will have to pay."

"And if I don't?" Kadare asked.

The police chief shrugged. "Then God help you. These men that have been killed have families. They must be taken care of." He crossed his arms. "That's the way it's done in Italy."

"You know, I don't really give a fuck how they do things in Italy." Kadare pulled a .45 and fired two rounds point-blank into De Luca's forehead. Lorik watched in disbelief as the back of the man's head exploded in a mixture of blood and brains, painting the wall in Lorik's office a grisly reddish-pink. The chief crumpled to the floor.

Lorik turned on Kadare. "What the fuck, Roan?" He looked from the chief back to Kadare.

Kadare returned the gun to his holster. "I eliminated an annoying mosquito."

"No. You did not." Lorik shook his head, his anxiety spiraling. "Tito De Luca is *protected*. When the Don finds out you just murdered his man, not to mention getting half the men killed that he loaned you, there will be no peace, no hiding. Only death."

Roan Kadare rolled his eyes. "Don't be dramatic." He sat behind the desk in Lorik's chair. "I'll pay him more money."

Lorik shook his head. "De Luca had a high position in one of the main crime families in Italy. They won't care about money. They will care about vengeance."

"So? Call him." Kadare shrugged. "I will talk to this don, man to man. He'll listen to reason."

Lorik turned away in disgust. How was he going to get out of this? He put Kadare and De Luca together. Would Don Vitale understand Lorik had nothing to do with killing the chief?

Probably not.

"We have to get rid of the body." The pool of blood spreading across the floor of his office would be relatively easy to clean. The walls, not so much. But what would they tell the Don? Half of his men were dead, and now the chief. Vitale would not be in a charitable mood, no matter how much money Kadare threw at him. A sense of helplessness enveloped Lorik.

He was so fucked.

37

Francesca counted the rounds in the magazine for a second time. Only five left. The second pistol had three. The sporadic gunfire outside the restaurant had dwindled to an occasional shot followed by return fire.

The front room was a war zone. Three employees had been killed—their bodies now lay on the tile floors, interspersed with broken wineglasses, plates, and scattered silverware. The large windows near the entrance were shattered, as were two of their prized Murano chandeliers. Bullet holes scarred several tables and chairs. The sound of automatic gunfire still rang in her ears.

She hadn't heard from Tomaso and Angelo in what seemed like an eternity. Was she now a widow?

Don't think like that.

Whatever the outcome, she vowed to never allow anyone to endanger her family again. If that required stockpiling weapons and training herself to kill, then so be it. Nothing meant more than family. The Madonna would understand.

Francesca shook her head to clear it of such thoughts. She needed to focus. Her phone vibrated. She glanced at the screen and her hopes soared. Ava was headed to the restaurant to help.

Crossing herself, she moved into position at the base of the reception desk and whispered a silent prayer for her husband and Angelo.

Pop! Pop! Another volley of gunfire serrated the night, then stilled. The urge to rush from her hiding place guns blazing overwhelmed her, but she stopped herself. What would that accomplish but her death?

She heard something behind her and spun, both pistols in hand.

"Gabby?" Francesca stared at her niece, crouched beside the back wall behind the bar.

Gabriela put a finger to her lips and looked both ways before darting the short distance to join Francesca. The two women embraced. Francesca pulled away first.

"You're supposed to be in Rome."

The younger woman's resolute gaze locked on hers. "I couldn't wait to come back. And now I know why." She gripped Francesca's hands in hers. "I'm needed here. I want to fight for my home—my family."

Francesca shook her head. "I know you do. But you can't. You have no training."

"Neither do you or Tomaso." Gabby eyed the pistols. "I didn't see him when I came in the back. Where is he?"

"I don't know." Francesca's nose burned with the effort to keep her tears at bay. "How did you get in? We barricaded the back door so no one could approach from the rear."

Gabby held up an old skeleton key. "I came in through the cellar. Don't worry," she said at the look on Francesca's face. "I secured the door behind me." The cellar was located on the side of the building. Hopefully no one saw her enter.

"Good. That's good. But you really, really shouldn't be here, *cara mia*. We are outgunned."

"What happened?" Gabby asked. "Is this because of what I saw on the beach?"

"Much has happened since Lucca." Francesca sighed. "Things have escalated."

"Obviously. Is this because of Ava?"

"No." Francesca shook her head. She wouldn't have her niece think badly of the woman who tried to save them. "She has worked tirelessly to keep us safe. We decided as a group to defend our town. She saw that we wouldn't change our minds, so she and her colleagues armed and trained us."

"Colleagues?"

"Five men and a woman. Professionals based in Greece. The head of the group employs the others in personal protection. The woman, Gina, is outside."

"They're bodyguards?"

Francesca shrugged. "I think so. All I know is that they fight for Scivoloso."

Gunshots erupted again, accompanied by return fire. Francesca winced.

"Is Ava here?" Gabby asked, trying to peer around the reception desk. Francesca grabbed her arm and pulled her back.

"Stay back," she warned. "It is too dangerous. Ava will be here soon."

"I want to help."

"You can't. These men are ruthless." This time, Francesca didn't hold back the tears. "We lost Opal, Derek, and Joseph."

"They're dead?" Disbelief filled Gabby's eyes. "But how?"

"They were shot to death. Murdered in cold blood." The tears flowed freely now. Francesca angrily wiped her cheeks.

"Bastards." Gabby's eyes reflected the pain and loss Francesca felt. "Then they must pay."

"We will remain here until Ava comes to help. Gina is holding off the gunmen, for now."

"How many are there?"

"I don't know. When they first attacked, we were able to fight them. We killed one and wounded two more. Opal and the others devised a plan to rush the two wounded gunmen—but there were more than we thought." Her words trailed off, the grief of losing long-time employees overwhelming.

"Where are the others?"

"They are hidden in the walk-in cooler. As long as we can hold off the gunmen, they'll be safe."

More gunfire could be heard outside the restaurant. Francesca moved to a crouch—Gabby did the same.

"Be ready to run," Francesca said.

"Let me take one." Gabby nodded toward the pistols. "Two women shooting is better than one, right?"

Francesca studied her. Would arming her hurt or help? "But you don't know how to use it and there are only a few bullets left."

"Teach me."

Francesca hesitated, then showed her niece how to fire a pistol.

***

Leine moved through the back alley toward the Mancinis' restaurant, following the sporadic gunfire. Gina had texted her position, so Leine knew which shots were coming from Kadare's men.

She slowed as she approached the rear entrance. The silhouette of a man wearing a backpack slipped behind the dumpster located to the left of the door. Gina was outside the front of the restaurant, meaning the man was likely a hostile. Leine kept to the shadows and waited.

Pop! The light above the door shattered and the alley went dark. A moment later, the silhouette emerged and moved to the rear door. In his hand was a shotgun. Leine moved closer, tracking him through her scope. He raised the shotgun and aimed the barrel at the door handle.

She hit him with a three-round burst. The man grunted and toppled to the ground. She scanned the area for more combatants, then moved to the body. Again, he carried no identification. Besides the shotgun, he wore a tac vest with a 9mm pistol, a combat knife, and extra mags. She pulled the pack open and found a breaching charge and a block of C-4, several flash bangs, and extra ammo.

Leine zipped the pack closed and slung it over her shoulder. Then she grabbed the shotgun and headed around the side of the building.

38

Leine stayed low and kept to the shadows as she skirted the restaurant. Security footage from the Mancinis' home showed two gunmen in position near the front. Gina was across the street, inside a bakery. The owner had closed his shop at the first sign of trouble, which meant there were no civilians to worry about. Leine texted Gina that she was there and sprinted across the street to the rear entrance. Gina cracked open the door, and Leine slipped inside.

"How many? Security footage shows two." Leine avoided stepping on the glass from the broken front window. No reason to alert the gunmen to her position. The yeasty scent of fresh bread still lingered in the cool air.

"Just the two that I know of. There are casualties inside the restaurant—they'd killed one gunman and wounded two before I got here."

"Do we know how many or who? Tomaso? Francesca?"

"Francesca's inside. She hasn't heard from Tomaso. When I try to draw the gunmen's fire, the rounds always come from two places." She moved to the side of the window and gestured to the same general areas Leine had seen on the video feed.

Leine shrugged off both packs and set them on the floor. She opened the one she'd taken off the gunman. "One of Kadare's men was about to breach the rear door of the restaurant. There's extra ammo, flash bangs, a breaching charge, and a block of C-4."

Gina nodded, her expression grim. "No one's reported explosions."

"Yet."

"Any more casualties?"

"Jorge and Nadia are taking care of things." Leine suppressed a twinge of guilt. It was too late for that. They needed to neutralize the threat. She could feel guilty all she wanted to later, once the rest of the town was safe.

Leine's phone buzzed with an incoming text. She read it and frowned. "It's Francesca. Gabby's inside the restaurant." What the hell was she doing back?

"The niece? I thought she was supposed to keep a low profile."

"So did I." Another text buzzed. Leine blew out a resigned sigh. "Francesca says she wants to fight."

"Does she have any experience?"

Leine gave her a look.

"Okay." Gina shrugged. "We will just have to deal with it."

"Francesca says she gave her a point-and-shoot primer on a pistol, so be aware. She says they're behind the receptionist's stand."

"How do you want to play this?"

"If there are only two gunmen, it should be easy to come in from behind and pick them off." Leine shrugged on her pack. "You're sure they're the only shooters out there?"

"As certain as I can be."

"All right. Which one do you want?"

The two women mapped out their attack, then loaded up on

extra ammunition. Leine grabbed the C-4 and detonators, along with two flash bangs, which she attached to her vest. She stashed the gunman's pack in a cupboard.

They exited through the back door and split up. Gina headed for the gunman behind several large planters, while Leine took the one using a hedge for cover.

Approaching from the rear, Leine identified her quarry crouched behind a boxwood hedge near the entrance to the restaurant. She hit him with a suppressed three-round burst to the back of the head. He grunted and slumped to the ground.

Leine raced along the hedge toward the restaurant, pausing long enough to text her position to both Francesca and Gina. Gina responded a few seconds later.

He moved position. Right 3 meters.

Just then, gunfire erupted near the second combatant's position. Keeping low, Leine raced toward the firefight. A round exploded off a nearby tree trunk, and Leine veered left.

Where'd that come from?

She ducked behind the thick trunk of an olive tree to regroup. A second round thudded into the bark, coming uncomfortably close.

Sniper. Was he using a thermal or night vision scope?

Leine grabbed one of the flash bangs from her vest, pulled the pin, and lobbed it toward the sniper. The grenade went off with a loud *bang* and a bright, white light. She broke cover and raced toward Gina's position. The sniper didn't fire.

NVG, then.

She took cover behind a concrete planter. Judging by the gunfire, there were at least two, maybe three gunmen pinning Gina down. Leine waited until one of them started shooting, revealing his position. She acquired the target and fired. Another round cracked into the planter, narrowly missing her.

Chips of concrete rained on her head. The sniper was back in business.

Gina fired at her assailants, spraying the area with rounds. Someone groaned. A branch snapped, followed by a muted thud. She'd hit one.

Automatic gunfire erupted inside the restaurant. Another gunman? She needed to get inside, ASAP. Leine shrugged off her pack and held it out so it resembled a silhouette. *Crack!* There was a brief flash from a building two streets over. A round tore through the pack.

The sniper had her pinned down.

Leine calculated the distance to the restaurant. Depending on the sniper's ability, she'd likely be dead before she made the door. She slid her phone from her back pocket and texted Francesca and Gina.

F: Turn on all outside lights. Clear the entrance. I'm coming in G: cover me.

More gunfire broke out inside the restaurant. Leine scanned her surroundings. She'd only have a short window to move. Hopefully, either Francesca or Gabby would be able to do as she asked.

Gina and the other gunman exchanged fire. Leine went low and sprinted to a tall laurel, closer to her attacker's position and out of the sniper's view. The sniper fired, but the round missed. Gina drew out the other gunman, giving Leine a clear shot. She fired, hitting him in the shoulder. He dropped back. Something moved in her periphery. She ducked and turned to secure the new target—a third gunman. He popped up to take a shot. Before he could open fire, Leine squeezed off three rounds. He went down.

Where were all the fighters coming from?

Leine had just reloaded when the outside lights blinked on. Gina was on her own. She took a deep breath, slid the second flash bang grenade from her vest, and ran to the front door of the restaurant.

She swung the door open, pulled the pin on the grenade, and tossed it into the main room. At the same time she dropped and rolled, averted her eyes, and covered her ears.

The grenade detonated. Leine leapt to her feet. A gunman had taken cover behind an upended table at the far end of the room and appeared disoriented. She fired, killing him instantly. There was a sound behind her, and she spun in place.

Gripping a 9mm pistol, Francesca stood behind the podium, eyes wide in a face drained of color. Leine scanned the restaurant for more threats. When she didn't find any, she crossed the room to the podium.

"I'm so glad to see you." Francesca's hands shook.

Leine gently unwound the other woman's fingers from the pistol grip, then wrapped her arm around her shoulders and guided her into the back room.

"Are you hurt?" Leine asked.

Francesca shook her head. "I don't think so."

"Where's Gabriela?"

Francesca gave Leine a blank stare. She turned to look behind her. "She was right there."

"Ava?" Gina called from the front of the restaurant.

"In the back room." Leine held Francesca by her shoulders. "Are there others here?" She'd seen the three bodies in the front room but didn't mention them.

"Yes. Oh, my God." Francesca ran to the cooler and ripped open the door as Gina walked into the back room. Four employees burst from the cooler. Francesca embraced each one.

None were Gabby.

"I take it your guy's been neutralized," Leine said to Gina.

Gina nodded. "Tactical error on his part. When you ran to

the front door the guy thought he could pick you off. I took him out."

"Thanks."

Gina glanced at the group assembled around Francesca. "Which one's Gabriela?"

"She isn't here. Francesca lost track of her during the gunfight." Leine called to Francesca. "Is there another way in or out of here?"

Francesca nodded. "The cellar. It's how Gabby got in without being seen."

"Take me there."

Francesca led Leine down an old wooden staircase to a cellar with a rock floor that stretched the length of the restaurant. Boxes of wine joined crates of root vegetables stacked against the chiseled rock walls. The heavy oak door had been reinforced with iron braces that looked centuries old.

Leine checked the door. "You keep this locked at all times?"

Francesca nodded. "Gabby kept her key."

"Looks like she left the way she came." Leine pointed to footprints in the dirt leading out the door.

Francesca met Leine's gaze. "She has a gun."

"Does she know how to use it?"

The other woman nodded. "I showed her how." She covered her mouth as she searched Leine's eyes. "What have I done? She thinks this is all her fault."

"Don't worry. We'll find her."

The two women rejoined Gina and the employees upstairs in the back room.

"There's a sniper outside. No one leaves here without Gina." The employees nodded that they understood. "Good. Gina, I'll text you when it's clear. Then take these folks to the farmhouse. I'll go after Gabby once I neutralize the sniper."

"Of course. Can I help?" Gina asked.

Leine pulled the C-4 from her pack. "I'm going to need a distraction."

LEINE MADE HER WAY ALONG THE STREET TOWARD THE BUILDING where she'd seen the rifle fire. The sniper could have moved his position, but more likely he'd stay put so he could pick off anyone who left the restaurant. Leine circumvented that possibility by leaving via the cellar and skirting the back of the building.

Gabby's disappearance was worrying. Her misplaced belief that everything was her fault was likely a powerful motivator that could prove deadly. For her.

But Leine had to focus on one threat at a time. Once she'd identified and neutralized the sniper, she could worry about Gabby.

The sniper's hide site turned out to be an historic building under restoration. Scaffolding made scaling the walls easy.

Leine climbed to the second highest floor, betting the sniper would have chosen the highest. She entered through a window covered with plastic sheeting and found herself inside a small anteroom. The stone walls, lack of furniture, and parquet flooring amplified the chill from the plunging temperature. Leine zipped her jacket. The smell of dust and solvent reminded her of an artist's studio, although there were no canvasses in sight.

She cracked open the door and peered down the darkened hallway. A stairwell could be seen at the end of the corridor. Her soft-soled shoes made no sound as she padded down the hall and slowly climbed the stairs.

The sound of something shifting on the dusty floor told her

someone or something was there. She climbed the rest of the way and paused to listen.

Wind shifted and rattled the plastic sheeting over the windows, but there was something else. The nerves at the back of her neck tingled. She scanned the room, her gaze landing on a dark shape on the floor near a slit in the sheeting.

The sniper.

She raised the MP5.

An explosion boomed in the distance. Gina had detonated the C-4. The shape moved. Leine sighted through the scope and pulled the trigger.

At the same instant, the sniper rolled right, leaving the rifle. Leine's round tore through the sheeting, missing her target. She moved forward, toward the sniper, scanning through the thermal scope.

There.

A canvas drop cloth draped over a pair of sawhorses quivered. Leine fired, stitching rounds through the canvas. She stepped behind a stack of bricks to reload.

Dead silence.

Sighting through the scope she moved left.

Something scraped across the floor. Leine dove behind a stone column as a muffled shot rang out. The bullet whizzed past and slammed into the wall a few feet away. The sniper had a sidearm.

Her back to the column, Leine waited for the shooter's next move. He was being judicious with his rounds. If he couldn't get a good shot at her, he'd likely be eyeing the entrance to the stairwell, hoping to escape and fight another day.

That wasn't going to happen.

She dropped and peered through the scope. The distance to the stairs was roughly nine feet of open space. Not good odds for the gunman. If he was good, he'd have more than one exit strategy.

The window? Leine shifted her line of sight to the wall that faced the street. The shorter distance would be tempting, although using the scaffolding would leave him open for too long. She came back to the stairwell and trained the MP5 on the open space between the sawhorse and the stairs.

The shooter was between a rock and a hard place. His main play would be to try to kill her and escape.

As if her opponent came to the same conclusion, something clattered across the floor toward the bank of windows. Leine averted her eyes. The flashbang detonated, and the room went bright. Ears ringing, she opened her eyes and sighted on the stairs. A dark shape darted from behind the sawhorses, crouched low, headed for the stairwell. Leine waited until he crossed her field of vision and fired.

The shape dropped to the floor. Leine moved quickly to the body and shot the gunman twice more to ensure he wouldn't be a problem. She pulled her penlight and directed the beam in the shooter's face.

It was Nestor.

39

———

Gabriela hurried down the street, the gun heavy in her hand. A cool mist had come in from the Mediterranean and enveloped the town, obscuring details and lending an eerie feel to a familiar place.

Francesca had shown her how the gun worked. There were three bullets left: two in the magazine and one still in the chamber. She'd also filled Gabby in on what had been happening—how Ava had dug deeper into who killed Eduardo, leading her to discover the Albanian thug, Lorik, extorting the businesses in town. She'd stopped him, but her actions led to another, larger threat to Ava and to Scivoloso—an old enemy who'd learned of her location.

Gabby's heart squeezed tight at the thought of her three friends being slaughtered and the danger the American woman and the whole town faced, making it hard to breathe.

All of this was her fault.

All of it.

If she hadn't witnessed those men kill Eduardo, none of this would be happening, and they would all be alive.

Except Eduardo.

She had to avenge their deaths. How could she live with herself if she didn't?

Gabby had a half-formed plan in mind when she left the restaurant during the chaos of the gunfight—find those responsible and kill them. She needed to help. She just didn't know how.

As she rounded the corner that led to the waterfront, a familiar silhouette walked under a streetlight half a block away. It was her cousin, Massimo. She hurried to catch him, waiting to get his attention until she was closer and her voice wouldn't carry.

"Massimo," she called, keeping her voice low. He turned.

"Gabby?" He stopped and waited for her. An emotion she couldn't identify crossed his face.

She'd always felt safe with him—not only because he was on the police force, but also because of his large frame and calming presence. He reminded her of a good-natured bear.

"Oh, Massimo. I'm so happy to see you." The relief at finding someone she knew left her knees weak. She hadn't realized how scared she was.

"What are you doing here?" He wrapped his arm around her shoulders and drew her into the shadow of a shuttered boutique. "It's too dangerous to be out here."

She gripped his hand. His skin, normally so warm and dry, was clammy and cold to the touch. Gabby gazed into his eyes, expecting warmth and familiarity. What she found wasn't that. The unsettling expression that met her eyes sent a chill down her spine. An odd mixture of excitement, confusion, and something darker didn't jibe with her cousin's normally easy-going nature. She let his hand drop from hers and stepped back.

"Are you feeling all right?" She kept the gun hidden behind her jacket.

"Of course." He pulled out his phone and typed something.

Gabby tried to see what he was writing, but he noticed and nonchalantly tipped the device to hide it from her.

She caught a glimpse of the text but wasn't able to read any of it. "What's going on? Has something happened?"

He shook his head. "No. But we need to get you to safety. Like I said, it's too dangerous out here." He grasped her arm and proceeded to guide her along the street.

"Wait." Gabby stopped. "I'm not going that way." By the look on his face, what she wanted didn't matter. He tugged her arm, but she stood her ground.

"Look," Massimo said, his annoyance plain at her disobeying him. "You have to come with me to the police station. It's the safest place right now. You'll have guards twenty-four seven."

Gabby wrenched her arm from his grasp. "I'm not going anywhere with you. And certainly not to the police station." Ava's warning not to talk to anyone, especially the local police, flickered through her mind. "For all I know, you're on side with the criminals."

A strange look crossed Massimo's face, telling her she'd hit a nerve. Shocked, she searched his eyes for the truth.

"Where is De Luca?" Gabby waved at the empty street, her anger rising. The chief of police should be taking the lead in repelling this horrible attack. "And the rest of the force? Shouldn't they be helping?"

"You don't know what you're talking about."

"Don't I? Since I've been back, I haven't seen one member of the local police defending the town. Come to think of it, my aunt never mentioned *any* of you doing anything to defend us."

Massimo's face flushed red. She'd hit another nerve.

"There wouldn't be a problem if you hadn't—" He stopped and looked away.

"If I hadn't what, Massimo?"

He turned back to her, his face a mask of anger. "If you

hadn't been dating that bastard informant, things would have been fine."

Disbelief shredded the last of her naiveté. "Eduardo?"

Massimo nodded.

"What do you mean, informant?" She glared at her cousin. "How did my dating him have anything to do with him being an informant?"

"Eduardo was going to go to the authorities."

"About what?"

"That isn't important."

"So, what, you and De Luca have some kind of illegal side business?" He remained silent. "It wasn't just you and the chief, was it?" That had to be it. Scivoloso's police force was on the take, and Eduardo had found out. Beautiful, principled, honest Eduardo. Indignation mixed with her anger and bubbled to the surface. "What was it? Bribes? Guns for hire? Were you in on the extortion, too?"

Massimo's eyes narrowed. "You'd better watch your mouth."

He straightened to his full height, obviously trying to intimidate her. It wouldn't work. Gabby had grown up around her male cousins. No man would intimidate her.

"Or what? You're going to kill me?"

Massimo opened his jacket, revealing a holstered gun. "I said, you need to watch your mouth."

Massimo was threatening her? She shook her head to clear it. This had to be a dream.

"Are you crazy? Massimo, it's me, Gabby."

"If you hadn't been dating Eduardo, you wouldn't have seen what you saw that night."

He knew? "How do you know I saw anything?"

He scoffed. "*Everyone* on the force knows you were there."

"Eduardo was *murdered.* I thought you two were friends." Tears filled Gabby's eyes. How could this be? Would he actually shoot her? Her whole world had changed in such a short time.

"He deserved it." Massimo's contemptuous tone surprised her. "He was going to put us all in prison. For what? No one got hurt."

"Until Eduardo." She spat on the ground. "You were part of it, weren't you? You benefited from protection money taken from people you've known all your life." Her tears forgotten, Gabby glared at her cousin. "How can you say no one was hurt?"

"Enough talk."

Massimo tried to grab her arm, but Gabby stepped back.

"You are going to come with me. Now." He reached for his gun.

Without thinking, Gabby raised hers and aimed it at him. "Don't."

He froze, then carefully brought his hands up. "Where did you get the gun?"

"That's none of your business." The gun barrel wavered—it was much more difficult to hold with one hand than she'd thought. She used both to steady the weapon.

Massimo lowered his voice and held out his hand. "Give me the gun, Gabby. You don't know what you're doing. Someone's going to get hurt." He took a step toward her.

Gabby re-gripped the gun and hardened her stance. "Don't come any closer."

He stopped and raised both hands again. His phone buzzed. For a moment, Gabby's attention shifted to his pocket. Massimo seized the moment and went for his gun.

Gabby fired.

The sound of the discharge cracked through the still evening air, its echo ricocheting off the buildings. Massimo clutched his chest as a dark stain bloomed on his white shirt. Wheezing, he sank to his knees.

"No!" Gabby rushed to him, but he collapsed in her arms. "No, no, no, no, no, no, no—" She cradled his head as his life ebbed. Tears spilled down her face as a sob escaped her, welling up from deep inside.

She'd just murdered a childhood friend.

40

———

L eine headed back to the park where Jorge and Nadia were still tending to the injured. Casualties had slowed to a trickle, giving everyone a shot of much-needed hope that the worst was over.

At last count, five townspeople had lost their lives—the three employees at the Mancinis' and two others. Manny was hanging on, but he needed a hospital, as did a few others. Sam and Zarko were coordinating transport to the nearest regional facility. Leine grabbed a bottled water and downed half. Her phone buzzed, and she glanced at the screen.

"Hey, Art."

"Good to hear your voice, Leine."

"Same. What happened with Alek?" They shouldn't have been blindsided by the attack with Alek reporting from Kadare's camp.

"I've got eyes on the villa. Lorik and Kadare came back with four of their crew. Alek's not with them." Sixteen of Kadare's crew were dead. Arming people in town had surprised the hired thugs—they came in expecting a slaughter. When that didn't happen, they took too long to recalibrate and lost.

"You sound worried." She walked to the Range Rover and leaned against the front fender.

"I called Lou to see if he'd heard anything from Alek, but he hasn't been able to contact him."

"You think he's been compromised?"

"Most likely. Nestor's return from the dead proved to Lorik and Kadare that Alek didn't carry out their orders. That marked Alek as a traitor."

"But Alek saved Nestor's life. Nestor knew what Kadare was like, that he'd eliminate anyone he deemed a traitor. Why turn on the one person who didn't want you dead?"

"Where was Nestor gonna go? He worked for criminals all his life."

"I'm sorry I didn't get to him sooner." Leine moved aside as Zarko and Sam helped Manny into the Rover.

"It doesn't look good for Alek, but that isn't your fault," Art said, preempting what she'd been about to say. "I should have had him kill Nestor when he had the chance."

Losing Alek and five people from town was too depressing. Time to change the subject. "Looks like Manny's going to make it." Some of Manny's coloring had returned and he was alert and responsive. "They're taking him and the others to the hospital."

"How many did we lose?"

"Five."

"Damn."

"I know." Leine's gut twisted.

"It could have been so much worse."

"Agreed."

"What's this about Gabby being back?" Art asked.

"She showed up at the restaurant to fight."

"Where is she now?"

"We don't know. She took off with a gun."

"That's a problem."

"Yeah. As soon as I'm done here, I'm going after her." Leine finished off the water and tossed the bottle into a box filled with empties. "Then we take this fight to Kadare. I refuse to involve these people any further."

"Kind of late, isn't it? I mean, they're already vested. They lost some of their own."

"That's why it's time for offense. But I'm taking it far away from here."

"I think you're underestimating your allies, but it's your op."

Leine ended the call and slid the phone into her back pocket. Time to find Gabriela.

GABBY HURRIED ALONG THE SIDEWALK, STOPPING TO LOOK BEHIND her as she ran. Memories from the night she watched Eduardo die slammed into her, ratcheting up the anxiety she already felt from killing Massimo. She didn't want to leave her cousin lying on the sidewalk. The internal struggle had been intense. Inevitably, she chose to leave. She couldn't call the police—they were now the enemy.

The *enemy*. She'd always taken the police's benevolence for granted—especially her cousin. In Scivoloso police were a force for good.

Until they weren't.

Who else couldn't she trust? Gabby wasn't normally paranoid, but ever since that night on the beach her mistrust of people had grown. The world was a dangerous place—even her beloved town.

She didn't like what she found.

Gabriela slowed at the end of the alley and peeked around the corner. She caught her breath. A shadowy figure walked toward her along the darkened street, but she couldn't make out who it was. Someone had shot the lights out, plunging the area into darkness, with ambient light from the stars the only illumination. Perhaps the person hadn't seen her. She ducked behind the corner, her mind spinning as she tried to figure out her next move.

The disposable cellphone Ava had given her buzzed with a text.

Don't move.

The message had to be from Ava—besides her aunt, she was the only person who knew the number.

Gabby replied with a thumbs-up emoji. Relief flooded through her. She was safe.

A second later, there was a *pffft* sound followed by a muffled thud. Gabby resisted the urge to peek around the corner. She assumed someone had been shot. The footsteps came closer. Heart racing, she searched for a place to hide. Her phone buzzed again.

Don't worry. It's me.

Gabby read the text but refused to believe it had come from Ava. What if someone had killed her and was now using the American's phone to lure Gabby to her death? She spotted a recessed doorway across the street and made a dash for it, flattening her back against the door.

As the footsteps grew closer, Gabby's heart raced faster. She squeezed her eyes closed, willing the person to pass by without seeing her. The footsteps stopped. Gabby's phone buzzed.

Gabby fumbled to turn off the phone's sound but was too late. The footsteps resumed their trajectory toward her. Tears welled in her eyes.

She was going to die.

"Gabriela?" A woman's voice.

And then Ava was there. Gabby couldn't hold back the sob as the American enfolded her in a hug.

"Shh. It's all right. I'm here."

Gabby buried her face in Ava's neck, her sobs quieting. After a few minutes Ava stepped back, her hands still holding Gabby's shoulders.

"You're not hurt?" Ava looked her over. All Gabby could do was shake her head. She finally found her voice a few minutes later.

"My cousin—he, he's—"

"The one that's on the police force?"

Gabby nodded. "He was taking bribes."

"Was?" Ava looked at her closely.

"I killed him."

Ava nodded, her expression unreadable. "Where's the gun?"

Gabby pulled the pistol from inside her coat and handed it to her. Ava wiped it off with the bottom section of her shirt, then slid the gun into a holster on her vest as she peered out from the doorway. She turned back to Gabby.

"He was going to shoot me." Gabriela searched the other woman's eyes for vindication. "My own cousin wanted to kill me." A fresh round of sobs wracked her body.

Ava took her arm and led her from the doorway. "We have to move. It's not safe here."

Gabriela followed, wiping at the tears on her face. "But where can we go?"

"I'm going to get you somewhere safe. Trust me."

"Are my aunt and uncle—?"

"Francesca is fine. We haven't heard from Tomaso."

Gabby stopped. "You mean he might be dead?"

"We haven't found him yet, so we don't know that."

The two women resumed walking. Ava peered around the corner then gestured for Gabby to follow. A man dressed in camouflage lay on his back on the sidewalk, obviously dead. Gabriela averted her gaze. "Did you—?"

Ava nodded. "He most likely would have killed you if he found you."

A frisson of fear scuttled down Gabby's spine. What if Tomaso had been murdered? "Nothing would stop my uncle from contacting my aunt if he was all right." The crushing guilt took her breath.

"We don't know that he's dead. Try not to think the worst, okay?"

Fifteen minutes later, they arrived at the park near the waterfront. Gabby took in the scene and turned to Ava. "How many have been hurt?"

"Last time I checked, about nine."

"And the dead?"

"Currently the count is five."

"Does that include the three at the restaurant?'

"Yes."

"Who are the others?"

Ava gave her their names. Both were people Gabby knew well who worked at restaurants in town. Despair hit her hard. Her knees grew weak, and she sat on a nearby bench.

"So much death."

"This isn't your fault, Gabriela. You didn't choose to see what you did."

"But I still saw it." She stared at the ground. "Nothing will ever be the same."

"You're right. But the town is still here, and most of the people. It's going to take some work, but it will be all right."

"I hope so." The way it felt right now, that wasn't possible.

41

Roan Kadare slammed his fist on the doorframe. "This. Is. Unacceptable." His tone grew louder with each word.

Lorik winced. At least the madman hadn't destroyed his precious Louis XV oak hall table with the mother-of-pearl inlay. Most anything else in the villa he could replace. The hall table was another matter.

"How many soldiers are left?" Kadare's chest heaved with each breath—his complexion resembled a ripe pomegranate.

If Lorik waited long enough, perhaps his exceedingly unwanted guest would keel over of a heart attack. Maybe a stroke.

"A dozen, give or take," he answered.

Kadare closed his eyes. "That fucking bitch."

"Indeed." Twelve out of the twenty-six men the Don had provided. It was a colossal understatement that the slaughter wouldn't go over well. If Kadare's health didn't fail him, Lorik was pretty sure the Italian boss would help things along. What was left of the local police force most likely didn't have Don Vitale's contact information—De Luca kept a tight rein on his people. Lorik had to distance himself from the bloodbath. He did not need to be on the wrong side of a powerful mafia leader.

But how?

Kadare narrowed his eyes and nodded toward the door. "Come with me."

Lorik followed Kadare outside. Several vehicles stood fueled and ready to go in the forecourt, awaiting the next phase in Kadare's war on the Leopard. A sea of brilliant white stars peppered the dark sky. Lorik took a deep breath of cool air and zipped his jacket closed against the chill.

God, he loved this place.

"Have you swept the villa for bugs?"

"Of course." Lorik hadn't, but Kadare didn't need to know that. Kadare's paranoia was wearing thin. Why couldn't the mad Albanian just die? Lorik had been sorely tempted to do it himself, but the question of fallout from Kadare's patron, Elvis Sadiki, stayed his hand. Even though Roan Kadare had made a mockery of Sadiki's word by escaping prison early, he was still part of his family.

Kadare nodded, apparently satisfied. "Bring me the traitor. I want to question him."

"I doubt he'll have anything more to say than what you've already extracted," Lorik warned. Aleksander had proved resilient in the face of Kadare's barbaric tactics. Lorik had left the session early, uncomfortable watching Kadare destroy the man who had been his bodyguard. His fears extended to the rest of the town. The possibility he would destroy Scivoloso in the name of vengeance didn't seem farfetched.

"He'll talk or he'll die."

Lorik sighed. He tried to reason with Kadare, but the more losses they sustained, the more Kadare wanted to kill the American woman, no matter what the cost. It was like trying to explain something to a drunk. And for what? He doubted Aleksander would give up one word of actionable information. He'd already proven to be a closed book. If anything, he'd lie to misdirect Kadare.

"Why not question the two prisoners?" Capturing Tomaso and Angelo had been one of the only positive developments in an otherwise ineffective offensive. "They might know where the Leopard is hiding."

Kadare's indifferent shrug told Lorik he wasn't operating in reality. Interrogating the prisoners should have been top of mind.

"Well, whatever you decide to do, you need to do it quickly. If he hasn't already, the Don will hear that his men were slaughtered. I doubt he'll be pleased."

"He'll send more."

"I'm sorry?"

Kadare pulled his .45 from his waistband and grinned. "The Don will send more of his men to vanquish the woman who is responsible for their deaths."

Stunned, Lorik stared at the man in front of him. Kadare had no concept of what would likely happen with the well-connected Italian. "You killed his main contact in Scivoloso—a police chief, I might add. Not only that, but your incessant need for revenge led to over half of his men being wiped out." He eyed the gun. Would Kadare shoot him? "He doesn't care about the Leopard. He cares about the man responsible for the bloodshed."

"Bah." Kadare waved away his explanation. "You don't know how powerful men think." He pointed at himself with his gun. "I know."

Lorik narrowed his eyes at the other man, wishing he'd pull the trigger. Instead of an equal, Kadare viewed Lorik as a subordinate. Well, there were ways to prove him wrong.

So many ways.

"I also know how I'm going to kill the Leopard."

"Oh? Please tell me of this miraculous plan." Kadare hadn't managed it yet. Why did he think he'd accomplish it now? Kadare's smile reminded Lorik of pictures he'd seen of a spotted hyena guarding a carcass.

"We'll use our prisoners to lure her here."

"And how will she know they're here?"

"You're going to tell her."

AT PIERRE'S INSISTENCE, SAM LOCATED AND ACQUIRED BOTH jammers before he transported him to the field hospital, which had been moved to the farmhouse's garage. Once Jorge patched him up and administered antibiotics, Pierre refused to leave, citing the need to maintain the team's comms. The town's survivors who didn't need a hospital congregated inside the farmhouse.

Anticipating another move from Roan Kadare, Gina, Sam, and Zarko retired to the library to clean weapons and reload. Leine and Art had just joined them to discuss how to proceed when her phone buzzed.

"Who was that?" Art asked as she ended the call. "I can tell by your face it's bad news."

"Lorik."

"What'd the little prick want? A ceasefire?"

"Not exactly. They have Tomaso and Angelo. Kadare wants to trade."

"Ah, shit." He let out a sigh. "Tomaso and Angelo for you?"

Leine nodded. "Interestingly enough, Lorik told me it was a trap and to be careful."

"Think you can trust him?"

"Probably not. But he assured me that Tomaso and Angelo are alive. That's something."

"Sure, but for how long?"

"I told him we needed proof of life before any kind of trade. He said he'd talk to Kadare. We don't have a lot of time to plan an attack."

Art gave her a look, then nodded. "Gina, Zarko—" They glanced up from reloading a pair of SMGs. He waved them over. "Get everyone in here for a brainstorming session."

Once the rest of the crew assembled, they hashed out a plan.

Afterward, Leine took Francesca and Gabby to a quiet place in the front room and told them that Tomaso was alive—for now. Francesca closed her eyes and sank onto the sofa with relief, while Gabby burst into tears.

"We're going to try to save him, but I can't make any promises that he'll survive."

Francesca put her hand on Leine's arm and looked in her eyes. "I know you'll do what you can. Thank you."

Gabby nodded through her tears. "Yes. Thank you so much for all you have done." She sat beside her aunt and wrapped her arms around her.

Leine left them alone. She didn't deserve their thanks, but she sure as hell was going to earn it now.

42

———

Leine scanned the forecourt of Lorik's villa through her NVGs, searching for perimeter guards. Two gunmen were in position at the entrance. She stepped back behind the cypress and checked the time. Ten minutes to go. She moved through the vineyard to a different vantage point to recce the west side of the building. Another guard leaned against the cellar door, smoking a cigarette.

"Two bogeys at the south entrance," she said into her mic. "One on the west sector, near the cellar." Leine had drawn a schematic of the security camera coverage and where the blind spots were so the team could take out the perimeter guards without alerting Lorik or Kadare. The plan was to leave the entrance guards alive until Leine and Zarko had breached the villa.

"Copy," Art replied.

"Bogey down, east sector," Gina reported.

There was a pause before Jorge chimed in. "Two down, north side."

"Bravo is in position," Sam drawled.

Leine dropped to a low crouch and sprinted to the villa,

pausing behind a stack of oak wine barrels. The armed guard at the cellar door took a drag off his cigarette and dropped it, then ground it out with his shoe. She drew a bead on him through the space between two barrels and fired. The suppressed round entered his forehead and his head snapped back. He dropped where he stood.

"West bogey down." Leine moved to the cellar door, slid her lock-picking tools from her back pocket, and went to work on the lock. Zarko materialized carrying a pack and a submachine gun. The lock disengaged, and Leine opened the door, then helped Zarko drag the dead gunman inside the cellar. She closed the door behind them.

A muffled groan erupted behind her. Leine pivoted and aimed her weapon. Someone lay huddled in a corner on the floor.

"Alek?"

The shape groaned and tried to move. She stepped closer. The bloodied, swollen face made it difficult, but not impossible, to tell who it was.

Leine shrugged off her pack and keyed her mic. "We've got Alek."

"Copy that," Art replied. "Status?"

"Anything broken?" Leine asked, keeping her voice low. She ran her hands over his extremities, searching for damage. Alek started to shake his head but winced in pain and abruptly stopped.

"No." Blood oozed from his mouth, and he spit on the floor.

"He's beat up but alive," she said into the mic.

"Delta." Art called out Jorge. "You're closest. Exfil ASAP."

"Delta copy."

"We still a go?" Zarko glanced at Leine.

She checked the time. Six minutes. "Affirmative." Zarko nodded and disappeared through the door leading into the villa.

"Have you seen Tomaso and Angelo?" Leine asked Alek as she pulled a bottle of water from her pack.

Alek attempted to say something, but the words came out garbled. Leine helped him sit up so he wouldn't choke on his blood.

"Upstairs," Alek managed.

She keyed her mic. "Precious cargo is inside the villa. I say again, precious cargo is inside the villa."

Art answered. "Copy that, Alpha. Tango, Bravo, continue as planned, but wait for Alpha's signal."

Sam and Zarko both copied.

Someone knocked at the cellar door. Leine moved closer. "Five-oh," she said in a low voice.

The person on the other side responded, "Six-two-four," answering the second half of the code. It was Jorge. Leine unlocked the door and let him in.

Jorge shrugged off his pack and knelt beside Alek.

"You good?" she asked.

Jorge nodded as he held the water bottle to Alek's lips. "We'll be out of here in under five."

Leine crossed the room to the door leading to the villa and cracked it open. When she didn't hear anything, she slipped through into the passageway and headed deeper inside.

She made it up the stone steps and along the entire length of the passage before she heard voices. Stealing closer to the kitchen, Leine used the shadows in the corridor for cover, allowing her an unobstructed view of the table that she'd hidden under when she last sneaked into the villa. Two men sat at the table smoking cigarettes—one faced the passageway, giving Leine a look at his unshaven face. The other had his back to her. Two AKs, two beers, and a roll of duct tape lay on the table between them.

"Why aren't we doing anything with him?" the one facing

the passageway asked in Italian. He took a drink from his beer and set it back on the table.

The other gunman shrugged. "Kadare says we need to keep him alive, for now."

The first man snorted. "After the failure of our last 'offensive' I'm not sure we should even be here."

"Offensive. That's a good word for it. What happened was offensive." Gunman number two flicked the ash from his cigarette onto the porcelain saucer they were using for an ashtray. "What can we do? Have you heard from Don Vitale?" The first gunman shook his head. "Neither have I. So we stay until we're told to do otherwise. Besides," he leaned closer, looking to each side as though someone might be listening. "Wouldn't you rather be down here guarding this guy than out there with the rest of those poor idiots?"

"You're right." The first gunman leaned back and raised his beer. "Either way, we get paid."

Leine shifted position for a wider view of the kitchen but couldn't see if Tomaso or Angelo were there. She raised the MP5 and stepped from the shadows. Angelo sat duct taped to a chair next to the fireplace. His eyes widened when he saw her. The gunman facing her glanced up and choked on his beer.

"Down the wrong pipe, eh?" The second gunman leaned over to slap his compatriot on the back.

"Not exactly."

At Leine's voice, the second gunman froze. The first stopped choking, regaining his breath.

"Slide those rifles across the floor to me. Now."

Angelo strained in his chair, making muffled noises through the duct tape covering his mouth. Leine shot him a look, and he quieted.

The first gunman gave the second a warning glance, adding a micro-shake of his head. Leine fired. The suppressed round slammed into the table between them, chipping the marble. Startled, both men jumped back.

"Don't even think about it, boys."

Gunman One raised his right hand and slowly reached for one of the AKs with his left. Gunman Two's body stiffened, telegraphing his intentions.

He dove for his weapon.

Pffffft. The round from Leine's MP5 carved a hole through the occipital ridge at the back of Two's head. Blood and brains sprayed across the table from the exit wound, spattering Gunman One. He watched in horror as Two slid off the chair onto the stone floor. Leine shifted her aim to the other gunman.

"Well?" she asked.

Both AKs clattered across the floor and came to rest at her feet.

"Good." She nodded at the roll of duct tape. "Would you mind?"

The surviving gunman grabbed the tape and tore off a long strip, then wound it around his ankles.

"Now the wrists."

Using his teeth, he did what he could. She walked over and finished the job, taping him to the chair and adding a piece to his mouth. Then she cut Angelo free.

Angelo peeled the duct tape from his mouth. "It's a trap," he whispered. "They're waiting for you."

"I know. Where's Tomaso?"

"Upstairs in the great room. Kadare's planned something, but I don't know what."

She activated her radio. "Half of the cargo is alive and in the southwest sector of the villa. I say again, half of the cargo is alive and well."

"He's crazy." Angelo circled his finger near his temple. "I have never seen a man so determined to kill someone."

"Are you hurt?" Leine asked.

Angelo shook his head. "Lorik interrogated us, but he just asked questions. He didn't do anything physical."

"He must have held back in case we demanded a video showing proof of life."

"Maybe." Angelo shrugged. "He took it easy on us, except when Kadare was watching, which wasn't long."

Something slammed behind them. Leine spun. The gunman she'd left alive had tipped over onto his back and was lying on the floor. He tried to call for help through the tape. His attempts were loud enough that someone in the next room could likely hear him. She shoved Angelo toward the passage leading to the cellar.

Footsteps from the interior of the villa pounded down the corridor toward them.

"Quickly. You need to—"

A gunman burst through the doorway. Leine shot him through the neck, and he fell in a heap on the stone floor.

"Get down," she yelled as she backtracked to the table. Angelo helped her tip the heavy piece onto its side, then dropped to his knees behind it.

Another gunman popped out from the doorway and sprayed the room with rounds. Bullets glanced off the marble top, no doubt chipping the stone, but at least the table provided temporary protection.

Leine waited for the lull indicating a reload before moving. The unmistakable snap of a magazine telegraphed the gunman's position. Leine popped up and relocated to the refrigerator, then aimed at a point forward of the doorway.

The gunman broke cover, his rifle aimed at the table. Leine dropped him. She waited to see if anyone else was coming but was met with silence. Leine peeked around the doorway into the dark corridor that led to the dining room and the foyer, but it was empty.

Leine ushered Angelo to the passageway. "Follow this corridor to the wine cellar. Wait there until someone comes for you. When you hear a knock at the door, use the words 'five-oh.' If the person on the other side answers 'Six-two-four,' it's safe to let them in."

Angelo repeated the instructions.

"Four bogeys down," Leine reported. "Half the cargo on its way for pickup."

"Copy, Alpha," Art replied. "See you on the other side."

Leine returned to the doorway that led to the rest of the villa and paused to listen once more. Again, silence. She moved down the hall, encountering no one. Bypassing the dining room, she headed for the foyer.

It was time to end Kadare.

Just then, Zarko's voice erupted through her earpiece.

"Tango to Alpha." His voice sounded a warning. "You'd better get up here."

43

———

Weapon held at high-ready, Leine raced to the foyer, encountering no opposition on the way. Zarko stood near the hall table.

"Got a bit of a situation here." He nodded toward the great room. "Take a look."

Leine glanced inside the huge, beam-ceilinged living area. Lorik sat at the grand piano, a cigarette smoldering in the crystal ashtray. Tomaso sat next to him on the same bench, his pasty complexion and wide eyes in direct contrast to Lorik's impassive expression. The piano blocked her view of both from the shoulders down. She started toward them, but Zarko held her back.

"You don't want to do that."

"Why not?"

"They're wired."

"They're—" She moved left so that she could get a partial view of Tomaso. A glimpse was all she needed. Black wires sprouted from a homemade suicide vest. "Oh, shit."

"But wait—there's more." Zarko pointed at a security camera mounted near the top of the fourteen-foot-tall ceiling.

"He's monitoring the feeds."

"Yeah."

"And we can't disable the camera because he'll blow the vest if the screen goes blank."

"I think that pretty much sums things up."

Art's voice broke through her earpiece. "Looks like the security guards at the entrance have been told to stand down. They're headed for a white pickup. Echo, you're on surveillance." He relayed the plate number.

"Copy, Charlie. On my way," Gina answered.

"Sounds like he's getting ready to blow the place. What about the rest of the house?" Leine asked Zarko.

"Clear."

Leine moved a distance away from the great room and pressed the transmit button on her radio. "Bravo, we need your expertise. How copy?"

"Good copy, Alpha," Sam replied. "Just finishing up here. Be there in a jiff."

"Use the cellar," Leine added.

"Alpha, Tango, sitrep." The tension in Art's voice stood in direct contrast to Sam's relaxed drawl. While Zarko explained the situation to him, Leine ran through scenarios in her mind, trying to land on something they could do to save Tomaso and Lorik, and protect her and Zarko. Then it hit her.

Leine waited for Zarko to finish, then pressed the transmit button on her radio. "Come in, Charlie."

"What do you need, Alpha?" Art answered. Leine explained her idea. "Got it. I'll notify Foxtrot."

Sam joined them a short time later.

"Think you can disarm a suicide vest?" she asked.

"Yes, ma'am. They're normally pretty basic, although they can be a bit touchy."

"Okay." She nodded toward the security camera near the

ceiling. "We can't do anything yet. I've got an idea that should work."

"Should?" Sam gave her a sidelong glance. "Meaning…"

"I can't guarantee anything." She shrugged. "Sorry. It's the best I can do."

"What if Kadare thinks you're already here?" Sam asked. "Won't he just do the deed and hope you get caught in the fallout? That boy wants you dead somethin' bad."

"I'm betting he won't waste his chance. He hasn't seen me yet."

Sam started for the far side of the foyer. "Then I suggest we search for more explosives while we wait."

A short time later, Pierre called.

"Foxtrot to Alpha, come in."

"Alpha copy."

"There's a gift for you outside the cellar."

"Copy that, Foxtrot." Leine sprinted through the kitchen and the corridor to the cellar and opened the door. A drone rested on the cobblestones. Pierre had attached one of the jammers they recovered from town to the underside. Leine detached the device from the drone.

"Alpha to Foxtrot. Package received."

"Copy, Alpha." The drone came to life and lifted off the ground, then whirred off, headed back to Pierre.

Leine returned to the foyer. Zarko and Sam hadn't found evidence of additional explosives, but that didn't mean a lot. Kadare could have planted IEDs that they'd missed. She assumed they were cellphone-activated and not on a timer, since he didn't know when or if she would show at the villa.

"We've got to move fast," Leine said. "As soon as I turn this on, Kadare's going to know exactly what we're doing. Not sure if he's got a backup, but I'm betting he does."

Sam nodded, his normally unworried expression grim. "You

two move away from the blast zone. No reason for everybody to turn into a jigsaw puzzle."

"I'm coming with you," Leine said. "It'll be faster getting them out with two of us."

"You sure?" Sam asked. "Seems like a shitty trade-off." He grinned at Zarko. Zarko rolled his eyes.

"Here goes nothing." Leine flicked the switch on the jammer, activating the device. A green light blinked on. She checked her cellphone. No service.

She and Sam started across the room. Exaggerating his movements, Lorik cut his eyes to the camera, obviously trying to warn them.

Leine got to the piano first. Lorik had a suicide belt wrapped around his waist. Neither he nor Tomaso held a dead man's switch. Leine ripped the duct tape first from Tomaso's mouth, then Lorik's, while Sam went to work on Tomaso's vest.

"What are you doing?" Lorik hissed. He nodded at the camera near the ceiling. "He'll see you and blow us all up."

"Not if he's using a cellphone to detonate, which appears to be the case since we're all still intact," Leine said. "We're jamming the signal. Are there more explosives?"

Lorik nodded. "The bench is a pressure plate."

"Ah. Good to know." Leine checked the bottom of the piano bench. A crudely made bomb was attached to the underside. She called to Zarko. "We need weight. They're sitting on a bomb."

"How heavy?"

Leine turned to the two men. "What do you weigh?"

Tomaso answered first. "Seventy-two kilos."

"About eighty, I think," replied Lorik.

She relayed the information to Zarko, then pulled out her phone. "What's your Wi-Fi password?" she asked Lorik. He gave her an incredulous look.

"You want to surf the internet?"

"The jammer only interferes with cellular networks," she explained. "We can still communicate via your wireless connection."

"Oh. Well, fine." He recited the password and Leine typed it into her phone. Nothing.

"It's not connecting," Leine said. "Kadare must have messed with that, too. We're flying blind until you defuse the two suicide bombs."

"No pressure." Sam isolated one of the connections on Tomaso's suicide vest and grabbed the wire cutters. He took a deep breath. "Been good workin' with ya."

Tomaso closed his eyes and muttered a prayer. Leine tensed. Santa's face leapt into her mind the same moment that Sam snipped the wire.

Nothing happened. Leine breathed a sigh of relief.

"Oh, thank *God*." Tomaso said with a nervous laugh. "I can move now, right?"

Sam and Leine turned at the same time and shouted in unison, "No!"

Startled, Tomaso froze.

"We still need your weight," Leine said. "Without it, the bomb you're sitting on will explode and kill everyone here."

"But won't the jammer stop Kadare from detonating it?"

"This type of explosive isn't connected to Kadare's cellphone," Sam explained. "A pressure plate explosive relies on a specific amount of weight to keep it from going off. If we removed you from the bench, it'd be *arrivederci, signore*." He nodded toward Leine. "And *signora*."

"You're doing great—just a little bit longer," Leine told Tomaso. "You, too, Sam."

"It ain't over yet." Sam moved behind Lorik to work on his device.

Zarko entered the room, pushing a wheelbarrow containing several oversized bottles of wine.

Lorik glanced at the contents with dismay. "Not the Goliaths."

Zarko gave him a look that bordered on incredulity. "Really? You do know we're talking about your life here, right?"

"You don't understand. The wine in those bottles is comprised of the best vintage ever seen from my vineyard. I spent over a thousand euros apiece to have the glass specially hand blown."

Shaking his head, Zarko left to search for more in case what he'd brought wasn't enough.

Lorik craned his neck, trying to see what Sam was doing behind him. "Promise me you won't endanger the wine."

"How long has it been?" Sam asked, ignoring Lorik's request.

Leine checked the time. "Eight minutes."

Sam brushed his hair back from his eyes. "Kadare's gotta know something's up by now. How long you think we've got before he tries comin' at us?"

"I don't know." She glanced out the picture windows at the darkness beyond. Having Art on overwatch and interconnecting comms with the rest of the team had been their ace in the hole. Now it was a crapshoot.

Headlights appeared in the distance. She grabbed a pair of binoculars from her pack and trained them on the possible threat. "There's an SUV on the road headed this way."

"Let's hope it's a civilian and they just drive past," Sam muttered.

Leine continued to watch the vehicle's progress. The SUV slowed as it approached the gate, disappearing from sight as it moved behind the perimeter fence. A few moments later, it reappeared and continued on its way.

"They drove past." She remained at the window, checking to make sure the vehicle kept moving.

"Almost there." Sam picked up the wire cutters again. "This one's the touchy one I told you about."

"Oh, great. Of course Kadare chose to have me wear the one that's hard to defuse." Lorik stared glumly at the giant wine bottles in the wheelbarrow sitting in his living room.

"What did you expect?" Leine asked from across the room. "He wasn't ever going to go into business with you, Lorik."

"Well, of course I know that *now*."

Something glinted in her periphery. Leine focused the binoculars on a dark section of the vineyard. "Lorik—did you recently add some kind of bird deterrent to the vineyard? Like metal wind chimes or strips?"

"Not recently, no. Why?"

"Hold on a minute. I think we may have company." A moment later, she saw it again.

The glint appeared to have moved several yards closer. "Yep. We've definitely got company."

"I just need a couple more minutes," Sam said.

"Copy that." Leine grabbed her MP5 and Zarko's long range rifle and redeployed to the entrance. She killed the lights in the great room and the foyer, then cut the ones to the landing outside. Sam turned on his penlight and held it with his teeth as he continued working.

Leine took a knee and cracked the front door open. She peered through the scope. Three dark figures moved purposefully through the vineyard toward the villa.

Boom! Something detonated to her left. Leine refocused her binoculars.

"What the hell was that?" Lorik asked.

Sam answered. "A little gift I planted for our erstwhile friends of the Albanian persuasion."

"I'm Albanian," Lorik reminded him.

"I know," Sam replied.

Leine located the blast area and confirmed the kill. "One down," she said loud enough for Sam to hear. "I got two more bogeys heading our way."

Zarko returned, carrying a large vase. He left it in the hallway and joined Leine at the entrance. She motioned to the two gunmen's positions. They were moving slower than before, obviously being careful where they stepped. Zarko nodded. She handed him the rifle and gestured for him to go left, while she covered the right.

They moved quickly, each taking cover behind the potted cypress trees, which stood on opposite sides of the patio. The support columns for the portico gave them partial cover from the side.

The wind picked up and raced through the vineyard, rattling dead leaves and moaning through tree branches. Leine focused on where she'd last seen movement. Before long, a figure broke cover from behind a fence post and ran forward in a crouch. Leine sighted on the figure through the scope and squeezed the trigger. The gunman dropped.

At first, the other gunman didn't shift position. Leine and Zarko stayed put, waiting for his next move. They didn't have long. Keeping low, the third gunman beat a hard retreat, back-tracking the way he came.

Boom!

Leine checked through the binoculars. Apparently, the gunman hadn't retraced his steps.

Zarko signaled that he'd keep watch. She nodded and slipped back inside the villa.

"How are we doing?" she asked.

Sam continued to work on Lorik's belt. "I should ask you the same thing."

"Your landmines worked like a charm. Three of Kadare's men are down."

"I aim to please."

BOOM!

This time, the detonation rocked the floor beneath their feet. Leine glanced at Sam. "How many mines did you plant?"

He frowned. "That sounded like the trip wire. Check the driveway."

Leine moved to the window and peered out. At the foot of the driveway a vehicle burned, its flames leaping and arcing into the deep night sky. "Affirmative. There's now a burning hulk of metal in the drive."

"Good to know." Sam leaned back and wiped his forehead with the back of his hand. "You can turn off the jammer now."

"You defused the belt?"

"Yeah."

Leine moved to the device, which she'd left on top of the piano, and flipped the switch to off. Lorik and Tomaso looked somewhat relieved, although they were still literally sitting on a bomb.

Sam lay on his back on the floor to get a better look at the bomb underneath the bench. "And now for explosive number three."

"Good luck. Let me know if you need anything." Leine returned to the front door, keying her mic as she did.

"Alpha to Charlie, how copy?"

"Good copy, Alpha. Glad to have you back. Tell Sam congratulations on a job well done. Looks like Kadare's falling back to regroup."

"How many are still out there?"

"There are two pickups besides the vehicle that just went boom."

"I suppose it's too much to ask if one of them was Kadare."

"That's a negative. He's in a second vehicle, heading west."

"Away from town?"

"Yep."

"Could he know the farmhouse's location?"

"Unknown. Let me check. Echo, how copy?" Art asked.

Gina replied, "The two gunmen in the white pickup are in position about a klick from base."

Kadare had found them. "Alpha to Charlie. I'm going to try to lure Kadare and his men away from there."

"Copy that, Alpha. I'll send support."

Zarko joined her inside the foyer.

"Stay here with Sam, in case he can't defuse the bench bomb. He'll need help putting weight on the pressure plate."

"You're going to need help."

"Yeah, I know. But right now I need to get Kadare to come after me."

"Maybe there's something else we can do other than use you for bait."

"This will be faster. It's me he wants." She headed for the front door.

Sam called after her. "Where you goin'?"

"Trust me."

44

———

Once Sam relayed where he'd planted the remaining explosives and Art gave the all-clear, Leine exited the villa through the front door and proceeded down the dark driveway. She skirted the burning SUV, briefly registering the flaming corpse in the driver's seat, and slipped through the gate, allowing the security camera to capture a partial image of her. Earlier that evening, Art had parked the Land Rover behind a metal shed across from the villa. She found the keys under the mat, climbed in, and drove by the villa's gate, ensuring a good camera shot of the Rover, in case Kadare hadn't noticed her leave the grounds.

Five minutes into her drive, Art's voice came over the radio.

"Charlie to Alpha. All vehicles positioned within range of the farmhouse are now leaving the vicinity. They're headed toward town."

"Good copy, Charlie."

Leine sent a group text, warning everyone still in town to stay indoors. As Kadare's main offensive had petered out, the town's survivors who didn't go to the farmhouse were sheltering in place until Art or Leine let them know it was safe.

Thirty-five minutes later, after performing a few evasive techniques to give her teammates time to get into position and hopefully make Kadare think she was worried about a tail, she pulled to the curb a block from the bookstore.

She exited the vehicle and walked along the darkened street to the bookstore, alert for anything unusual. Luring Kadare to her home turf was the only way she could think of to get him out in the open, allowing her to finally put an end to the insanity. The man was obviously past reasoning—his intent to burn everything to the ground told her that. But it also made it easier to play him—he allowed his emotions to drive his actions, like Leine had when she'd been dead set against the town's involvement. She didn't want to think about what could have happened if Art and Manny hadn't talked her into enlisting their help. Yes, there were five dead, but it could have been so much worse.

Leine took a deep breath and exhaled. She assumed Kadare had men watching the bookstore. The body armor she wore wouldn't protect her against anything larger than a 9mm, and certainly wouldn't shield her from a head shot. Gina and Jorge were in position watching the store, and Pierre's drone was monitoring the town from overhead, but that didn't mean they'd be fast enough to detect the threat of a hidden gunman before he fired a shot.

Pfffft. The distinctive hiss of a suppressed round being discharged echoed through her earpiece, followed by a thud.

Leine's heartrate skyrocketed. Had one of them been shot? "Delta, Echo, report."

Gina answered a second later. "Bogey down. He was on the roof across the street with a rifle."

"Copy that, Echo. Thanks."

Leine entered the bookstore, closing the door behind her. The fresh scent of new wood hit her hard, reminding her that her dream of a peaceful retirement was just that—a dream. She cleared the store and the rooms upstairs. Although security footage hadn't shown anyone entering the building, redundancy never hurt.

"Clear," she reported.

"Copy."

She returned to the back room and took a moment to stretch her neck muscles to relieve the tension. At her request, the installer had kept the original flooring covering the trap door—she cited an interest in keeping at least some of the original architecture intact—and he'd obliged.

The trap door swung up easily, revealing the canvas bag filled with weapons. The crash of waves against the rocks below greeted her, along with a cool breeze and the brackish scent of the sea. Leine pulled the bag free and selected what she needed, then closed the hatch, making sure to position the latch so that the door wouldn't break away if she somehow stepped on it. Then she accessed the bookstore's security feeds on her phone.

And waited.

The gunman on the roof had enough time to take the shot before Gina neutralized him. Obviously, Kadare didn't want her killed on sight.

He wanted her for himself.

Come and get me.

IN A PARTICULARLY FOUL MOOD, ROAN KADARE SCANNED THE security footage on his phone as he and his driver raced toward Scivoloso. Not only had the American bitch thwarted his efforts to blow her and the villa to pieces, she'd recovered the traitor, Aleksander, alive, and her explosives expert had defused the bombs and saved both Lorik's and the restaurant owner's lives.

He'd had one of De Luca's men install a camera with a view

of the American's bookshop, and stationed a sniper on the roof facing the store in the likely event that the Leopard's allies came to her aid. But first, he had a surprise for her.

No one made a fool of Roan Kadare—especially not the Leopard. His anger toward the American woman seethed through him, blotting out all thought but revenge.

Something moved in the footage—a shadow? He enlarged the picture and froze. "She just walked into the bookstore." His anger growing, he glared at his driver—one of the Don's men who'd survived both offensives. He'd turned out to be the most loyal. "What happened to the sniper? He should have checked in." He needed the sniper for surveillance, as well. Kadare's plan had no room for mistakes.

The driver stared ahead as he drove. "Maybe his comms are down. The target has both jammers."

"Your men need to be careful." Kadare slammed his fist on the console. "I sent three killers—the best—to the bookstore before and they disappeared."

The man nodded. "They've been warned." The tattoo of the cross on his neck marked him as a member of the mafia's northern branch. As Lorik had predicted, the Don had been most unhappy about the massacre and refused to send more men. Kadare had insisted the surviving gunmen stay to fight, citing the amount of money the Don charged for their services. The mafia boss had relented but warned him he would be on the hook for taking care of the deceased men's families.

Not that he would honor the request.

The driver's phone vibrated, and he frowned at the screen.

"What?" Anger radiated off Kadare. The Don's men had been ordered to communicate directly with him.

"One of our men is reporting they found our guy."

"Well? Is he dead?"

"I don't know." The driver squinted at his screen. "Affirmative. He's dead."

"How the hell did she manage to kill him?" Kadare visibly seethed. Radio discipline among the men had been shit from the beginning. "She must have been on the roof."

"She just entered the bookstore. It had to be someone else."

"We don't know how long he's been dead. She could have killed him on the roof and easily taken the stairs to the street." Kadare pounded the console. His head felt as though it was going to explode. "Dammit. Get me to town. I'll take care of it."

"I don't think—" the gunman began.

"That's right. You don't. I do the thinking. Drive me there. Now."

45

———

Leine shifted position in the dark hallway. She'd cut power to her building and was using the night scope with a pair of NVGs for backup. She didn't know if Kadare had the same capabilities, but the flash bang on her tac vest would take care of them if he did.

"White Hilux approaching," Pierre reported. His drone had a bird's-eye-view of the roads in and around town. Leine monitored the security feed on her phone. Three minutes later, a Hilux pickup rolled slowly past the entrance, then disappeared. She didn't pick it up on the next feed, which meant the truck had either stopped between cameras, or had turned off the main street. She checked the cameras stationed along the feeder roads.

Nothing.

"Echo to Alpha, how copy?" Gina's voice cut through the silence.

"Good copy, Echo. What've you got?"

"That truck that just drove by only had one occupant."

"Kadare?"

"Negative."

"Copy that, Echo." Where was Kadare?

Several minutes ticked by. Every nerve at attention, Leine took a deep breath, exhaled, and closed her eyes to listen.

Antsy, she keyed her mic.

"Anything?"

"Negative," Gina replied.

Pierre added, "I found the pickup, but there's no one in it."

"Want me to recce the area, see if I can flush him out?" Zarko asked.

Art answered. "Echo, Foxtrot, keep an eye out for another sniper. Tango, go ahead."

"Copy that." Zarko replied.

What the hell was Kadare up to?

Leine closed her eyes again, reaching out with her senses, hoping to catch something—a change in air pressure, a sound, a scent...

There.

Leine stepped back from the landing. She'd heard something but couldn't be certain which direction the sound came from.

There it was again. A scraping sound in the other room.

"Foxtrot to Alpha, come in." The stress in Pierre's voice was obvious. "Bogeys on the back of the building. I say again, bogeys climbing up the rear wall of your building."

Something crashed through the window behind Leine. She spun and fired. A man dressed in black carrying a submachine gun crumpled to the floor. There was another crash—this time downstairs. Leine vaulted over the dead gunman to the window to see how many more were coming. Two dark figures attached to climbing gear on the rear wall waited their turn. A rigid hull inflatable boat bobbed on the waves, a short distance from shore. Leine leaned out the window and picked off the men on the wall. The RHIB moved farther from shore, making a shot iffy. She fell back and moved to the landing.

Footsteps thudded across the main floor below her, telling her there were multiple hostiles. Leine stepped behind the door to one of the bedrooms and calmed her breathing.

"Clear," a man shouted below her in Italian. It sounded like he was at the front of the store.

More footsteps, followed by something heavy crashing to the floor. A bookshelf? A table?

"Clear," another man called from the back room. There was a pause, then a shout. "She's upstairs!" He must have seen his now-dead comrades hanging outside the window, or the man in the boat had warned them.

A stair squeaked as someone started for the upper level. Leine leaned against the wall in the second bedroom and waited. She'd positioned the door so there was a gap near the frame, giving her a good view of the landing. The gunman was cautious—the barrel of his gun appeared first. She waited to see which direction he chose.

He turned toward the opposite bedroom, where the dead gunman lay on the floor under the window. She slipped from behind the door and shot him twice in the back of the head. She moved to slow the man's descent to the floor, but the sound alerted the others below that something had happened. She took his comms and melted back into the shadows.

"Bibi—come in." Another gunman—the echo of his voice was audible from below. "Bibi, come in."

"Alpha, you copy?" Art's voice in her other ear. She keyed her mic, letting him know she was alive.

"*Merda.*" The man's voice in her other ear shifted into low. "Man down."

Keeping the enemy's earpiece in place, she moved to the landing. Now that they knew she'd compromised one of their teammates they'd likely switch to hand signals, but there was a chance that someone else on their network might not be aware and break radio silence.

Weapon raised, she hugged the wall and slowly descended. Halfway to the bottom, a gunman popped around the corner. Leine fired, hitting him in the shoulder. He fell back with a grunt. A stair squeaked behind her, and she turned.

She was too late.

46

Leine came to, her head pounding like tympani. She tried to move, but the duct tape around her wrists and ankles made that difficult. Squinting against the light of the floor lamp, she assessed her situation.

It wasn't good.

A man kitted out in tactical gear held her at gunpoint, while a stocky man with a crimson red face, a dark buzz cut, and expensive-looking hiking boots paced the room. A roll of duct tape sat on the counter to her right. Next to that were her NVGs, her radio, a nail gun, and compressor. The floor installer must have forgotten to take his equipment with him when he left. Her cellphone was on one of the window ledges that hadn't been breached in the assault.

"You must be Roan," she said as she tested the strength of her duct-taped wrists. Three bodies in such a small space had increased the temperature. The odor wafting from the two men wasn't pleasant.

Startled, the stocky man stopped pacing and turned toward her. A cruel smile curved his lips.

"You've decided to join us, I see."

Leine gave the other gunman a sidelong glance. "No thanks to your muscle here. It feels like there's a full orchestra performing Vivaldi inside my head. You know, head injuries are nothing to play with."

Kadare's smile widened. "And that's just the start."

Leine turned her head toward the gunman. "You came through the window?" The gunman glanced at Kadare before he nodded. "Were you driving the white pickup?"

"Don't answer that," Kadare snapped. The gunman fell silent.

"Can I ask how you were able to enter the bookstore without getting shot?" she asked Kadare. Had his men killed Gina? Where was Zarko?

"That I will answer because it's ingenious, if I may say so." He nodded toward the trap door. "I have to thank you. It's not every day that my quarry provides a direct route. I'm just sorry I don't have the gift of time. I really hoped that you'd suffer."

Leine gave the trap door a quick once-over. He hadn't engaged the latch. She returned her attention to her captor. The tape around her wrist had stretched a fraction. She continued to work it back and forth.

"How did you manage to get enough men together who knew how to climb? I assume you thought your scheme to blow the villa was going to work."

"I had a plan B. Several of the men are ex-commandos. It would have been a shame not to use their abilities."

Touché. "So, you got me. You certainly went to a lot of trouble. What could you possibly gain from destroying the town?" She needed to keep him talking, give Art and the team enough time to mount a counteroffensive.

He cocked his head. "It's not the town I care about. It's you, of course. Lorik showed me your weakness. You care about the people here."

"You did all this for me? Aww. I feel so special. I guess I should thank you."

Kadare's face grew an even darker shade of crimson. "Shut the fuck up."

"Looks like I hit a nerve." *Careful, Leine. You don't want to speed up his timeline.*

He seized the roll of duct tape from the counter and ripped off a piece, which he then slapped across her mouth, using a little too much force. He threw the tape back on the counter and, fists clenched, resumed his pacing.

So much for her idea to spin him up and make him do something stupid she could exploit.

He nodded at the man holding her at gunpoint. "Cover the front door."

"You sure?"

Kadare narrowed his eyes. "Of course I'm sure. She's taped to the fucking chair."

The gunman gave him a quick nod and disappeared through the door.

Kadare pulled up the footstool and had a seat. "Now, before I end this, I want to tell you something you may take with you to the grave." He leaned closer.

Leine's stomach rolled at his robust body odor.

"Back in the day, when I thought you'd been wiped off the face of the earth, I did a little digging into your past. I think they call it closure. You'd murdered two men I admired most. My brother and Nico Abramov. They were both family. My only family. Do you want to know what I found?"

When Leine didn't respond, he continued.

"I found out that you were recruited at the tender age of sixteen by the head of a shadowy group of operatives. I also learned you'd been left an orphan. But when I tried to find out more about your parents and how they died, I was only able to discover information about your mother." He made a moue. "Pity she died so young. It must have been difficult."

Where the hell was he going with this? Leine narrowed her eyes.

"I couldn't find anything on your father for the longest time. But then I had a breakthrough. A serendipitous meeting, you might say."

He had her attention.

"One day, as I was destroying yet another group of thugs trying to replace me in the arms race hierarchy, I came across a dossier in a safe. This was not just any dossier." He stared pointedly at Leine. "It was all about your father. It seems that he'd infiltrated the organization I was in the process of destroying. They'd known, of course, and had him executed on the spot." He leaned forward. "Apparently, he worked for the same organization that you eventually did, doing much the same work. Isn't that interesting?"

Old memories flooded her mind of pleading with her old boss, Eric, for information about her father. He'd never given her anything.

If what Kadare said was true, then Eric had known exactly how her father died.

The bastard had just decided not to tell her.

"And you know the best part?" Kadare grinned. In a low voice, he said, "Someone inside your organization tipped them off. Someone with the initials E.M."

His words landed like a wrecking ball to the gut. Everything tumbled into place. Eric's lies—that he wanted to help her find out the details of her father's death, that he'd randomly seen her at the shooting range and thought she'd be a good addition to his team of assassins, that he loved her and wanted to be a father to their daughter, April. Leine's own father had warned her not to pursue his line of work under any circumstances. Had Eric told her father he had his eye on his daughter? A distant memory surfaced of her father talking heatedly on the phone, pushing back on something about Leine. She'd thought he was trying to keep her from joining the ROTC at school.

Had he been arguing with Eric?

Leine fought to control the inferno of feelings that surfaced. Her rage had nowhere to go. Eric was long dead.

"I see I've hit a nerve." Kadare smiled and walked to the counter, skirting the trap door. He picked up the nail gun. Leine braced for the pain about to come.

Kadare returned to his original position in front of her, this time stepping foot on the trap door. Nothing happened.

C'mon, just a little closer.

With a flourish, he sat back down on the footstool. "Are we ready?"

Just then, Leine's phone erupted in a familiar tone. Kadare twisted on the stool to see where the sound was coming from.

"Expecting a call?" He put down the nail gun and crossed the room to look at the screen. Again, he missed the trap door.

A string of curses floated through her mind.

"Who's Santa?"

Leine kept her expression impassive. No sense giving him the idea of killing someone she cared about.

Kadare picked up her phone and swiped the screen. The notification stopped. "Oh, well. Whoever it is, they're too late." He turned back, continuing to swipe at the screen as he did. This time he stepped wide, hitting the mark. For a brief second the trap door held, then, with a sharp *crack!* the breakaway ledge collapsed. Kadare disappeared down the chute, his screams cut short.

Just like that, he was gone.

Footsteps pounded toward her from the front of the store. She ripped her left hand free from the tape and lunged for the nail gun, landing on her side, still attached to the chair. Her fingers curled around the handle, and she twisted toward the doorway. The gunman burst through and she rapid-fired the gun.

Not entirely accurate, nails shot every which way. One speared his neck. He gurgled as he slapped his hand over the wound. A second later, his body jerked, and his eyelids fluttered. His eyeballs rolled back in his head, and he toppled forward onto the floor, a twelve-inch throwing knife protruding from his back.

Gina stood several feet from him, a second knife ready in her hand. She ran to Leine and cut her free, then helped her to her feet. "Are you all right?"

Leine peeled the remnants of tape from her ankles and wrists. "Thanks to your stellar throwing skills."

"Looks like you did some damage yourself," Gina said, glancing at the nail protruding from the gunman's neck. Blood from both the nail and the knife wounds puddled beneath him.

"What happened to Kadare?"

Leine gestured toward the gaping hole in the floor. "He took an unexpected trip."

"I see."

"There's a pair of NVGs on the counter." Leine peered down the dark crevasse. The waves weren't as loud as before, and she could just make out a sliver of pale white sand below. The tide was out. Gina found the NVGs and gave them to her. At the bottom of the crevasse, a pair of feet in expensive-looking hiking boots glowed acid green.

"Is he dead?"

"He's not napping," Leine said. "How many others were there?"

"Pierre tracked the RHIB with the drone. There was only one

guy manning the boat. The rest were direct ops. We didn't see any others after neutralizing the sniper."

"Everyone's all right?"

Gina nodded. "We're all good. No more casualties, at least on our side."

Leine turned back to the dead gunmen on her fresh, new wood floor and sighed in dismay. It had been like pulling teeth getting the installer back the last time. No way would he be able to repair the damage before Santa arrived. There had to be something else she could do to cover up the stains. The trap door would take time to repair, too.

She cocked her head to the side. There *was* one possibility. She glanced at Gina.

"How are your painting skills?"

47

———

The next day, Leine went to visit Manny in the hospital. His color looked better, and he was awake and responsive. He'd been rushed into surgery to repair the gunshot wound, although his oxygen levels had been dangerously low. It was touch and go for a while, but the doctors were able to stabilize him and complete the surgery.

Leine brought a bottle of Lorik's wine to share. Manny's eyes lit up.

"You are an angel," he said as he accepted a glass.

"What did the docs say? You going to be dancing the cha-cha soon?"

Manny smiled and sipped his wine. "You know, getting shot may have been one of the best things that ever happened to me."

"You're kidding, right?"

He shook his head. "I might never have gotten to know Nadia. That woman is fierce, not to mention a wonderful cook."

"Why, Manny—you old dog. Putting the moves on the local widow?"

He arched a bushy eyebrow. "Who said anything about me putting on the moves? It was all her doing."

Leine smiled. "Good for you."

Manny set his glass on the bedtable. "I hear that Kadare met his end in a most inopportune way. Someone mentioned a trap door in the back room of your store?" He smiled at her silence and leaned his head back on the pillow, satisfaction obvious on his face. "So this is how you disposed of the assassins."

"You said it, I didn't." She looked through a couple of get-well cards displayed on his bedside table. "Looks like you've got a lot of friends wishing you well." She turned one of them toward Manny. "'To Manny. My old friend and loyal consigliere. All the best, Don Vitale'?"

Manny shrugged. "It was another time. Another life."

Leine returned the card to its place on the table. "I know all about that."

His eyes sparkled at their shared secret. "Yes. I suppose you do. I only wish I would have known earlier that Don Vitale was the source of Kadare's gunmen. I might have saved us a war."

"Water under the bridge. There's no use thinking about what could have been."

He took another drink of wine, savoring the taste. "When is your Santa coming? It's soon, yes?"

"Tomorrow."

"Will you stay in Scivoloso?"

Leine shrugged. "I haven't decided. We'll see how things go tomorrow." The danger of enemies from her old life finding her again was something she didn't want to revisit on the good people of Scivoloso. Much as she loved the idea of retiring and running a bookstore in a small Italian town, the reality was that she was a danger to anyone and everything with whom she came into contact. Santa knew the risks and decided to take the chance.

The people of Scivoloso deserved to live in peace.

"Well, whatever you decide, keep us in your thoughts. And

know that everyone in Scivoloso, to a man and woman, would be proud to have you as their neighbor."

"Thanks, Manny. You don't know how much I appreciate that." Leine drained the last of her wine and said goodbye, leaving the bottle for Manny to finish.

On the drive home, her phone buzzed. She put the caller on speaker.

"Ava. It's Lorik."

"What do you want?" He'd left several messages telling her he wanted to meet. She hadn't called him back—Leine wasn't fond of people who played both sides.

"You haven't answered any of my calls." His petulant tone didn't do him any favors.

"I've been busy."

"I need your help."

"That's nice."

"You owe me."

"I what?"

"Who gave you the extra guns to arm the good people of Scivoloso?"

"I didn't ask you to."

"What about when I gave you Nestor?"

"Nestor almost got me killed."

"That never would have happened if you had done the job yourself."

"I don't recall that being part of the deal. If you wanted him dead, you should have taken care of it." A flicker of anger rose in her chest. "If you'd really wanted to help, you would have taken out Kadare before he destroyed half the town."

"If I had done as you say, I'd be marked for death. You don't fuck with a fellow countryman. Especially one as connected as Kadare. Besides, there weren't many chances. His paranoia knew no bounds. Just ask Aleksander."

Leine ignored his jab about Lou's plant. Thankfully, they'd gotten to him in time. Alek was damaged but would heal, eventually. "Speaking of the dead, how is Kadare's demise playing back home?" She'd need to be prepared in case Kadare's patron wanted to avenge his death.

"Word is that you did what needed to be done. Roan Kadare was out of control. Like a mad dog, he had to be put down. I doubt there will be repercussions."

"Good to know. So, what did you want to tell me?"

"Can we meet?"

"I'd rather not."

"Fine." He sighed. "I've been in contact with Don Vitale. He's demanding reparations for the men he lost."

"How does that even remotely have anything to do with me?"

"He says he'll cover the costs if you'll meet with him."

"Not an option, Lorik."

"He assures me this is about business. A friend of his has interceded for you, and he's interested in speaking to you."

"What on earth for?"

"I believe he wants to hire you."

Leine rolled her eyes. "Tell him I'm retired."

"But—"

"Goodbye, Lorik."

"Wait."

It was Leine's turn to sigh. "Yes?"

"What the fuck am I supposed to do? I don't have the kind of money he's demanding."

"That's not my problem."

"He's going to expect something."

"I seem to remember a huge bottle of award-winning wine in a one-of-a-kind, hand-blown bottle back at your villa. I'm sure the gesture would go a long way toward appeasement."

"Are you out of your mind? Those bottles are...they're..."

"Rare? Unique? Sounds like something a discerning Italian businessman would enjoy, don't you think?"

Lorik answered with a frustrated groan. "Fine. I'll have one delivered."

"I think it would go over better if you personally delivered it to him. Who knows? You might make a friend."

Lorik didn't reply right away, as though the little hamster wheels needed time to turn inside his head.

"That's actually not a bad idea." He hesitated before continuing. "I need to ask your opinion on something."

"Be quick. I'm almost to my destination."

"I've been thinking about our earlier conversation when we discussed giving something of value to the people of Scivoloso for their contributions."

"You're not seriously considering extorting them again? That's a lose-lose, Lorik. Remember? They won't stand for it."

"No, no, no. Nothing like that. I want to open the villa to the public. Hold concerts, weddings, that kind of thing. What do you think?"

"I think that's a great idea, except why would anyone from Scivoloso trust you? You were on the wrong side of the war, buddy."

"This is where I thought you might be able to help."

"Ah. You want me to vouch for you. After all they've been through?" Leine rolled her eyes. "That's a hard no."

"I am a changed man. I promise. I want to contribute, be a part of things."

"They probably won't buy it. Just a warning."

"I want to try. The villa and vineyard are everything to me. If that means I must humble myself to make a legitimate living, then so be it."

"I just don't think I can, Lorik. Sorry."

"All I'm asking for is a second chance."

Damn. He'd hit on the one thing that she cared deeply about. Second chances.

She sighed. "Fine. Don't make me regret this."

"I promise you won't. Thank you."

"How are you at advertising?"

"Advertising?"

"How else will you attract people to the villa?"

"I hadn't thought about it. This is a new idea."

"Tell you what. Why don't you call a town meeting, get their input? I guarantee it'll be easier to promote with them on your side."

"Will you be there?"

"Afraid not. But I will talk to a couple of people on your behalf."

"Again, thank you."

Leine ended the call and glanced at the time. Only hours until Santa landed. Happiness pulsed through her at the thought of seeing him again, replacing the stress of the last several weeks. She turned right onto the road to Scivoloso and headed for the bookstore to make sure everything was in place.

48

Leine opened the door to the bookstore and stepped aside so that Santa could enter. The sweet scent of lavender greeted them, emanating from strategically placed bundles of the dried flowers—a gift from Nadia. Sunlight shone through the squeaky-clean picture window and the new glass door, highlighting the new flooring.

"Nice." Santa took in the filled bookshelves and the display of leather notebooks, pens, and greeting cards. "You did all this?"

"I had help." She nodded toward the pack on his shoulder. "Let's put your gear away and you can freshen up. Then we'll take a little walk."

"Great."

Leine led him into the back, relieved that the paint on the mandala had dried in time. Gina had proven adept at creating the perfect design to cover the blood stains left by Kadare's driver.

"That's different." Santa studied the giant symbol. "I like it."

Leine started up the stairs and Santa stopped. "Is that what I think it is?" He pointed to a bullet hole in the wall near the third tread.

Of course he'd zero in on the one she hadn't had time to repair. "Oh? I hadn't noticed." She continued to the upper floor without a backward glance. Santa followed.

He set his pack on the bench at the foot of the bed. She showed him where the bathroom was and waited while he washed the transatlantic flight away. When he returned, he wore only a towel and a smile.

She smiled back. The walk could wait.

THEY HELD HANDS AS THEY WALKED THE STREETS OF SCIVOLOSO. Several townspeople greeted them both with a wave and a smile.

"You seem to have made a lot of friends," Santa remarked after the fourth or fifth person had come up to give her a hug. She'd told him that everyone knew her as Ava, and he went along with it, understanding Leine's need for anonymity. Not that the name change had done any good. Kadare had found her anyway.

She took him for a stroll along the Path of Love for the cool breeze and crashing waves, avoiding the secret walkway where Gabby had witnessed the death of her fiancé—the start of trouble that Leine should have had the sense to avoid.

But ignoring a problem just wasn't her. If someone was in trouble, she was always going to be the one to help.

Santa pulled her over to sit on a bench with a view of the sea. He wrapped his arm around her shoulders.

"You seem pensive," he said. "You're happy to see me, right?"

She covered his hand with hers and smiled. "More than you know." She sighed. "I'm just not sure this is the right place for us."

Santa gazed at the sea. "Something happened here that you're not telling me, didn't it?"

"Why do you say that?"

He smiled. "Because I know you, for one thing. For another, there were a lot of damn people out fixing things."

"Can't it just be civic pride?"

"Oh. Right. Replacing all the glass in the streetlights? Okay, I'll give you that. But what about the broken plate glass window and all those mysterious patches on the wall inside the gelateria?" He'd remarked on the different shade of stone where someone had filled in the gouges along the lower wall created by the rounds from Nadia's AK-47. Thankfully, the tile flooring and dark grout hadn't absorbed the gunman's blood and was easily cleaned. When he asked her about them, Nadia just shrugged and mentioned something vague about never using the same moving company to transport equipment again.

"And?"

"And the fresh patches all over your bookstore. The rigged trap door, the new flooring. If I looked hard enough, I bet I'd find more booby traps. There was a brass casing behind the dresser in the bedroom." He gave her a sidelong glance. "C'mon, Leine. What happened?"

Leine studied the clouds scudding past, trying to decide how much to tell him. Finally, she turned and looked him in the eyes.

"It's a long story, but you deserve to know what you're getting into." She recounted what happened, from Gabriela banging on her door that night, all the way through two days prior, when she'd almost died in her own back room.

When she'd finished, Santa was quiet for a long time.

"Where's Art and his crew now?"

"They went back to Greece yesterday."

He nodded and grew silent again. Leine gazed at the frothy white waves relentlessly hurling themselves against the rocks below. Was she doomed to live the rest of her life alone? She wouldn't blame him if he decided to cut bait. Being with her wasn't anyone's idea of a picnic.

Finally, he appeared to have come to some conclusion. He pulled her close and kissed the top of her head.

"If you don't think Scivoloso is right for us, then we look for somewhere else that is."

She held his gaze. "We might never be able to stay anywhere for long. You know that, right? I've got a lot of enemies who would like to see me dead."

"Yeah, yeah. I know. Your life is a series of terminal threats." He shrugged. "I'm all in, Leine. Whatever happens. I know how to handle myself. I have a few enemies, too. Most of them are in prison right now, but there'll come a day when someone gets out and comes looking for revenge. You still want to chance being with me?"

She leaned over and they shared a slow, languorous kiss. She broke away first and snuggled deeper into his arms.

"That's a chance I'm more than willing to take."

YOUR EXCLUSIVE FREE BOOK IS WAITING...

Find out the full story behind what happened between Leine Basso and Roan Kadare's older brother, Fatos. Download your exclusive copy of Making Leine : bitly.DVBReaderList *(and bonus short Bad Spirits, a Kate Jones Thriller)*

ACKNOWLEDGMENTS

I'd like to thank the following people for their help and support in writing *Terminal Threat*: first reader and partner extraordinaire, Mark Lindstrom, for your unconditional support, fabulous dinners, and wicked sense of humor; early readers Ruth Ross, Ali Mosa, Jenni Conner, Michelle Van Berkom, and Brian Yelland—I owe you all dinner and drinks for unfettered access to your varied life experiences and help; and Stephen England for copy edits. Big thanks go to the infamous ARTeam—you all are so dedicated and go the extra mile, always. My books are so much better because of your attention to detail. And, last but not least, special thanks goes to TSODA134 (a.k.a. SFD, or Special Forces Dude) for double-checking my use of weapons and military tactics, and providing great suggestions for my characters.

Any mistakes are entirely the fault of this author.

*Writing is never a solitary endeavor.

ABOUT THE AUTHOR

DV Berkom is the USA Today bestselling author of action-packed, riveting action-adventure and crime thrillers. Known for creating resilient, kick-ass female characters and page-turning plots, her love of the genre stems from a lifelong addiction to reading spy novels, thrillers, and action/adventure stories.

A restless soul and adventurer at heart, she spent years moving throughout the US and traveling to exotic locations before she wrote her first novel and was hooked. More than twenty books later, she now makes her home in the Pacific Northwest with her husband, Mark, and several imaginary characters who like to tell her what to do. Her most recent books include the Leine Basso thrillers *Terminal Threat, Fatal Objective, A Plague of Traitors, Shadow of the Jaguar,* and *Dakota Burn.* DV's currently hard at work on her next book.

For more information, visit her website at www.dvberkom.com. To be the first to hear about new releases and subscriber-only offers, go to: bit.ly/DVB_RL

ALSO BY D.V. BERKOM

LEINE BASSO CRIME THRILLER SERIES:

A Killing Truth

Serial Date

Bad Traffick

The Body Market

Cargo

The Last Deception

Dark Return

Absolution

Dakota Burn

Shadow of the Jaguar

A Plague of Traitors

Fatal Objective

Terminal Threat

KATE JONES ADVENTURE THRILLER SERIES:

Kate Jones Thriller Series Vol. 1

Cruising for Death

Yucatán Dead

A One Way Ticket to Dead

Vigilante Dead

CLAIRE WHITCOMB WESTERNS:

Retribution

Gunslinger

Legend